"You have the most incredible eyes I have ever seen."

Lucy smirked. "At least that you know of, Missing Memory Guy."

It wasn't every day a woman got to sit so close to a half-naked man. Or smell his interesting cologne.

Pleased with her lusty thoughts, Lucy was startled by a thunk of Truvin's knuckle.

"Earth to Lucy." His smile flashed the whitest teeth. "I'm the one with memory loss, remember?"

Feeling the blush creep up her neck, Lucy blew out a breath. It was growing hot in here.

"Your mouth is very sensual," he said. "Lush and pink."

Compelled, Lucy leaned in and kissed him. A short but well-placed kiss on his mouth. The connection sparkled in her chest. And that sparkle shimmered out to the surface of her skin.

"Oh." She pulled back and suppressed a smile. "I'm sorry." The tickle on Truvin's mouth worked to flush her smile to the surface. "Oh, I'm not—"

And then he leaned in to finish what she had only begun.

Tentative at first, he glided his mouth across hers before pressing. Testing. Feeling. As if it was his first kiss.

And maybe it was. The first he could remember.

Books by Michele Hauf

Silhouette Nocturne

From the Dark #3
Familiar Stranger #21
Kiss Me Deadly #24
His Forgotten Forever #44

*Bewitching the Dark

MICHELE HAUF

has been writing for over a decade and has published historical, fantasy and paranormal romance. A good, strong heroine, action, adventure and a touch of romance make for her favorite kind of story. (And if it's set in France, all the better.) She lives with her family in Minnesota, and loves the four seasons, even if one of them lasts six months and can be colder than a deep freeze. You can find out more about her at www.michelehauf.com.

HIS FORGOTTEN
FOREVER

×××

MICHELE HAUF

Silhouette Books

nocturne™

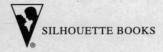 SILHOUETTE BOOKS

ISBN-13: 978-0-373-61791-3
ISBN-10:   0-373-61791-7

HIS FORGOTTEN FOREVER

Copyright © 2008 by Michele Hauf

www.silhouettenocturne.com

Printed in U.S.A.

Dear Reader,

This story is the third in the BEWITCHING THE DARK series, which pits witches and vampires against one another. Truvin Stone, the hero, made an appearance in *Kiss Me Deadly* (Sept '07). He may have seemed villainous, but trust me, he had good reason, for taking on the challenge of defying a powerful vampire leader.

When I began writing this story, I rented *Unknown White Male,* a documentary about a man who had amnesia. Incredibly, they began to film the subject almost immediately after he lost his memory, and followed him for years as he sought to gain back his memories. Film critics are skeptical that perhaps the documentary is an elaborate hoax, and they are not all convinced the subject did actually lose his memory. I found it very believable, and one very significant idea emerged for me after watching it—if you have no memories, how then can you even know to miss them? We can say, "I would miss this," or "I would miss that," but that is because we have our memories, and know to miss them. But if you haven't any memories, then your world is a blank slate. Anything can happen. And to discover you are a vampire?

I hope you enjoy this story! And do take a moment to wonder about the magic of memories.

Michele

To Pat and Mickey Svedahl

Chapter 1

The ache between his ears is what startled him to consciousness. Felt as if his skull had been drilled with something hard. Eyes falling over the wall against which one shoulder leaned, he noted the streak of murky crimson on the tar-stained cinder block.

Blood?

Posted halfway down the alley, a streetlight touched the edge of the shadows where he crouched. A roaming feel over his scalp located the ache, there at his right temple. His fingers slipped away with blood on them.

He figured his head had been rammed into the wall. By…someone else? But why? Or maybe he had tripped, fallen forward and hadn't had a chance to catch himself before his skull connected to the wall of—where was he?

Close by, cars rolled over the tarmac, kicking up slushy white noise. Horns honked. A velvet-gray sky, illuminated by city lights, loomed overhead. He must be sitting behind a building, perhaps a retail business.

A fishy odor tendriled beneath his nostrils. Listening more acutely, he could pick out the clang of pots, perhaps cooking knives slicing across cutting boards, and the muffled gabble of kitchen staff. Must be a restaurant nearby.

There, at the end of the alley, he heard a man's loafers shuffle over the wet pavement and the muffled click of a woman's heels walking double time beside him. She gave an audible shiver and cursed the winter chill.

Shuffling about to sit, he shook his head, which cleared away the bits of haze that fogged his brain.

But the fog did not completely recede. It seemed he could not get his bearings, could not…grasp on to any mental affirmation of his situation.

"Where am I? Who the hell did this to me?"

Or was it as he'd thought? He'd fallen?

Blood glinted in the light as he turned his fingers before him. A conclusion sprang to the fore of his brain. *Mugged.*

He did a sensory appraisal over the rest of his body. Nothing else hurt like his head did. Must have been punched or hit with something.

He wore black leather ankle-height boots, which were soaked from the snowy slush pushed up along the building wall. His gray trousers were crisply seamed, but also drawing up the wet. A white dress shirt bore a dribble of crimson down the front. A suit coat to match his trousers had been tugged down to his elbows.

Were these his clothes? They didn't strike him as familiar. Why did he feel so separate from reality? As if he stood off to the side, a stranger observing the man sitting on the ground.

A quick pat over the trousers found nothing in the pockets, or anything in the coat pockets. No ID or wallet. Not a cell phone or even car keys.

"Robbed," he said resolutely. "Dash it."

An odd taste swirled over his tongue. A slide of his finger across his bottom lip discovered blood. Must have been punched on the jaw. A tongue test didn't sense any loose teeth, nor did his jaw ache as did his forehead.

The chill air began to permeate the thin shirt he wore and he realized he sat surrounded by snowy slush. When had it snowed? It was winter?

Of course it was winter. But why didn't that mean anything to him? Was this a dream? Truly, did he stand outside himself, watching the horror? Would he wake to find himself safely tucked in a warm bed?

The ache at his temple pulsed, as if to answer, *No, this is happening.*

"Right. Wonder how much the bastard got from me."

Pushing up by the wall, he surprised himself that he didn't wobble and felt quite agile. May have been a quick hit-and-dash robbery, no struggle. He couldn't have seen it coming.

Had he blocked out memory of a traumatic event?

Logically, he knew it was possible, that a hit to the head could fuck with a man's memory. But…he knew things. It was winter. He was in a big city. It was night. And he was obviously hungry, for the restaurant smells stirred an aching want for sustenance, though the sensation sat higher than his stomach, and seemed to prod him right beneath the heart.

He stood in the slush-soaked alley looking from one end to the other. A parking lot one way, the bright neon lights of a main street the other way.

Had he been on his way home? This building he stood behind, had he come out of it, or was he on his way inside? What was the place?

He searched the nondescript cinder-block wall. The black metal door was marked with a painted white 4D. Five steps away a dingy green Dumpster displayed the name of a garbage company.

Clasping a hand over his heart, he panicked at the thud of his pulse. He didn't feel attached to this place. Where did he belong?

The horrifying sensation of unknowing put him out of his senses. Briefly, he lost control. His body wavered. Catching his palm against the wall, he stopped himself from keeling forward as the world suddenly took a dive into darkness. Blinking, he fought the wooziness.

And a moment of clarity emerged.

Obviously he needed to contact the police. If his wallet had been stolen, he didn't relish the weeks and months it might take to clear his name of identity theft.

You don't know *your name, buddy. How would you know if someone stole your identity?*

Christ, what was his name?

A twist of his boot crinkled a small square of yellow paper. It sat on the underside of his boot toe—as if he'd stepped on it. He bent to pluck it off.

The first word had begun to blur from the snow, yet he could easily read the small fancy writing.

"Go to the Saint Paul cathedral. Now." He flicked the paper with a finger. "Huh. Saint Paul?"

What sort of thief robbed a man, then asked to meet him at a church?

Yet recognition surfaced. *Saint Paul.* That was a city in…Minnesota. The capital. Yes, he was here in Saint Paul. *I know it.*

Staggering forward, he moved toward the end of the alley. Slush splashed with his tromping steps. Shrugging the coat up over his shoulders lessened the chill. A delivery truck cruised past the end of the alley, splattering gray snow to the toes of his boots.

His surroundings did not appear familiar. To search the sky, he could not pick out a major building, but he could see the base of many. Deep within the city, then, for to be farther out, he might have seen whole buildings and perhaps recognized a landmark.

Casing his periphery, he reasoned that most people weren't intimate with the alleys of a big city.

I live here. That fact felt real, like it was truth. But where? How to get home, to be *safe.*

A tickling cry formed at the back of his throat, but he swallowed the urge. He was a man. Men didn't panic. *Even men who had lost their identities.* He'd figure this out.

Walking a cobbled sidewalk, he followed the curving line of a large building toward an intersection. A glance up and behind saw a massive lighted sign for the Xcel Energy Center. The flashing marquee advertised the Dixie Chicks in two weeks. Tickets still available.

A country-rock band.

"I know things," he muttered. He recognized the band. "So why don't I know my name?"

Perhaps he required a hospital more than the police? Could emergency-room professionals snap their fingers and give him back the vital memory—the very knowing—that eluded him?

High above the buildings across the street, he sighted a gold cross, seeming to float in the sky, lit from below by spotlights.

"Saint Paul's Cathedral," he muttered, and picked up his pace. The cathedral was huge, a city icon. "I know. Yes, I recognize it."

Compelled for no other reason than at least he could fit one and one together—note, and the actual church—he jogged across the street, avoiding a speeding cab that honked as it passed.

There, he hadn't lost his memory. He was...

He was...a man...racing toward the refuge of the holy. A man who didn't want to consider the details he couldn't touch right now.

What would he do when he encountered the thief? Was he able to throw a punch?

He coiled his fingers into a fist, and felt his forearm all the way up to the bicep tighten. Yes, he had muscles. But did he know how to use them? was the question.

Should have found the police. What could go wrong in a church?

And who was to say the note had been written by the thief? A witness might have left it there. Someone who had observed the violence but was then too afraid to deal with an injured man. That made little sense. Why then ask the injured man to walk blocks away to a cathedral? Wouldn't it have been easier, and more Good Samaritanish, to simply call for the cops?

He stopped on the sidewalk before the cathedral. Preceded by a huge snow-littered lawn, it sat upon a hill. Half a mile to his right a busy freeway hummed with activity.

Should he go inside? It didn't feel right.

Apprehension tightened his jaw, and again he tasted the blood on his lip. Yet when the tip of his tongue probed the wet inner surface of his mouth, he found no lacerations.

"How can I fear," he muttered, "when I don't know my own courage?"

And so he stepped forward, taking the hill in sure, determined strides. Bounding up the granite steps, he then entered the dark, cool building.

The cathedral was open, but there was no one inside the narthex as he wandered in, slowing his pace in reverence to the silence. Low lighting fell across the dark wood floor and walls. Open doors to the sanctuary revealed dozens of candles glittering up by the altar, and there, along the sides in the various shrines.

Someone had to be here to tend the candles.

He entered the vast sanctuary. Walking across the back of the room, he noted now that two or three people did sit in the wooden folding chairs toward the front. Choosing the left aisle that paralleled the dozens of rows of wooden chairs, he wandered around behind the first marble pillar.

For a moment, he breathed in the dark and cool quiet. Alone with no thoughts.

What thoughts can you have? What thoughts have *you had?*

A strange, unfamiliar vulnerability nagged at him. *You are stronger than this.*

Physically or mentally?

"This way." A voice, female, and utterly unexpected, set him to alert.

He tightened both hands into fists, the act of which startled him so thoroughly, he stepped backward and his shoulder hit a marble pillar.

"Who's there?" he whispered. Heartbeats worked a furious pace. Darting his gaze up and down the wooden chairs and along the tiled floor, he spied no one. "I...I found the note."

Determination, and an innate refusal to step back from the unknown, fortified his courage. He stepped down the aisle, toward the back of the cathedral where he had entered, passing another marble pillar.

So he was a curious man. It felt right.

Maybe not so much curious as bold?

A wisp of long black hair fluttered from behind a pillar just ahead. A woman? Couldn't be his thief. No woman could overpower him. He didn't think—no, he *knew* he was not gullible to feminine charms. Maybe she had witnessed the crime. And, frightened, and knowing her own inability to help, she'd chosen to lure him here where the holy might grant her confidence.

He quickened his pace. For a few steps the dizziness he'd felt in the alley again threatened. He slapped a palm to the marble, finding it as cold as the outdoors.

"Where are you?" he called in a whisper. Incense hung in the air, and seeped into his pores, escalating the woozy swirl in his brain.

Two columns ahead, he spied long fingers dash out and coaxed him to follow. "Truvin," the soft voice sang.

What had she called him? Truvin? Not a name he'd heard before. Was it even a name? No, she must have said something else.

"If you saw what happened, you can help me. I need some answers," he said, and charged onward.

A welcome rage of heat fired in his core. He may not know who he was, but he did know that he would not be toyed with.

An angel stood in the doorway out to the narthex. Tall, lithe and gorgeous. Long hair streamed from her scalp as heavy as black velvet. The tresses glowed blue with flashes of candlelight, and there was a sparkle in her eyes, palest blue and washed with more ethereal white.

She wore white slacks and a fitted blazer of the same fabric. And those lips, palest pink—he must have kissed those lips. The feeling radiated deep within him, and it wasn't a random idea. He *knew* he had kissed her.

But what was her name?

"What are you playing, darling? Don't fright. I'm in no condition to do you harm. And I would not." Or would he? The fact he'd even said such disturbed, but briefly. "Did you leave me that note?"

She nodded, and coaxed him closer with a crook of a narrow forefinger. Then she slipped out of sight.

He dashed through the doorway and to the right. An elaborate iron gate opened to a baptistry.

"Do you know me?" he tried. "I'm sorry, but I don't recall. My brain's not working properly right now."

She glided backward, stepping around a freestanding baptismal font carved from a deeply veined pale marble. The water inside wavered. Curving around to the other side of the basin, she then stopped and merely stared at him.

A study in understated sensuality, her pale lips pursed, a perfect bow. Standing more than ten feet from her, he could scent her; it was different than the incense. A dark, musky smell topped with an even darker note of smoke and earth. Silently, she tempted. In a church, of all places.

Held in the angel's eyes, he disregarded suspicions of robbery, and moved toward the font.

"What did you call me? I can't seem to place my name."

"You don't remember?" Her eyes darted to look over his right shoulder.

He didn't hear the others come up behind him, yet the scent of aggression stabbed at him with an acrid tongue.

Arms wrenched back and behind him, heat burned along his shoulder blades as his muscles were stretched awkwardly. Two large men secured him. A hand slapped across his mouth to contain his shout.

As he protested and tried to kick backward, a man in a white cassock and white stole, Bible in one hand and his other raised to make the sign of the cross, appeared before the baptismal font.

"*Ego te baptizo in nominee Patris, et Filii, et Spiritus Sancti.* I baptize thee—"

What the hell?

Pushed forward, his face broke the surface of the water inside the font.

"—in the name of the Father and of the Son and the Holy Spirit—"

Grabbed by the hair at the back of his head, he was brought up, sputtering and choking.

He cast a watery sneer to the woman, but she merely dipped a finger into the baptismal waters, avoiding his pleading gaze. He wanted to shout, "Who are you people?" but the hand over his mouth held tight.

"I baptize you, Truvin Maximilien Stone."

And his attackers again plunged him forward into the holy water. His face hit the base of the font. His nose cracked. Were they going to drown him in a baptismal font? What kind of sacrilegious criminals were these people?

When he began to choke and swallow water, he was pulled up. Gasping, he spat and heaved in for air.

"May God bless you and keep you and make His face shine upon you," the priest pronounced. He then reached to make the sign of the cross before his forehead. "Go with God, until…otherwise inclined."

His aggressors dropped him before the font. He collapsed, groping for the edge of the solid marble bowl, but landed in a sprawl on his chest. Water pooled below his face. The icy chill of the outdoor air trickled across his wet scalp.

Spitting out water, he shook his head. Had he just been baptized? Forcibly?

"You've ten minutes, Truvin." The female voice.

Even while he fought with the craziness of the situation, he sensed action was required. The overwhelming understanding that he was in danger fired his adrenaline. He pushed up, staggered and began to weave between the marble columns, not seeing the dark-haired angel, but sensing she ran ahead of him.

"Then we come after you," she announced. "With a cross."

"With a—? What in hell?" Standing in the open doorway before the street, he touched the unreal terror that stirred his blood, and made him want to run.

Run? From what? A cross? But why?

"Run, Truvin," came the voice from somewhere above and behind. "Run!"

And for some crazy reason, he did.

Chapter 2

Short, black-lacquered fingernails caressed the air before pale blue eyes rimmed in thick black eyeliner. "The night is my haven," the young man announced dramatically for the camera focused on him.

The glare of the handheld spotlight glinted on the silver skull jewelry that wrapped the man's fingers, ears and both nostrils. "The shadows of midnight cradle me in acceptance and undying love."

"I thought the night was your hunting ground, a crimson torment of beating pulses and hot blood?" Lucy Morgan, who held the microphone, tilted a raised eyebrow over her shoulder to the camera.

Her interview subject, clad in black pants, beruffled black shirt, long black coat, dyed black hair and more pewter skulls and chains than you could shake a stick at, was a self-proclaimed child of the night.

"I gain acceptance through blood. Love equals sacrifice." He nodded solemnly, thick clumps of hair falling over his pale cheek. With both hands, he made the sign of the devil and crossed them over his chest.

Yikes. This assignment was getting too whacked even for Lucy.

"Great. Love it." Lucy tugged up the collar of her blouse. No, she wasn't afraid of getting bitten, but she wouldn't discount the chance of being gnawed by this ridiculous excuse for a vampire.

She swung around, her practiced on-camera smile dropping, and spoke directly to the camera. "Let's wrap this up. I've had enough."

"I thought you wanted to witness the blood exchange?" the child of the night begged as Lucy began to march toward her car.

Rich, the cameraman, followed. He'd parked behind her on the street out front of the Scarlet nightclub.

"Don't have the appetite for it tonight," she called to Mr. Tall, Dark and Deluded. "Thanks for the interview. Best of luck with your…" Your stay on the mental ward, she thought, but waved off the dismissal with a sigh.

To Rich, who snapped his digital camcorder shut and tugged off his earphones, she said, "I am so over this job. I'm a smart girl. I graduated from college. I can work mathematical formulas, debate the effects of global warming on climate and produce my own news spots. So why do I always get stuck with the wacko assignments?"

"All our assignments are whacked, Lucy. It *is* what the show is about."

Folding the handheld spotlight and tucking it away in the trunk, Rich accepted the wireless microphone from Lucy, who slapped it into his palm a little harder than necessary.

"Who proves myths to be myth, anyway?" she challenged.

Tossing her purse in through the open passenger-side window, she dug for her keys in the deep pocket of her wool houndstooth coat.

"We should be busting them. Finding the real vampires. Instead, I get Child of the Night over there who really needs a new dye job, and can you get any more cliché? Look at all that black. And the fake fangs? Want to bet he found those in a box of Count Chocula?"

"They were better than that chick at the bookstore last week. I could see the seams in the plastic on hers."

Lucy smirked and crossed her arms over her chest. Leaning against the back of her car, she stabbed the curb with the spike of her red-heeled Louboutin.

"I'm sorry, Rich, I think this is a wrap on the entire assignment. I've enough information to prove that vampires are a bunch of wannabes. Not that there was ever a way to prove them real in the first place. God, I hate my job."

"Yeah, but you look good on camera, Lucy."

"I couldn't care less about my appearance. Why am I not saving the world? Where did I take a wrong turn?"

She realized she'd slipped into poor-pitiful-Lucy mode, and quickly shoved that from her demeanor.

Standing up straight and peering over the muted black facade of the nightclub, she asked Rich, "You heading home to the wife?"

"Probably need to pick up some flowers on the way. This is the third day in a row we've done the night shift. I'll e-mail you the footage tomorrow morning."

"Thanks. I appreciate your help. Tell the wife I loved those blondie brownies she sent with you last week. See you at the studio."

Lucy slid behind the wheel of her red Audi and shifted into

Drive. The avenue headed toward home was a few blocks north, paralleling the now-defunct Soo rail line.

Scratching the nonexistent itch on the side of her neck, she signaled and turned into a residential section.

Despite the fact she possessed zero belief in vampires, she always felt crawly after interviewing a subject. A desperate soul-searching for a means to belong. For connection, even if that connection did mean a risk to AIDS and other blood-related diseases. Poor bastards.

"I am so ready to ditch this gig. Creatures of the night, rejoice! Lucy Morgan is no longer on your trail."

Though, she did have one more interview scheduled.

But after the rumor she'd heard in the office this afternoon, well…she was ready to give up the day job entirely.

Thing is, she wasn't sure what she'd give it up for. Philanthropy wasn't one of those jobs a person dived into without the funds to begin with. And yet, it remained a persistent goal in her life—to help others.

Right now, her life seemed in stasis. She'd been reporting for the local cable channel KSNW5 for two years now, after a one-year internship and a failed few years at getting a marketing career going. Sure, she had control issues. Turns out marketing wasn't exactly a job designed for individuals; it was more a group talent.

Journalism had been a fluke, really. Following a year out in the big world on her own, trying to kick-start her career, and after her mother's sudden death, Lucy had literally stalled. She'd had a tendency to focus solely on the goal, not noticing the world that moved around her. And then when her mother had died, she'd been forced to look beyond herself, to embrace the life around her.

An uncle had hooked her up with KSNW5 after she'd expressed a need to get back into the nine-to-five bustle.

Now, she occasionally hosted and did field reporting for the biweekly program *Myth: Confirmed*. Yeah, it was like that other myth-busting show on the major network, except they confirmed the myth instead of proving it to be a bust.

But recently, the station manager decided their small efforts were going nowhere fast. It hadn't been spoken out loud, but whispers seemed unanimous—*Myth: Confirmed* was going to be canned.

"After I gave them two years of stalking through forests in search of Big Foot and werewolves, and flipping freakin' buttered toast to the floor. And now vampires! I have spent three weeks on this idiot assignment," Lucy muttered tightly as she signaled and turned right.

Oh sure, that'll be an easy myth to confirm, she'd thought. As expected, her research turned up nuts, freaks and vampire wannabes. Not that she had thought to find a real vampire in the mix. And how would she really know?

The challenge to her assignments had once been making them fun, self-effacing and more than a little snarky. But she'd lost all enthusiasm for snark lately.

"I need…what do I need?" she muttered. "You don't need anything, Lucy. Think of those who really are in need. The homeless. The wounded and the sick. Tomorrow morning I'm going to find me a homeless guy and take him out to breakfast."

Okay, maybe she wouldn't dive in quite so fast. Small steps to start, like handing out ten-dollar bills to the panhandlers who stalked the intersections on Highway 94.

Admittedly, she was more a behind-the-scenes volunteer. She enjoyed working on the fund-raising committee for the Red Cross, and hosting local charity events. She liked the satisfaction of planning, organizing and seeing her efforts spark others to charity.

Swerving to avoid a poodle that jogged across the street—the white fluff ball blended smoothly with the snow plowed up a foot high along the curb—she turned sharply down a dark street and let out a cry when a blurry figure collided with the hood of her car.

Had she hit him? She wasn't driving more than twenty miles an hour, and—no, it was some joker. He'd slapped the hood with his fists.

"Get a life, buddy!"

He hit the top of her car now, and beat against her windshield. A microcrack fractured across the glass.

"Or…maybe I'll drive quickly away," Lucy amended.

Thank God, her doors were locked. She gripped the peridot rosary she kept wrapped around the stick shift. While not a bad neighborhood, it was a major metropolitan suburb—the loonies were everywhere.

Shaking her head and shouting, "No money in here!"—which was pitifully true—she drove onward.

When the passenger window shattered into a rain of safety glass, she slammed on the brakes—and then realized her mistake.

She had stopped just long enough for the crazy man to reach inside, pull up the lock, and open the door and get inside.

"Drive!" he shouted and reached over to turn the steering wheel toward the street. "Now!"

"I—" Wasn't about to argue when he growled at her. The guy could have a gun. She wasn't keen on taking a bullet. Who would help the homeless then? "I don't have cash. But you can take my purse—"

"Get this car moving!"

A dash of blood glistened on his forehead. He was wet and huffing, as if he'd been running.

Lucy stepped on the accelerator, not sure why she complied, but cursing her need to please even as her heart sank in dread.

Fingers wrapping about the steering wheel, she searched for strength. But her foot pressed harder on the accelerator and the car picked up speed.

"Left!" he ordered. "Quickly, they're after me."

"They? Who?"

It was all she could do to concentrate on driving, and not hit anyone. Though it was close to nine o'clock, there were kids bundled up in snowsuits playing in front yards beneath the streetlights.

"Do you need a ride to the hospital? You're bleeding. Are you homeless?"

"Shut up and don't bloody slow down."

"All right, but where are we—"

He grabbed her jacket lapel and twisted so it tightened around her neck. Lucy gripped the steering wheel, but her foot pulled back from the accelerator.

"Foot on the gas. Pedal to the metal." His voice was deep and angry and he smelled like blood and snow. "Someone's after me. I don't know why. I'm not going to hurt you—watch out!"

She hadn't realized she'd boarded the bridge that led to a stretch of warehouses along the river. The Audi broke through the wooden barrier. Airborne, the vehicle soared through the crisp winter night.

Lucy screamed. She grabbed for the man's arm, but he'd let her go. This was not happening.

She was going to die before she accomplished a single life goal.

The seat belt was stuck. Truvin couldn't release it, and the more he pulled on the belt the more it seemed to tighten. The car had landed in a huge snowbank, pushed up alongside the shore of a stream.

Total distance of the drop had to be less than ten feet, but he'd felt the impact of landing in every bone of his body.

The woman behind the wheel was unconscious. Or maybe dead? Her air bag had deployed and now it hung deflated over the steering wheel and across her lap. His own air bag had not deployed, but he was okay. Head hadn't even hit the windshield. Weird luck.

Or was it?

"What have I done?"

He could not be responsible for the death of an innocent. That wasn't—*he* wasn't that kind of person. As far as he knew.

He'd scared her by jumping in and demanding she drive him away from the goons who had been pursuing him through the streets of Saint Paul. He should have been more careful. Should not have gotten someone else involved. She would still be alive had he not commandeered her car.

There had been three of them; two men and the same woman he remembered from the cathedral, except she'd worn a long black leather duster and her hair had been secured behind her head.

Why had they been chasing him? It was as if they'd given him a head start...to what?

"Darling, are you all right? Talk to me. Please don't be dead."

A heaving gasp from her alleviated his worry. Alive.

He shook her shoulder, and then decided he shouldn't move her too much. Not until he could be sure she wasn't injured.

The snowbank had been plowed up from the parking lot below, sitting behind a stretch of warehouses. No streetlights. Not a populated area. It was likely no one had witnessed their accident.

Had they given his pursuers the slip?

"My...my car," she murmured.

"Good, you're awake. Don't speak," he said as he crawled up to sit on his knees and look her over. "I'm not going to hurt you."

He peeled back the air bag and inspected her without touching. No blood, but there could be internal injuries. Bruises across her forearms showed where the air bag must have hit as she braced for the fall.

"I'm sorry," he muttered, feeling it a miserable cop-out, but rattled, himself. "I was being chased."

"Who…who are you? Where are we? We went over a bridge!"

"And landed a snowbank."

She tilted a look out the driver's-side window. "We're not dead. I saw my life flash before my eyes. And it wasn't the least interesting." Wide green eyes turned on him and blinked, then her eyelids fluttered. "You're not hurt?"

"I'll survive. How are you? We need to get you home and cleaned up and warm," he said. "You live close by?"

"Is this the old crossing bridge?"

"I have no idea. There are a stretch of warehouses, and I think… Is that a dock out there?"

"Sounds like the bridge. I'm a few blocks away. Didn't anyone see us go over? Why aren't the police here?"

"Not sure. Do you have a cell phone?"

"Sent it in for repair a few days ago. We can walk to my house."

"Are you sure? Can you walk? Let me carry you."

She shoved away his hands. "Don't touch me. I can walk. I just…need to get my bearings."

"Right. Sorry."

Bearings. A grasp on reality. Something he couldn't yet accomplish. "I know the feeling. Just sit until you feel ready to move."

"Who are you?"

"Who are you?" he volleyed back.

She stroked a hand across her forehead, pushing away a thick spill of chestnut hair, and looked him over. Her pupils were wide. Dilated? Couldn't be a good thing. "Lucy Morgan. And you?"

"Truvin…Stone. I think."

She lifted a brow. "You *think?*"

Chapter 3

The light post in the front yard of the house across the street cast a blue haze across Truvin's hand.

Right now, he listened without trying to appear to be listening as Lucy talked to the police dispatcher on the phone. He'd remained in the same place since she'd invited him into her house, standing just inside the front door, which boasted a gorgeous emerald and azure stained-glass window.

Initially he'd been reluctant to cross the threshold, but, like a child being coaxed out from the rain, he'd relented at her insistent invitation. It felt strange to enter the home of someone he had forcibly, well, *almost* kidnapped. He hadn't meant to be cruel.

Was it because cruelty came easily to him?

No, he wouldn't consider it. The man he was, or should be, was not violent. He didn't *feel* violent.

But until he could grasp some bearings, he'd stand back,

practice politeness, and not get in this woman's way. He had to admit it felt comforting to be around another person who hadn't the mind to drown him in holy water.

What the hell had that been about?

Lucy explained to the dispatcher that she'd run off the road and over the bridge. The relief in her voice was obvious as she repeated that a tow truck would be sent out for her car. She gave her name and address and all sorts of information.

At his ankle, a cat meowed. Thin and slick, it flicked its tail, sneered a toothy, hissing growl up at him, and then scampered off.

Hanging up the phone, Lucy sighed. Attention focused on the black refrigerator door before her, she shrugged a hand through her tousle of hair. It was thick and shiny. Truvin found himself wondering at the exact color of the long curls as they tumbled down her back. Not really red. More a deep chestnut, like stained cherrywood.

When she turned, her heavy-lidded eyes held a weak glimmer. She had been through a lot this evening. "They're sending out a tow truck."

"I heard."

From her position in the entrance to the kitchen, she gazed across the floor. "This has been one of my more interesting days. And that's saying a lot."

"I didn't hear you tell the police a man had carjacked you."

"Didn't think it necessary. You were being chased. You were desperate. Hell, I would have done the same thing in your position. Heck of a lot of safety I offered, landing on top of a snowbank. Wasn't that a strange bit of luck? Whew. Karma is really working overtime tonight."

He nodded. Safety. What did that feel like?

Actually, it felt like this. Standing in a home that wasn't his own, but the cozy furnishings, quiet light and ambient scent of vanilla did make him feel welcome. And though he didn't know the woman, she was all he could connect to. And right now, connection felt safe.

Yet he felt unsure how to make things right, because they needed to be right. He could feel the woman's anxiety radiate from her, even at this distance.

"I need something warm to drink. Coffee, or no, chai. Want something?" she offered. "I've got rum. Pour a little of that in your chai and you'll be feeling much better in no time."

"I...er, probably should be going."

Lucy sorted through the kitchen cupboard and pulled down a round tin.

"And you," Truvin offered. "At the least you should go to the emergency room to get looked over. I've heard that having an air bag can be as dangerous as not having one. You've bruises on your arms. And you may have pulled muscles, or even broken bones."

"If I wasn't so tired, I'd probably do just that." She lifted an arm to examine the purple bruise on the underside of her wrist. "But there's the issue of having no vehicle to get me to the E.R. The walk from where we landed wore me out, so I think I'll sleep it off. Doesn't feel as if anything is broken, just bruised and battered."

"You could call a cab?"

She dismissed the suggestion with a wave of her hand. "I'm fine, really. What about you?"

She dangled a coffee mug from a long finger. For the first time, he noticed she stood in bare feet, rumpled gray skirt and a ruffled sleeveless green shirt that matched her eyes. Even if they were tired, her eyes reached out to him, offering an intangible warmth.

"You look—" she quirked a chevron brow that highlighted one gorgeous, heavy-lidded eye "—not as shaken as you should be after an accident. Did you check yourself over for bruises? I could swear you were bleeding when you jumped in the car."

Truvin swiped a couple fingers across his temple. No blood. Where his skull had connected with the bowl of the baptismal font, it didn't even ache. Must be all the adrenaline rushing through his system, numbing his pain receptors.

"Sit down," she said. "Please, I won't let you leave until you've had a few moments to relax and get your wits about you. I'll have you know I'm a reporter, and we don't let mysteries like this slip between our fingers. A strange man flags me down, jumps into my car and presses me to a high-speed chase? Who the heck was after you?"

The water faucet splashed on and she held the coffee cup underneath the stream.

"I have no idea."

Setting the cups of water in the microwave, she turned it on. Her fingers brushed the dirt smudges littering the ruffles that veed down her silk shirt—dirt from *his* hands.

It hadn't been an act of violence, his clutching her in the car, but one of desperation. He knew that instinctively. After the crash, he had feared for her safety. And he'd needed her help.

Really? Would he seek help from a woman? Didn't feel right. But how he knew that eluded him.

Sitting still was out of the question. Truvin paced before the sofa, hands shoved in his trouser pockets. *Truvin Maximilien Stone*. Quite the mouthful. And even unspoken, it was still a brainful.

He startled when the white cat pounced at his ankles. "What the hell?"

"That's Tabitha," Lucy called from the kitchen. "She's curious. Not a threat. So, how can a man be chased without knowing what the reason is?"

"I don't know. I…don't remember. Though I'm sure I was mugged. I knew that I didn't want whoever those nuts were to catch me."

"You should let me take a look at that abrasion on your forehead."

The microwave dinged and Truvin jumped. Yeah, he was skittish, and damp, and exhausted.

Lucy stirred the spicy powder from a tin container into the mugs.

"Smells good," he called from the living room.

"Chai. You can smell it all the way in there? Huh. It'll warm you up, and then you can be on your way. Sure you don't want a shot of rum in yours?"

"Go for it," he said. "Sounds good to me."

A few moments later, she carried both cups out into the living room.

Now that she got right up to him, he noticed how tall she was. And beneath the rumpled clothing, her body advertised a landscape any man would like to glide his hands over. Not a single straight line, all curves and rises and—what was he thinking?

She's been too kind to you. Don't muck it up now.

Truvin averted his eyes to the mug she offered him.

"Have a seat."

He accepted the mug, and a brown and gold cat jumped onto his lap. A wide-jawed hiss wasn't nearly so intimidating as the solid weight of the thing. "Another one?"

"Toast," she said. "Not a threat either." She patted the fat tabby on his generous behind and it sprang to the floor. "And Tony is around somewhere, but he won't come out of hiding when he knows there's a stranger in the house."

"And what's Tony's threat level?"

"Oh, it's up there."

"Right." Truvin sipped the chai. Felt good, the warm liquid spilling down the back of his throat; he could even taste the rum. Not bad. "So are you, like, the crazy cat lady?"

She smirked at his forthright deduction. He hadn't meant it as a slam. "I'm big on helping others. I…have a tendency to take in strays."

"I've noticed."

Lucy realized that she'd done it again. Taken in another stray. A much larger, and infinitely more handsome stray than she'd ever rescued from an alley or the tangled remains of a neighbor's abandoned volleyball net.

"How can you be so calm?" he asked, sipping the chai. "My irrational behavior could have gotten you killed. Both of us."

"But we are alive. It's water under the bridge now—oh, that was so bad, wasn't it? I can't believe I've just walked away from a crash. Maybe I'm high on the thrill of it."

Lucy settled onto the overstuffed velvet chaise and pulled a chenille blanket over her lower legs, bare, but for nylons. She sipped the hot drink and studied her guest.

His cheekbones were blades, his eyes jewels of an indistinguishable color, maybe blue, but with an intriguing glint of gold. A mix of blond and brown hair tousled about his head, short along the sides and longer on the top. Everything about his face was bold and inviting. A far cry from her gothic interview earlier, and thank the Lord for that.

"When you told me your name—" she leaned forward on the chair "—why did you say you *think* that's your name? You don't know?"

"They said it when I was in the cathedral—as if it was my name. Truvin Maximilien Stone. Though, it doesn't *feel* like my name."

"They? The people who were chasing you?"

He slid to the edge of the couch, and cocked a look toward the front door where the stained glass filtered in muted colors. Ready to dash? Not, Lucy hoped, until she'd gotten the scoop on his fascinating predicament.

"This is what I know," he said. "I woke an hour or two ago, sitting in an alley behind a building that might have been a restaurant. I don't know how I got there, or how I got this lump on my head. I'm sure I was mugged. There was a note stuck to my shoe. Told me to go to Saint Paul's Cathedral."

"And you…did?"

He shrugged. "Yeah. Bad move on my part."

"Huh. Where's the bruise?"

He touched his forehead. "Right here. Or at least, that's where it hurt. And it was bleeding."

"Yes, it was." Lucy leaned forward. "But now it's as if it was never there. Are you sure it wasn't higher up? Maybe in the hairline?"

Though the light was dim—she'd left the kitchen light on, which glowed into the living room—she couldn't see a mark on his forehead, save a bit of dirt. And she wasn't so bold as to touch him and look for a bruise.

Not yet.

Of course, he couldn't be in his right mind. He might have thought he'd felt blood, seen it on his hands, and if he'd been hit on the head, suspected that's where the blood had come from. And she, freaked by a sudden carjacking, probably thought she saw something as well.

"I feel as if someone is after me." His voice sounded so small, and not because it was, but because a palpable fear stripped it bare. "Hell, it's not every day a man wakes without memory of his life, is forcibly baptized and then veers off a bridge on a high-speed chase. Anyway. The name doesn't feel like it's mine."

"It's unique. I've never heard it before."

"Do I look like a Truvin to you?"

She smiled and cupped the mug in both palms. The rum worked wonders to ease her shivers and notch down the strange exhilaration of surviving the crash. "You do. Sort of powerful, yet thoughtful. That's what Truvin sounds like to me."

He tilted a noncommittal nod.

"But you said something strange. Forcibly baptized? You lost me on that part."

"That's the part that loses me, as well. So I go to the church, right?" He splayed his palms upward, long fingers, and one silver ring around his thumb. Sexy. "And there's this woman, gorgeous, long black hair—obviously waiting for me—who sneaks around the pews and tells me to follow her."

"Which you do."

"Which I do. Because, I don't know why. I don't know anything. And at the moment, I identified with the cathedral and maybe I had hoped the woman had witnessed the mugging. I felt like she could help me."

"You said she was gorgeous?"

He paused midsip and eyed her over the rim of the mug. Now, *there* was a sexy stare. Soft, yet intense. And his mouth. What kind of kiss could that full mouth deliver?

"Just wondering," Lucy said. She'd known the man less than half an hour and already she was contemplating how good a kisser he might be. Par for the course.

"She was pretty," he answered. "Sort of ethereal, in a way. Dressed fancy, but businesslike. Slim."

He tilted a look at Lucy, taking in her shape stretched along the chaise. "I think I prefer them well rounded myself."

"Because you know yourself so well right now?" She crossed her legs and eased her less-than-slim hips forward a bit to relax. "So this gorgeous chick leads you into the church and then…?"

"I'm attacked from behind and held over a baptismal font. A priest appears from out of nowhere and says the rites of baptism, and then they dunk me in the font. And the weird thing? The priest ended by saying, 'Go with God…until otherwise inclined.'"

The story grew more incredible with each word he uttered. Yet Lucy couldn't get enough. What a fascinating find. A stranger with a mysterious life, and handsome to boot! Who cared that he was instrumental in totaling her car, she wanted to hear more.

On the other hand, hadn't she had enough from the wackos?

Well, not the gorgeous ones. At least, not until she'd finished her chai.

"Then the woman said something like they'd give me a head start, and that I'd better not stop running." He settled back into the piles of decorative pillows on the sofa and wobbled the mug on his palm. "You got a clue about any of what I've told you?"

Invited to a mystery. Now this was getting better.

"The facts are sketchy. And if you don't know who you are, then that's going to make tracing your whereabouts difficult. I think the key is to discover what put you in the alley in the first place. Do you know where you were?"

"I walked around the Xcel center. There was a seafood restaurant close by where I woke up, but I didn't remark any of the building fronts."

"Hmm, could have been the Lighthouse. They have delicious mahimahi. But I've not heard of any vigilante baptisms going on in the Cathedral Hill area. Sounds so…"

"Fucked up. Sorry." He shrugged a hand through his hair. "Shouldn't speak like that around a lady. It just came out."

"I'm not breakable. And I can swear with the best of them."

"Until otherwise inclined," he said thoughtfully. "What do

you think that means? I can't imagine that's the usual way to end a baptism ritual."

"Does sound very odd. Almost as if he thought you'd stray. More chai?"

"Thanks, but no, darling. I think I'll be flying on this stuff for a while as it is."

"It does have caffeine."

"And rum," he said with a wink.

A knee-quivering, nipple-tightening morsel of a wink. Lucy coached herself not to sigh audibly. Was it getting hot in here?

"What time is it, anyway?" he wondered.

"Close to midnight."

"I should leave. It isn't right for me to intrude like this."

She stood and followed him to the door, noticing that he initially wobbled, but with a long stride found his pace. "You're not steady on your feet yet. You can stay a while longer. I promise not to give you any more caffeine, and I can put away the cats if they make you nervous."

"I really shouldn't."

He backed up to the door and Lucy stepped a little closer than was friendly—she'd learned the technique through reporting; always get close to the subject. If you invade their personal space there is an initial moment when they helplessly drop their defenses. Move in during that key moment, and the subject will spill all the details.

Here stood a handsome man. And Lucy, invading his personal space—and surprising herself in the process.

Handsome, yes, but more importantly, a lost man who needed help solving a mysterious evening. And she did like to help others. Especially strays. With a little love and tenderness, they could come back from just about anything.

But a forced baptism? She didn't know what to think of that.

"Where will you go? If you don't know who you are?"

"Not sure." He spread a palm over his chest, not stepping away from her blatant closeness, and perhaps curious about her intrusion. "I suppose I should return to the alley and look around for a wallet or some identification."

"Not a good idea. Whoever was chasing you might be lurking there, waiting for you."

"You're pretty up on your skulking about."

"I watch crime shows whenever I can. I know it's never wise to return to the scene of the crime so quickly. On the other hand, if you were robbed, if you go to the police they may have already recovered your valuables, which could provide answers to your identity."

"And what if my identity is featured on a wanted poster?"

She was about to say "impossible," but stopped herself. Just because he was handsome didn't make him a saint. And yet he could be an average citizen attacked and then...baptized. That was too weird to comprehend.

She'd always been a good judge of people, and this man was not a criminal. Criminals didn't wear expensive suits and worry that they were intruding. He was so lost even he couldn't realize how lost he was.

Stepping back, Lucy offered, "You hungry?"

He studied the white cat that curled about her ankle. "I think so. Maybe I could borrow a couple bucks from you to stop at a fast-food place?"

"They're all closed this late at night. What if I pop a pizza in the oven while I take a shower and then give you a turn at the shower, how does that sound?"

Truvin leaned closer. He smelled of dirt and ice thanks to their climb down the snowbank, as did she. Yet there was the slightest trace of perfume—incense, it had to be. From the cathedral?

His eyes searched hers. A few crinkles at the corners of each prompted Lucy to wonder at his age. "Why do you trust me? I could have gotten you killed."

"You weren't the one driving. I should have paid better attention to the road. I've always been pretty trusting. My downfall, if you look over my history of failed relationships."

"You've had a lot?"

"Don't we all?"

"Er...I...don't know." He winced, and she felt for his lack of history. The man had no memory of his past. It was too incredible to comprehend.

What she wouldn't give to obliterate a few months from her past, at least the parts that had found her talking to fake vampires and fishing for the swamp monster.

"Here's the deal." She strolled into the kitchen and pulled a pizza from the freezer. "I'm desperate for a shower after that graceless descent from the accident scene. And I'm starving. You watch the pizza while I shower, then I feed you, wash and dry your clothes, and send you on your merry yet mindless way."

She set the oven timer and slid the pizza inside, onto the rack.

"You possess a strange sense of charm, Lucy, you know that?"

"I've never been able to pass a stray cat without taking it in to feed for a few days. Which reminds me, when the buzzer on the oven sounds, look out for Tony. He likes to jump onto the stove top and peek inside."

One last look over the man who stood in the center of the living room casting a blank glance about, decided her. He was lost. He didn't know who he was. The least she could do was feed him.

But what sane woman would dare take a shower with a stranger in the house?

There was a lock on the inside of the bathroom door. And

she had Tony, vicious attack-cat extraordinaire, who was probably hiding under the bed right now, because he hated visitors.

"You can use the phone to call the police if you change your mind," Lucy said, and left a perfect stranger to his own devices while she went and got naked in the next room.

Once inside the bathroom, she shuffled through the top drawer and pulled out a small black canister of pepper spray.

"Just in case."

Chapter 4

Truvin noted the scatter of items on the kitchen table first off. A monarch butterfly had been pinned to a narrow sectioned board, wings spread and delicate antennae curling about the long pins.

"Butterflies. In the winter?"

A startling sense of familiarity surfaced. He traced the shape of the upper wing, knowing not to touch, for the scaled surface was very delicate. Something about the pinned insect spoke to him. But he couldn't grasp a reason why.

Everything inside his brain was so inaccessible. "Damn frustrating."

The night sky shone black through the window. His gaze moved over an assortment of potted plants on the ledge before the bay window. They weren't the usual leafy plants. Cactuses? Not many had spiky appendages. Succulents, perhaps. Did he have a green thumb, to know such?

On the short counter between the fridge and the stove top

a big clear plastic container held Kitty Nummies, according to the handwritten label.

Truvin glanced out to the living room. The white cat sat on the couch, its luminescent green eyes glowing at him.

"Tabitha, Toast and Tony," he muttered. "And…Truvin. Hell, she really is the crazy cat lady. And I'm one of her latest saves. Not that you didn't invite yourself into her life by literally kidnapping her, eh?"

He sensed the need to make an escape, to be alone and to sort through this eerie stall of memory he couldn't seem to kick-start. But she'd gone to the trouble of making him food—red sauce and cheese spiced the air—so he figured he shouldn't just disappear.

Truvin studied the melting mozzarella ooze across the pepperoni through the oven door. He wondered what pizza tasted like. He had no idea. Yet certainly he knew it was a popular food.

Hmm… He was hungry. But for what, he couldn't place. Seafood?

"You don't know who the hell you are," he said to the reflection in the black glass oven door. "What have you lost? Are you an arsehole or a good guy? Were you mugged or were you such a jerk that the attack was warranted? Do you have family?"

Did he really care? Not terribly. The question regarding family faded as quickly as he'd spoken it.

"One way of finding out."

He startled to find Lucy standing in the archway to the kitchen. She'd donned pink sweatpants and a clingy gray shirt that emphasized gorgeous full breasts. A gentle curve rounded her hips, and her legs weren't stick thin, but muscled with strength. Wet hair hung in thick chunks over one shoulder, the color of it twice as dark as when dry.

"Finding out what?" he asked.

"Let me see your hand."

Though he didn't offer, she clutched his left hand and looked it over. The connection shocked him, but in a good way. Nice to feel the warmth of another person against his skin. Was it because he missed it? Who usually held his hand?

"No ring," she said.

"You mean a wedding ring? Could have been stolen."

"Maybe. But the one on your right thumb is still there. Looks like silver." She rubbed the base of the ring finger on his left hand. "No indent. I know some married men don't wear rings, but you'd think there'd be an indent if you had slipped it off for...well, you know."

A blush rosed her cheeks and Truvin marveled at the burgeoning color. He wanted to touch her cheek, but couldn't summon a good excuse to do so. So instead, he pressed his free palm to his chest. Heartbeats thudded and he felt...not so much aroused as...awakened.

This must be what a first date felt like. Awkward, and yet every word spoken and movement made was something he wanted to record and save so he'd always have it.

"So maybe not married," she said. A little too eagerly. And now she held his hand sandwiched between both of hers, as if a keepsake. "Sorry." She dropped his hand.

Truvin twisted the silver ring on his thumb. A wedding band that he'd moved to a different finger? No, the size was wrong. "I don't feel married."

"You don't?" Again, eager. Such marvelous green eyes. Bright and clear. Bewitching.

"What does married feel like?" he wondered aloud. "And kids? Could I be a father? How old am I?"

"How old do you feel?"

Running a hand back through his hair, he took assessment. Sleek, but thick hair, tousled from his evening adventure. He couldn't be over forty, for it might be thinning then. Was he in his thirties? He felt…vigorous. Like he could run a marathon. And he had run from the cathedral, quite a distance, and at a good clip. Hmm. Maybe he was in his twenties?

"I'm guessing late twenties, early thirties," Lucy said. "You have the slightest creases at the corners of your eyes, but they are hardly wrinkles. Your skin is clear and healthy. And I bet that silk shirt fits so well because of the muscles beneath. But there are probably not a lot of twenty-year-olds who can afford such an expensive suit. Zegna, is my guess."

He smoothed a palm over the trousers. Yes, the weave was fine and even after everything he'd been through tonight, the fabric had not creased.

"Probably not American," she prompted. "I detect the slightest British accent."

"Really? You're the one who talks with an accent."

"Scandinavian. Very common in the Minnesota tundra. But back to you. Besides the accent, you're handsome," Lucy noted with another delightful blush. "You must have a girlfriend. Someone who may be missing you right now. You really do need to go to the police. They could search their databases, check if a missing person has been reported."

"True. But what if I'm a bad guy?"

"I don't get why that concerns you so much. If you don't have a clue who you are, why is the first thing to trouble you that you might have committed a crime?"

"I did carjack you. Doesn't bode well for my morals."

A shrug of her shoulder sifted some of her wet hair across her cheek. Truvin shoved a hand in his front pocket to avoid touching her. It was almost as if he could sense the pulse of her. Did he hear her heartbeats?

No. Had to be his own. No one could hear another person's heartbeats without skin-on-skin contact.

"If my mother taught me one thing," Lucy said, "it was kindness."

"Was?"

"She's dead. I won't see her again until after forever."

"After forever?"

"Yeah. She always made me promise I'd enjoy forever. Used to call me the princess of forever. There'd be plenty of time after that for reunions, meaning, I'd be in her arms again in heaven."

"Forever is a long time."

"Not if it's only for a lifetime."

The fat brown and gold cat thundered into the kitchen and did a base-saving slide into the cat-food bowl.

"Toast, mind your manners."

The oven buzzer rang and Lucy grabbed a pot holder from the counter.

"Just because I'm kind to a stranger doesn't mean I trust him. Even if you are bad, you don't know it, so I should have nothing to fear from you."

"Distorted logic at its finest. Most definitely the crazy cat lady."

"Yeah, well, I can't deny I like my strays. But it's not my problem if others don't get it. Is it so wrong to want to care?"

"Not at all. I'm sorry, I guess I'm being leery. Is that how I normally am? Leery? Who can know? And is this what my future holds? Forever asking questions, when I may already have an answer, yet I can't touch it?"

"Asking questions will be good," Lucy offered. "Maybe it will jar your memory. And eating. Tastes are good harbingers of memory. Sit."

He sat down and inhaled the garlic and pepperoni. Not an ounce of saliva to prove he wanted to take a bite. But this was good. A new adventure. Trying pizza.

"Here's a plate. I've Pepsi or apple juice."

"Juice, please."

"You sure?"

He shrugged. "It was a gut reaction to the choice you gave me. That's all I know."

Lucy placed a tall glass before him and slid onto the chair opposite his before the narrow oval table. After a bite of pizza she smiled and wiped her mouth. "A man without history. His brain so fresh and unmolded. I could do things with you."

He lifted a brow, giving it a lascivious waggle. Well, he wasn't dead, and flirting felt good right now. As if he was actually someone who knew what he wanted and why.

This new memory of connecting with Lucy felt playful and right. The levity served to relax his tight shoulders. *Just take it in. It's all new, so sit back and experience.*

"What's a Zegna?" he wondered as he lifted the pizza to his mouth.

"Designer men's suit. Italian. Very expensive. Check the inside of your sleeve."

He turned back the suit sleeve to reveal a black label sewn inside.

"What did I tell you? I did a short stint as a fashion editor at a local magazine. You're clean and shaven and it looks like you've had a manicure. Metrosexual."

"Is that something like homosexual?"

"Nope. It's a straight man who likes to take care of himself, and who spends a lot of money to do so. Nice skin, spendy haircuts, manscaping, fine clothes and lifestyle, you know."

"Actually, I don't. And I'm not even going to broach manscaping. There's nothing wrong with a man taking care of himself, is there?"

"Absolutely not. Just makes me think you might be rich. And that you can't possibly be single. My bet is that your honey is missing you right now."

"For what it's worth, I don't feel as if I have someone to go home to. I know I must have a home. But probably there isn't a honey."

"Good. Er, I mean, well, okay. So…good." She made a goofy face, then proceeded to eat, very seriously. "You going to try it?"

"Never had pizza before. That I recall. Here goes."

One bite of the pizza and he felt like gagging it up. Salty pepperoni slipped through grease. Bland tomato sauce–coated dry crust. It didn't taste awful; it just didn't taste like anything he wanted to put in his mouth again. Maybe he wasn't as hungry as he'd thought.

Truvin pushed his plate away and instead drank the juice. It was probably not his favorite, he guessed, but it served to wash away the pizza.

"So what do you do, Lucy? That is, when you're not pinning butterflies, or rescuing felines or being hijacked by crazy amnesiac men with a death wish."

"I'm a reporter for a local cable channel. KSNW5. Heard of it?"

"Last television show I remember is…hell, I don't remember any TV."

"You're not missing much."

"What sort of reporting do you do?"

She set down her slice and slid her eyes toward the plants on the windowsill. A silly tickle curved one side of her mouth. Truvin liked her profile, all eyes and lips and cheekbones. The curve of her jaw where it met her neck screamed for attention. A kiss. Long, lingering, and accompanied by a gliding lash of his tongue to taste her gorgeous freckled flesh.

"At the moment…" she said, "vampires. Please don't hold that against me."

"Vampires?"

"I'm with a program that confirms myths and legends. We

present the alleged facts for a certain myth being real, and then bust them to prove it's all a hoax. I've been researching the local vampire scene for the past few weeks, but today I found out the channel might ax the show."

"Vampires not a popular subject?"

"Actually, they're enormously popular. But we're competing with a much larger show that gets national viewing. And that show actually claims to bust myths. You know, prove they're real? Which is a hell of a lot more interesting than coming out and saying, yep, it's all a myth, like you suspected. So, our little program isn't necessary."

"I'm sure the vampires will be relieved."

"You're being snarky."

"So I am. What's snarky?"

"Eat, Truvin."

"I wonder what I do. Workwise."

"You've no clue whatsoever?"

Truvin paused from drinking and really connected to her gaze. "No."

Framed by newly dry springy curls of chestnut hair, her wide eyes drew him in. It was as if he could find something in there. Or was it that he needed so much, he sought it in every kind glance she gave him?

"You have the most incredible eyes I have ever seen."

"At least that you know, Missing-Memory Guy." She laughed and grabbed another slice. "I thought you were hungry."

"I am." He shoved back in his chair and, pushing up his shirtsleeves, clutched his arms across his stomach. "But for some reason that stuff doesn't appeal to me."

"Not a pizza fan, eh? I can make something else. Toast. A frozen dinner. Soup?"

"Don't worry about it. You've been far too kind."

"And now you're going to say you should leave."

"That would be the polite thing to do."

"Where will you go? Really, I wish you'd stay here for the night. Take a shower and sleep on the couch. I insist."

"I could be an ax murderer."

"Do you remember where your ax is?"

"Lucy."

"So I'm trusting. And maybe I'm a fool for it, though, I do have pepper spray in my back pocket. But do you want to know a secret about me?"

"I'm game." At the least he'd learn *someone's* secrets.

"I crave adventure. The unknown. And having a gorgeous man sit at my table and flirt with me is making me very happy. And, hey, you never know, I could have a concussion from the crash. I probably need someone to stay with me tonight to make sure I wake up in the morning."

"Sounds a little needy. Maybe I'm the one who should be careful of you," he said in a light tone.

She was harmless, he could sense that. Though, she did like to kill butterflies. And pepper spray? Ouch.

"My threat level is zero. Unless I'm provoked. Then I'm a nine. There are towels in the bathroom. I set some out. If you'll set your clothes outside the door, I'll get them in the wash, and you can tool around in a bathrobe. Deal?"

"I think this suit may require dry cleaning."

"I have Woolite. Not sure about the bloodstain, though. Did you bite your lip?"

She leaned forward to inspect, and Truvin touched his lip. Didn't feel swollen or bitten. In fact, to assess, nothing on his entire head hurt anymore. He couldn't even feel the egg on his temple he'd felt sure was there earlier. And hadn't his nose cracked when he'd been plunged into the baptismal font?

"Guess I'm a survivor," he said, a little uneasy, but not sure how to process the whole night.

Maybe she was right. What he needed was a shower. And some rest.

"I can make a doctor's appointment for you tomorrow," she offered. "For the amnesia thing. I don't imagine you remember who your doctor is?"

"Nope. But that would be nice of you. And I should stop by the police station. Okay, darling, I'll take you up on the offer."

When he emerged from the bathroom, white terry bathrobe wrapped around his body, Lucy greeted him with a weary yawn and pointed toward the living room.

"It's not a Hide-A-Bed, but I put some sheets and blankets on it for you." Another yawn. "I have some sweatpants I can offer you to sleep in."

"That would be great, darling."

The lights were out, save for a small lamp to the side of the sofa that put out a minuscule glow. Truvin wandered into the room, feeling his sense of displacement strangely absent. The dark and quiet settled his thoughts. Perhaps because he knew this place now. It felt safe.

Yawning, he was intent on sleep, and not worrying about the night's events until morning.

Another yawn preceded Lucy's return. She handed him a folded pair of plaid flannel pants. "You do have a girlfriend."

"Huh?"

"You keep calling me darling. Probably because you're used to calling someone else the pet name, don't you think?"

He hadn't realized he'd been calling her the name. "I suppose I can't rule that out. Do you want me to stop calling you darling?"

"No, I like it." Her sleepy smile was *that close* to luring him to actually touching her this time. Everything about her pleaded at him, heartbeats, warm scent and drowsy voice. "It's after midnight. Nearly three, actually."

"And you're tired. Thank you for everything, dar—Lucy. I promise I won't come after you with an ax in the middle of the night."

"I'm locking my bedroom door anyway. Gotta keep the cats inside. See you in the morning. I don't have to work tomorrow until late in the afternoon, so we can spend the day finding your life. Night."

He waved a little as she turned and with a whistle, called the white cat, which had been hiding behind the sofa, to follow her down the hardwood-floored hallway to where her bedroom must be.

"Finding my life," he repeated her ominous words. Sounded a monumental task.

How did amnesiacs get back their memory if they had no one who knew them to recite details of their past? It was too much to think about, and honestly, he didn't care.

He dropped down the end of the flannel sweatpants and tugged them up his legs. Fit loose, but they had a drawstring, which he tightened. His body was toned and he must work out, because his delts and pecs were defined and he had a decent six-pack.

Clean-shaven, and probably that was clear gloss on his fingernails.

He sat on the sofa. The thick quilts welcomed with a warm snug. But he didn't feel like sleep yet.

He reached over to turn off the lamp. The room went completely black for a moment, then moonlight streaming in through the blinds illuminated the edge of the sofa and the glass coffee table.

There were four paperback novels scattered on the table. Truvin reached for one. It wasn't difficult to read the lurid pink script in the darkness. *A Vampire's Heart,* read the title. And the others had equally sensational titles: *Night Lover, Love Me, Immortal* and *Dark Rapture.*

"She did say she was researching vampires. Strange chick."

But nice, as her mother had taught her.

How many women would invite a strange man into their home and give him berth on their couch for the night? Very few, he felt sure. And those that would were probably desperate or needy or—hell, what had he gotten himself into?

Rising, Truvin padded through the beam of gray-white moonlight and into the kitchen. It was darker in here and smelled like garlic and tomato sauce and Kitty Nummies. The pinned butterfly had been set beside the potted plants. He reached to touch a delicate wing.

"Butterflies. Fluttering away from…" He lost the thought. It was there, and then like the winged insect, gone in a flutter.

Strange. Had that been the beginning of a memory?

He stared hard at the orange and black monarch, willing the thought to return, but he succeeded only in a tight jaw.

Peering through the window, he could make out the shadows and curves of what might be a lush summertime garden retreat in the backyard. Now it was blanketed with snow. A stone faerie attempted to take flight from the center of a birdbath, but would not be granted freedom.

Smirking at his fantastical thoughts, he turned and, sidestepping the cat bowls on the floor, paused in the center of the kitchen. Staring down at the bowls, he marveled that he'd avoided them. Anyone walking through the room might have stumbled over them, even in broad daylight.

Curious.

Back in the living room, he wandered his gaze across the walls. The wall to his right held a glass-encased dragonfly and another a yellow-winged butterfly. Must have an interest in entomology. Or else Miss Lucy Morgan simply enjoyed killing small things.

Darling?

Why had he so casually used that moniker for his rescuing nightingale?

There was no denying he got a weird vibe from his hostess. Weird, yet beguiling. And why was that? She was gorgeous. Touching her became the foremost thought whenever she stood close to him. And he sensed she was single. Three cats. Zero men.

So why not touch?

Wandering down the hallway, he passed what looked like a yellow evening gown in a plastic bag, hung over the corner of a door frame. Must have plans to go out soon? He bet yellow looked amazing against her skin tone and with those electric-green eyes. And hugging those ridiculously tempting curves.

To his left, the hallway ended at a door. He paused when he heard a cat's snarl. If it made too much noise it would wake up Lucy. Probably not a good idea to repay his hostess's kindness by creeping about her house and listening at her door.

Backing up, Truvin returned to the sofa.

He settled in, covering his legs, then rubbed his temple. Being plunged into a font of holy water, and his blubbering underwater protests returned.

That was the strangest part. Had he—when he'd had his memory—arranged for a baptism? It was possible. Adults were baptized all the time. Had he never been baptized? Did he need to be saved? But why the violence and the obvious threat?

And yet his attackers apparently knew him, to name him during the baptism.

Who was the gorgeous angel whose eyes had seemed to glow as if an ethereal creature? He'd felt a connection to her.

You have kissed her.

Hell, he was tired. Tomorrow, he would attempt to learn who he was.

Chapter 5

Lucy spent the morning on the phone, verifying one final interview with a woman who claimed to be a witch who hunted vampires. Hell, she wasn't going to quit anything without at least finishing the project assigned to her. And a vampire slayer? How could she resist?

Rich had sent her the video from yesterday's interview, but she didn't open the file. Maybe this afternoon she'd have a few minutes to check it out. Right now she was on all-systems-go mode and determined to do some good for the stranger out in the living room.

The tow company called to let her know her car had been taken to the auto-body shop on Franklin Avenue. A call there discovered minimal damage to her car, but the undercarriage had taken a beating and a new muffler was a must. She'd have to arrange for a rental for a few days.

She canceled her appointment for a teeth cleaning with the

dentist; she could reschedule. That left her free to take Truvin to the doctor, from whom she'd secured an appointment for tomorrow afternoon. It was her own doctor, and she'd explained she might have an amnesia patient on her hands.

Dr. Schwan didn't specialize in neurological disorders, but she would do an initial examination and recommend Truvin to a specialist. She also recommended they go to the police. If the man had any sort of record, they might be able to identify him. The doctor followed that with a warning that she certainly hoped Lucy had not taken in a complete stranger.

Of course she hadn't *taken him in.* That implied allowing one to stay for a while. It had been less than a day.

Lucy considered calling the police station to report a possible *found* missing person, but then decided that was Truvin's call.

Truvin. She liked the name. It was original, and she couldn't guess at its nationality. Like the man. He seemed to have a British accent, but she couldn't begin to place it; it could very well be Irish or Scottish for all she knew. He appeared to be your average Midwesterner, make that gorgeous, possibly rich, Midwesterner. He could definitely make some bucks modeling for magazines should he not remember what he really did for a living.

Or maybe he was a model?

"You're a dreamer, Lucy," she chided her active imagination. "They don't get models here in Minnesota unless they're in rehab or making a movie. Just help the man to sort out his life, don't start picking out floral arrangements and ordering the wedding stationery."

Of which, she had a tendency to do too early in any relationship. Which also explained why her relationships were few and brisk. But certainly, she did know the exact stationery she planned to use should a wedding ever become a reality.

"You did teach the princess of forever kindness, Mom," she

said, smiling at the memories of her mother's laughter. "But you died too quickly to teach me dating skills."

Lucy had been fifteen when breast cancer claimed her mother's life. Fortunately, they'd had the period talk, but it hadn't yet progressed to boys and sex. "How can a girl have forever if she can't even get beyond the third date?"

"Maybe if she'd quit talking to herself…" Lucy answered her own angsting heart. "What are you doing? This is not about you, it's about him."

Right. Nothing would get done if she sat moping over her pitiful lack of love life. It was almost nine. Time to go scramble up some eggs and see if her guest was awake.

"Still sleeping?"

Lucy tiptoed over to the couch and looked over the stretch of limbs snuggled there. He wore no shirt and the old sweatpants she'd almost tossed because too much washing had shrunk them beyond hope for enclosing her thighs.

The man had no clue who he was. Completely moldable and free for her to do with as she pleased. Ah, such evil plans she could form. So what if there was a wife? Lucy suspected there was not. But how could someone so handsome *not* be attached to someone model-like and probably freaking like crazy right now because she couldn't find him?

As if Lucy could relate to missing a lover.

Sighing, she decided her decision to dump the day job was a good one. Some time off from reporting might be exactly what the doctor ordered, if it allowed her time to pursue a relationship.

His eyes flashed open. Truvin let out a panicked noise and gripped Lucy by the throat.

"Whoa! Wait," she managed to say. He cut off her air supply with an iron grip. "Tru-Truvin?"

He released her with a shove and snapped up into a pace

across the living-room floor. Long, lean legs moved him swiftly, a caged panther seeking escape. Pushing a hand over his scalp, he then exclaimed, "Sorry. I felt you were a threat."

Tilting her head to ease a palm along her neck, Lucy collapsed onto the couch. "That's the first time I've ever been considered a threat to a guy."

The caged beast stopped pacing. "You were right there in my face, and—sorry." He shook his head and paced into the kitchen.

Lucy heard the water flick on.

"I have a tendency to be snoopy," she called to him. "I'm curious about you."

He stood in the archway to the kitchen, one arm high against the wall. Water trickled down his face. He had no idea how nummy he looked standing there in the dull morning shadows. Tight muscles wrapped his abs, and his bare chest stretched into a long and lean torso.

"I should get out of your hair today."

"Only if you promise to return. I made a doctor's appointment for you, but not until tomorrow afternoon. Dr. Schwan is very busy, but good."

"What will I do until tomorrow afternoon? I can't stay here, Lucy. It's not fair to you."

"I'll decide what's fair."

She got up and slid past him into the kitchen. Nice move, Lucy, slide up close to the half-naked man with no memory. Give him some new memories to think about, eh?

"Breakfast?" she offered. The way to a man's heart. "And then later this afternoon, I have an appointment with a witch. You can tag along if you like."

"A witch? I thought you were doing vampires?"

"I am. This alleged witch claims to hunt vampires. It's kooky stuff, I know, but she might be quotable. And if she's not too wacky, I could get some good footage of her. Though, I promised Rich the day off today…"

"I thought you said the show was ending?"

"A rumor. But until it becomes fact, Lucy Morgan never gives up on an assignment, as bizarre and life draining as it has become."

"Life draining? That can't be good."

"It's the people. I think I've spoken to enough pale-faced Goths who wear vials of blood around their neck and hang around graveyards for a lifetime. I don't like to judge, and I don't. Heck, if there were real vampires, I would have a hard time believing they'd dress in black and live such joyless lives. I mean, if you had to survive centuries, you've got to smile once in a while, am I right?"

"No coffins for Lucy."

"Exactly."

"But evening gowns?"

"You saw the dress in the hall? I need to take that to the dry cleaner. Hosted a charity event for the Red Cross the other evening. Now sit down. I'm making breakfast."

Truvin strode back to the couch and plopped down, hiking his feet up on the coffee table. "I feel so useless. I should be doing something. Trying to figure out what's missing. But how do I do that?"

Lucy set a carton of Egg Beaters on the table, and then dug around in the odds-and-ends drawer for a spatula. "Can you type?"

"I have no idea."

Right. Lost his memory, Lucy.

"You could go online. In fact, we'll both do so after we eat. I can look up amnesia. See if we can figure you out. Then we can Google your name."

He was paging through one of her romance novels when she walked into the living room. Sprawled on the couch, his legs crossed and no shirt on—perfect pecs, don't look, Lucy—he looked as if he belonged on one of the paperback covers.

"You like these things?" he wondered.

"That *thing* is a vampire romance. And actually, they're research. I wanted insight into why they're so popular. What is it about a vampire that women find sexy?"

"Vampire romance." He sat up and set the book on the coffee table. "Isn't that an oxymoron? I don't understand how a bloodsucking creature who wants to bite you on the neck is in any way romantic."

"I would have agreed, until I read a few." Strolling back into the kitchen, Lucy pulled out a frying pan. "Women are attracted to the fantasy of a man who never ages, and who possesses a remarkable sexual appetite. It's the whole living-forever-and-having-everything-you-could-ever-wish-for thing."

Which, now she considered it, didn't sound so bad, if one ruled out the need for drinking blood. There was that.

"Sex with vampires? Lucy." He followed her into the kitchen and propped an elbow on the door frame.

"Hey, I said it was a fantasy. Fantasies are dreams that never come true, otherwise they'd be called reality, right?"

"You want to live forever?"

Lucy missed the burner with the pan, and made a great clatter. She couldn't take her eyes from the hard body stretched before her. He took up the whole doorway with his pose, arm stretched above his head and hip cocked just so. "No. I, er…I once did. When I was a kid."

"That's right, the princess of forever."

"My mother gave me the royal title." She shrugged and focused fiercely on the pan of sizzling eggs. "I lost both my father and my mother before I was eighteen. Guess I wanted the power to give forever to people so they wouldn't leave me. You know?"

"That's very sad. Do I have a mother?"

She smirked. "Of course you do. Everyone has a mother. She's probably alive. We've already determined you can't be that old."

He shrugged, dismissing the notion easily. "Pay attention to the eggs, Lucy. What? Do I have a strange growth?"

"You work out."

"You think so?" He stroked a palm down his abs. His perfectly hard, tight abs. He hadn't seen sunlight to judge the pale flesh, but that was expected here in the great tundra. Each of his fingers rolled slowly across the six-pack, feeling, mapping out the body as if for the first time.

Lucy would like a chance at that sensory mapping. Just one touch?

"Got any tattoos?" She tried to focus on the pan. "Any distinguishing marks that may tell us a little more about you?"

"Didn't check." He turned his bare back to her. "See anything?"

"No." Just a broad, muscled back that begged for her fingernails or a good tongue tickle. "No tattoos. Unless you've one on your ass?" She drew in the corner of her lower lip. Pretty please?

"Doubt it." Truvin sat at the table and assumed an easy sit, slightly relaxed, and one foot up on another chair. "You got any tattoos?" he wondered.

"I do. The month following my mother's death." She lifted her top to reveal the orange and black monarch tattoo on her stomach, to the left of her belly button.

"Nice. You like butterflies? Because it's hard to know for sure."

"Adore them. I plant my garden in the summer specifically to attract them. There are days I can sit out back and admire entire flocks for hours."

"And yet for as much as you love them, you also kill them."

She delivered an evil smirk. "That I do."

"Anything else I should know about your sanguine habits, Miss Morgan?"

"Only that I once snapped the head off a chicken. My grandma was trying to teach the princess that life wasn't always rosy. Sometimes you've got to snap a few necks if you want to eat."

"Again, sanguine, but strangely charming. You're a woman who can fend for herself."

"Yep." She stirred the eggs, suddenly tasting regret. If she could fend for herself, did that mean she'd never need a man?

She did want a man. *God, Lucy, when did you stop caring about yourself so much?* It's always been about everyone else. And somewhere along the journey, Lucy had forgotten to put herself on the list.

"What was the schedule for today?"

"Huh? Oh. I'm thinking an afternoon of shopping to get you some clothes. Is that okay?"

"I'm all yours. But I don't feel hungry for eggs."

"You didn't eat last night. Are you sure, or are you just afraid to eat the crazy cat lady's cooking?"

He chuckled. "Not at all, darling. Why don't you allow me to take you out for a nice lunch to show you my appreciation. Maybe my stomach will lure me to what I most crave."

"That offer would be lovely, if I didn't know you were robbed last night and haven't a penny to your name."

"And I'll take that as my cue to extricate myself from this conversation. I think I'll get dressed."

"I went over your shirt with Woolite and got most of the bloodstain out, but you need to give it a few hours to dry. Your suit looks good, too. At least I don't think I shrunk it. Feel free to use the bathroom and comb or whatever else you need."

"Thanks, Lucy." He touched her shoulder, pushing aside her

hair. "I appreciate your generosity. And I will make this up to you when I figure out exactly who I am."

"Even if you're an ax murderer?"

"Even so."

Chapter 6

After breakfast, at which, Lucy felt sure Truvin merely moved the eggs around on the plate to make it look as though he'd tried them, she invited him into her bedroom-slash-office to do some online sleuthing.

The room was huge, which is what had sold Lucy on this narrow little house in the Mac-Grove neighborhood of Saint Paul. It made up the entire back end of her house, which was boxcar-like in shape. Her queen bed filled one corner, while this nook held a desk, a file cabinet, her Mac computer and a picture window that looked out over the neighbor's crumbling brick garden wall but five feet away.

She settled into her office chair and motioned for Truvin to pull up the padded round vanity chair. It was pink damask, but he didn't comment.

The last time she'd had a man in her bedroom, well, it hadn't been *that* long ago, but it had been uneventful, to say the least.

Was it because she needed to control the outcome of every moment of her life? She couldn't be comfortable with a naked man unless she had that condom in hand, first off, and though the subject of past sexual diseases was distasteful, it was really for her own good. Talking about STDs while rolling on a man's condom did tend to turn him off.

Note to Lucy: chill.

"So—" she flexed her fingers over the keyboard and waited for the Safari browser to fire up "—amnesia."

She Googled the word and it brought up tens of thousands of hits. The first entry was Wikipedia—which she knew could be unreliable—but she read the first line anyway. "Amnesia is a condition in which the memory is disturbed."

"I could have told you that." Truvin tapped the LED screen. "I don't have much faith in these machines. Good old-fashioned newspapers and books are much better."

Interesting. "So you're an old-fashioned kind of guy, eh?"

"I guess I am. What's that?" He slid forward to study the screen, his knee nudging her thigh.

He leaned in, propping an elbow on the desk. The thick veins on his arms drew attention to the muscle. He wore her sweats still—and no shirt—because he was waiting for his clothes to dry. Had to get the guy some clothes.

Or not.

It wasn't every day a woman got to sit so close to a half-naked man. Or smell him. Lucy could only smell remnants of her mint soap on him now. But earlier, when she'd been scrubbing his shirt, she'd inhaled an interesting cologne caught in the fibers. It had a root-beer tinge, maybe sassafras?

Mmm, she'd take some sass with that fras any day.

Pleased with her lusty thoughts, Lucy was startled by a thunk of Truvin's knuckle to her forehead.

"Earth to Lucy." His smile flashed the whitest teeth. "I'm the one with memory loss, remember? Now focus."

"Right. What did you say?"

She read the term he pointed to on the screen. "Traumatic amnesia, associated with a hit or bump to the head."

"Sounds like me. Does it say how to get it back?"

He was so eager. It suddenly hit Lucy hard how displaced the man must feel. To not remember a single thing about his life? And what about that missing wife or girlfriend? Here Lucy was literally keeping the guy captive—no, that wasn't true. He hadn't anywhere else to go. He needed her.

Lucy straightened on the chair and lifted her chin.

"Lucy? Don't you feel well today?"

"Sorry." Just helping another stray find a life. And it felt good. She scrolled through Google. "I was trying to relate to how you feel."

"Lost. Angry. Freaked. Indifferent."

"Indifferent?"

"Yes, it's like some things don't really matter. You wondered about my family, but to be honest, I'm not all that concerned."

"Probably because you've an entire world to wonder about. There's too much to attract your concern."

He clasped her hand and brought it to his mouth, holding it there below his breaths. "You're very kind, Lucy. I was lucky to have stumbled onto you."

"You mean carjacked me."

"I'll pay you for the car repairs. Promise. I'm sure I must have cash stashed somewhere if you think my suit is so expensive."

"Don't worry about it, Truvin. I can afford it." A small lie. She had a vacation fund. And if cozying up to a handsome man wasn't considered a vacation, well, then sign her up for the workhouse right now. "You need more clothes. Maybe driving around the city might stir up memories?"

"It's worth a try. But your car?"

"I've arranged to pick up a rental in a few hours. After the interview, we've got a date at MOA, what do you say?"

"MOA?"

"Mall of America. It's a huge shopping center that attracts tourists from far and wide? Never mind, you probably had someone shop for you. Most rich guys do."

She clicked back to Google and typed in Truvin's name. "What did you say your middle name was?"

"They called me Truvin Maximilien Stone."

Not a single hit came up, though the screen did prompt to verify if she meant Truman instead of Truvin.

"That's depressing," he muttered. "I don't exist on the computer either?"

"If you were never big on technology, it's entirely possible you're not out in cyberspace."

She tried his name again without the middle name. Two miserable hits. "This one is, like…" She opened the page and scanned the list of names. "It's an eighteenth-century roll of villagers in an English town. It lists the name Truvin Stonewall. Hmm… Dead end. Well, if you don't exist today, you probably will if whoever stole your wallet goes on a shopping spree."

At his miserable groan, Lucy notched up the empathy level a bit. "Sorry. That's only if you were carrying plastic. You seem like a cash man to me."

"I do?"

"Yes, old-fashioned. Practical. Considerate."

Unreal blue eyes took in her features. It was as if he was scanning her, recording her for later reference. Lucy felt a blush rise. It spread down her neck and across her clavicle, prickling defiantly.

"You seem to know more about me than I know myself," he offered. "Do you have some ability to read people?"

"Only everyone else on this planet but myself."

Now he roved his gaze from her face and down her body. His closeness didn't make her in the least comfortable. Yet, to be studied so carefully didn't so much as scare her as loosen her within her skin.

Feeling the blush creep up her neck, Lucy blew out a breath. It was growing hot in here. And the stranger sitting next to her was probably more aware of that than he let on. But she couldn't look away.

Nor did he. Now she studied his eyes, the blue irises were speckled with a darker spot of amber. They were like cat's eyes, almost changing to gold with an intensity that made her think of a predatory stare from a beast waiting to pounce.

His nostrils flared. Lucy parted her lips.

"Your mouth is very sensual," he said. "Lush and pink."

Oh yeah?

Compelled, Lucy leaned in and kissed him. A short but well-placed kiss to his mouth. He didn't react, but he didn't need to. The connection sparkled in Lucy's chest. And that sparkle shimmered out to the surface of her skin. *Alive.* Is this what she'd been denying herself in favor of a career?

Silly girl, Lucy.

"Oh." She pulled back and suppressed a smile. "I'm sorry." The tickle on Truvin's mouth worked to flush her smile to the surface. "Oh, hell, I'm not sorry. I wanted to do that. And you were so close to me. You're...not angry with me?"

"Not at all. It was far too quick a morsel to even register a minor grudge."

And then he leaned in to finish what she had only begun.

Tentative at first, he glided his mouth across hers before pressing. Testing. Feeling. As if his first kiss.

And maybe it was. The first he could remember.

There before the hum of the computer monitor, Lucy

touched a sweetness she had thought lost to her. It wasn't about the world and all its needy homeless and strays right now. This kiss belonged to her. And Truvin. And it was a shame she couldn't see it through.

He's not yours. He could very well be married. Don't do this, Lucy. Do you want to risk the hurt?

The rental shop sent a courtesy car to pick up Lucy. While she was gone, Truvin donned the dress shirt and suit he'd worn last night. Lucy's efforts had proven worthy. There were no signs of the dirty ring around the pants hem from the snow. A faint trail of pink dashed down the front left side of the shirt, but he covered it by keeping the suit coat buttoned.

I was hurt, he decided. For where else would the bloodstain have come from?

Closer inspection in the mirror didn't locate a trace of a cut or wound on his head. He even peeled back his lower lip to check. Maybe he had bitten his lip?

Could he have possibly injured his attacker?

"I hope I gave him hell."

Scrutinizing his reflection, he unbuttoned the coat. Too fussy. Was he the fussy kind? The suit fit snug at the shoulders. The shirt had definitely shrunk a bit, for it tugged at the buttons across his chest.

"She's right, I do need some clothes." He flicked off the bathroom light and strolled out to wait for Lucy's return.

Running his tongue across his teeth—he'd borrowed her toothbrush, she'd never notice—he contemplated that brief kiss earlier.

It had been difficult to simply kiss. To not draw her into his arms and begin to slip off her clothing. The woman oozed a sort of pheromone that hooked into his flesh and compelled him forward. Yet, he had managed to keep the kiss only a little less than chaste.

And it all happened quick. There was no patience around Lucy. The woman was a reactor, not a thinker.

"Could use another of those kisses."

In fact, he felt sure he couldn't be married, for he sensed something akin to craving Lucy. The feel of her mouth against his had felt so new, exciting and surreal. It was as if he had never before kissed a woman.

To consider his situation, everything was new to him. Even brushing his teeth. The taste of the minty toothpaste had cut sharply in his nostrils. The swish of the water rinsing his mouth clean. And to shower, the water skimming his muscles, it was quite the exhilarating sensation.

It was as if he'd forgotten the pleasure of simple things along with his memory. Yet for all purposes he could function as a normal adult. Talk, read and dress himself. He knew right from wrong.

"I wonder if I can drive a car."

Perhaps a drive through the city would spark his memory. If he asked around at the businesses in the area where he'd woken in the alley someone might recognize him.

"Worth a try."

Outside, a car horn honked, and he glanced out the window. Lucy stood near the hood of a black Taurus, waving.

"Like one of those fifties sex goddesses," he said as he headed outside. "Gorgeously curved, red-lipstick smile and breasts bigger than a handful. Nice."

And then he checked himself. "I know about fifties sex goddesses?"

The afternoon was growing long, and the sun hadn't made an effort this dreary winter day. Truvin took in the passing landscape as Lucy navigated Grand Avenue. He hadn't argued overmuch when she'd suggested they leave the driving to her.

That way Truvin could keep an eye on the surroundings. See if something caught his eye.

She had been more than a little reluctant to hand over the keys. He'd give her that.

Her witch lived in a brightly painted Victorian house just off the main avenue. This part of the city was completely unfamiliar to Truvin, though he got a sense of its yuppie charm. Quaint, painted streetlights and high-end clothing boutiques and innumerable cafés and coffee shops paralleled him to either side.

None of the storefronts jumped out at him as familiar. Not even the Starbucks Lucy pointed out. No, he wasn't even familiar with—what Lucy explained to be—the most popular coffee shop in America. Which didn't bode well for his condition.

Either that, or he didn't do coffee. Which was entirely possible. Heck, if he was a Brit, probably tea was his drink of choice. Either that, or ale. And didn't a pint sound ducky about now?

"We're here. Want to sit in the car or come in with me?"

"And miss meeting a real witch?" Truvin opened the car door and sprang out.

Before Lucy landed on the top step, the front door swung open. Inside stood a woman who looked exactly as expected. A lacy black dress dipped to below her knees. Red-and-black horizontal-striped hose wrapped her long legs. An Andes ridge of silver rings climbed the edge of both ears, and one nostril. Unnatural blackest-black hair capped a heart-shaped pale face, obviously made so with powder and makeup, because even here in Minnesota the sun did occasionally pop out. Goth, to the nines.

Save for the fuzzy green turtle slippers on her feet.

Threat level: less than zero. It was her mental stability Lucy wished she had a read on.

Her voice was a kooky mixture of helium and aggressive need as she grabbed Lucy's hand to shake it. "It's so nice to meet you, Lucy Morgan. You know, Morgan is a common surname for witches? I did an article for *Witch* magazine on the craft and genealogy last year. Uffda, but that got a lot of e-mails. I felt like a star with all the attention. Oh, and who is this?"

Lucy tugged her hand from the *alleged* witch's grasp and stepped back to her partner, whom she was now glad to have invited along.

"He's a friend interning on the show with me, so I thought I'd invite him along to watch the interview process. Truvin, this is Midge Olson."

"Midge?" He offered a hand, and Midge shook it eagerly.

"Ya, you betcha." Her violet-rimmed eyes alighted and a brilliant smile cracked the black lipstick to reveal pale pink creases beneath. Even the turtles at her toes seemed to perk at Truvin's presence. "Come in, the two of you. I've hawthorn tea in the parlor."

"Hawthorn tea?" Truvin gave Lucy an utterly what-the-hell-kind-of-crazy-house-have-we-ventured-into look, and, gliding a hand along her waist, escorted her inside to the parlor.

Intrigued to have his teasing confidence at her side, Lucy was surprisingly relieved the parlor was more a little old lady's retreat, complete with white lace doilies on the red velvet chair and sofa arms, than a gothic torture mansion.

Not that she expected Midge to be of the torture persuasion. Lucy was open-minded about alternative lifestyles—at least, those that did not involve living naked in a forest or sucking blood for kicks. Wicca was a completely acceptable religion to Lucy, though her Catholic parents would turn over in their graves at such an insight. But real witches that could fly and cast spells with a twinkle of their noses or a snap of their fingers? Not so much belief in that.

"Truvin. That's an old English surname, don't ya know," Midge offered.

The witch flounced onto a chinoiserie chair, her tulle black skirts splaying in an artfully decadent manner. Were it not for the turtle slippers, Lucy felt the woman had a great witch thing going, as far as fashion.

"So this is all anonymous, right?" she asked Lucy. "I don't want to be named on the show. A witch has to keep her privacy. Uffda, the fallout if my elders found out."

Uffda, and ya, you betcha. A charming accent. Brought back memories of Lucy's grandparents, and summers spent at Lake Itasca fishing and camping. This may be the first Scandinavian witch Lucy had ever encountered.

Not that she chatted with witches on a regular basis.

"Of course, Midge. This is a preliminary interview to see if I can use some facts for the program. I want your spin on vampires and why you think they exist."

"*Think* they exist?" Midge set down her teacup with a clink and leaned an elbow onto her knee. She hooked a finger encrusted with a strange articulated dragon ring at Lucy to lean in closer. With a dramatic not-quite-whisper, she announced, "I hunt them, sweetie, so trust me, they do exist."

"How does one hunt a vampire?" Truvin asked. "With stakes and garlic?"

"That's good backup," Midge replied enthusiastically. "But for us witches it's easy, don't you know." She waggled a forefinger before her face. "It's all in the tip of my finger."

Oh great. Lucy's heart dropped. Another whack job. This one thinks she's Samantha Stevens with a death wish for vampires. Not that she hadn't expected something of the sort, but the tea service really had thrown her for a loop. Threat level soared up a few notches.

Lucy tilted back all the tea in one swallow. "Don't tell me, you zap them with your magical powers?"

"Oh, Lucy, you surprise me." Her accent was beginning to grate on Lucy's nerves. "I know this show confirms the non-existence of what you believe to be mythical creatures, but I had thought you were open-minded when we spoke on the phone."

"I am. And trust me, I want to hear what you have to say. But I own all eight seasons of *Bewitched* and—"

"Bewitched?" Truvin wondered.

"A ridiculous television show from the seventies that touted witches as domestic housefraus with over-the-top powers," Lucy said.

"And silly polyester dresses," Midge chimed in. "It doesn't work like that." She sighed, took another sip of tea. "All right, I'm only going to say this once, so you'd better take notes, because I don't repeat myself."

Lucy made a point of whipping out her notebook and pen from her purse, but she was already planning a quick escape. There were better ways to spend an evening. Shopping on the arm of a handsome man, being one of those ways. "Go ahead."

"Vampires and witches are mortal enemies," Midge said. "They've been so ever since the great Protection spell was cast in the fourteenth century."

"And what does that spell do?"

"It succeeded in making the blood of all witches poison to the vampire. The vampires were this close to enslaving all our kind, and some head witch decided she'd had enough. Thus, the Protection spell. Now all it takes is one little drop of blood—" she held up her finger and pressed the tip so the flesh deepened to crimson "—and *wham, pouf!* They're ash."

Truvin noticeably flinched and settled deeper into the doily-backed sofa.

"I see," Lucy offered, because that's all she could summon for such a far-out story.

"Wouldn't a vampire be smart enough to stay away from a witch?" Truvin posited.

"Of course! But how to know a witch on sight?" Midge's dark eyes twinkled. "It isn't so easy as making string-bean hot dish, don't you know."

Lucy held back a response that Midge's Goth attire wasn't helping in the Remaining Covert category.

"Isn't easy for a witch to find a vampire, either," Midge continued. "Heck, even vampires can't tell one from another without actually touching. It's called the shimmer."

"A shimmer of what?" Lucy wondered, now a little interested, even though she wasn't buying it for a minute. The girl did have a way about her, though.

"When two vampires touch they call it the shimmer. Supposed to be some kind of vibration that moves through their system and tells them they are touching one of their own kind."

"But a witch doesn't get the shimmer?"

"Uffda, no. A witch has to have the Sight to really see a vampire. Which, let me tell you, isn't something any of us has, or would risk having—save the one. And she's a real badass, you know what I mean? Sold her soul to Himself to obtain the Sight."

"Himself?" Truvin rubbed his palms over his knees. "Let me guess. Would that be old Lucifer himself?"

"You betcha."

Truvin flashed a knowing grin at Lucy. They were both thinking the same thing. Damn, but those blue eyes begged for some kind of surrender.

"Anyway," Midge continued, "the rest of us have to track

mortal victims of a vampire bite to then trail the vampire to his lair. It's tough, but satisfying to see them fry. As soon as witch's blood touches vampire flesh it sizzles and burrows deep into their system. It literally eats away their insides. It's very fast. *Boom!*"

Lucy and Truvin both jumped.

"They're ash within minutes." Midge picked up her teacup and swallowed down the contents, ending it with a sweet black-lipstick smile for her guests.

"I see." Lucy looked to Truvin, who delivered her the coolest, most utterly undisturbed expression possible, considering the circumstances. "So what you're saying is there is no proof a person is a vampire until they've done the deed of biting a victim, and that act has to be witnessed by someone?"

"Exactly." Midge picked up the teapot. "More tea? You're looking rather pale, Mr. Truvin. I've some lunch meat in the fridge. I can make a mean ham-and-cream-cheese rollup. Do you like pickles? Homemade lefse, too, don't you know."

"Thanks, but no."

"He's been sick," Lucy tossed in, seeing opportunity for escape. "I think we should be going. I do appreciate your time."

She stood, and when Midge grabbed her hand and turned it palm up, she tried to tug it back. The witch held firm as she traced the lines on Lucy's palm.

"An interesting lifeline," Midge said. "Split in two, but overlapping." She released Lucy's hand. "Two lifetimes for you, I think. You've a great adventure ahead of you."

"Does that include vampires?" Truvin said, unable to hide the smirk in his tone.

"Maybe." A secretive smile tickled Midge's lips. "Can I see yours, Mr. Truvin?"

With a shrug, Truvin splayed out his palm, which Midge

leaned over, but did not touch as she had Lucy's hand. "That's curious. The lines of your palm are worn. Kind of like my great-grandmother's hands. I could never do a good reading on her because of it. How old are you?"

Truvin tucked his hand in his pocket, and nudged Lucy to start walking toward the door. "Old enough to know palm reading is a bunch of hooey. Thank you, Midge."

Once back in the car, Truvin studied his palm. And Lucy chuckled out the laughter that had been pent up since meeting Midge.

"I'm sorry about that. It's not as if I expected something serious, but sometimes the subjects really do throw you for a loop. We should have asked for a blood sample, though, eh? Just in case we run into any vampires?"

Truvin didn't answer, because his attention remained on his palm.

"Must be lovers," Midge mused as the Taurus drove off. "I do love me a handsome British hunk. Though he could use some sun. And she's gorgeous, too. TV personalities. What do you expect?"

Shutting the door, and almost getting her turtle slippers stuck in the door, Midge tromped back to clean up the tea service.

Truvin's hand had been slightly interesting, but she'd seen hands without definite lines before—of course, they were usually the sixty-and-older set. Work, stress and lifestyle made people's palms very different.

It was Lucy's hand that had really intrigued. Of course, she'd seen two lifelines before, on others. But never overlapping, as Lucy's had. It was almost as if she would become two people. Split personality?

"Hope she doesn't get in an accident. And I sure hope she uses me as an expert on the show."

Midge bristled to imagine being on TV. Of course, it would all be anonymous. Maybe they'd film her in shadow. But she'd have to put out the word it was really her. Then everyone would know she was important. And maybe she'd gain some friends.

"Cool."

Chapter 7

"**W**hy do they call it the Mall of America?" Truvin wondered as he ambled down the crowded carpeted hallway, Lucy's hand clasped in his.

"Because it attracts all of America. They organize tours and even get whole flights from Japan to shop this place. Nuts, if you ask me. Right ahead is the men's suit store. High-class stuff, which I do believe is your style."

"I have no cash, Lucy, let's go budget."

"Don't worry about it, I've got this—"

Truvin paused before a store called Hot Topic and eyed a long black highwayman's coat hanging above a pair of glossy black leather boots. A white ruffled shirt snuck out at collar and wrist. "In here, Lucy."

He ran a palm over the coat, marveling at the silver buttons; they had little skulls on them, which he didn't particularly care for, but he did like the style and cut of the coat.

"This is so not you," Lucy said, even as he tugged the coat over his shoulders. "This store is for Goths, Truvin, and it's mostly teenage stuff."

"But I like this. Rather smart and it's heavy, so it would be warm for the weather." The coat sleeves fell to his wrists and the skirt of it didn't billow out quite so much as he would have liked, but it would serve. "And the shirt, too."

"You're serious?"

He leaned in and kissed her on the cheek. "Not my style?"

"Maybe I guessed wrong, but I don't think a man who wears Zegna would be caught dead in a store like this."

"Perhaps I'm turning over a new leaf."

The scent of her tempted him in for one more kiss to her cheek. He lingered. There at her jaw was where her scent was strongest. A delicious sensory repast to add to his memory bank, lacking as it was.

Lucy sighed. He'd won her over. He liked that she didn't seem to hang on to anything negative too long. Very easy-going, yet not a pushover.

Truvin picked out a few shirts, a loose white silk one, and a different black shirt that fit tightly and had a few buckles at the left side of the torso.

He handed the stuff to the salesclerk who wore more nose, eyebrow and lip rings than the jewelry display at the end of the counter.

"You should try on the corset, darling," Truvin said, pointing out the spiderweb-black corset that zipped up the front.

"I'll hold out for Victoria's Secret," Lucy said and handed over her credit card.

The Men's Wearhouse intrigued Truvin as much as Hot Topic had. He picked out an Italian number in a smoky shade of gray with the finest pinstriping. A fitted white shirt had to be taken out over the pecs, much to the salesgirl's delight. And the crocodile loafers contrasted to the black Doc Martens they'd picked up from a shop a few stores down.

Lucy's credit card was about two thousand dollars heavier, but she could manage it. So her vacation plans to Hawaii would have to be put off a few more years. It was worth it to see the satisfaction on Truvin's face. To know she was helping someone who truly needed it.

And what about yourself, girlfriend?

That was easy. Spending time with Truvin boasted her ego immensely.

Wait—you need a man to make you feel good?

She shook her head at her chiding conscious. She did not *need* a man. But what woman could deny it was fun spending time with one? As they walked he clasped her hand, as if they had done so a thousand times before. They were comfortable with one another. And there was no denying the burgeoning attraction she felt for him. He felt it, too. No man looked a woman so directly in the eye unless he was contemplating something more than a chaste friendship.

And they'd kissed! Lucy was ready for the next level, like a real intense make-out session. But she didn't want to push. It had to come at Truvin's pace.

He wore a gray cashmere sweater and soft black pants home, which Lucy was glad for. The Gothwear was sexy on him, but not so enticing as snug-fitting pants and a sweater. The way the material conformed to his muscles absolutely screamed for her to touch.

And maybe later, she would do just that.

On the way home, Lucy detoured toward Saint Paul's Cathedral. Truvin wanted to go inside alone, which was fine with her, because this wasn't a parking space. She intended to idle until she saw a cop, and then circle the block.

"Five minutes," Truvin said, and took off.

The man had the sexiest walk. Like a feline pacing the sidewalk. Each step placed center of his gravity, as if to keep his trail as narrow and inconspicuous as possible. It worked to sway him slightly as he strode, and gave him a confidence of self that would surprise the world if they knew how little the man did know of himself.

Threat level? Less than zero.

Threat of seduction? Off the charts.

"What are you doing, Lucy?" Catching her forehead in a palm, she drew her fingers down her face, dipping her littlest into the corner of her mouth. "Are you falling for a man whose only interest in you is shelter and clothing? It's been but a day!"

No, there was more between them. And while Lucy knew that Truvin might have a woman somewhere—hell, there could be a family—she couldn't deny her attraction to him. He'd lingered after that kiss to her cheek. It had been more than a polite closeness.

The idea of becoming the *other woman* had never appealed to her. Affairs were definitely not her thing. But this *thing* going on between her and Truvin didn't feel sneaky or forbidden. Which made her believe that perhaps Truvin was free for the taking.

Truvin slung his suit coat over one arm. Though Lucy had said it could go over the sweater, he was a little warm, and eager to breathe in the fresh night air. It was cold—in the twenties, as Lucy had remarked—but for some reason he couldn't summon a single shiver.

As he neared the cathedral, visions of last night, running frantically away from the great building, flashed in his brain.

And then the flash of something more disturbing stopped him on the granite front steps to the church.

Run, Truvin.

In his mind, he stared at the woman who had whispered that entreaty to escape. Long black skirts cinched at the waist fluttered across the grass. Her curling black hair fell over narrow shoulders. When last he'd seen her, she had been gasping for breath. Or had she been wearing white and standing behind the baptismal font?

Startled out of the visual reverie, Truvin cast a glance over his shoulder.

What the hell had that been about? It was almost like his experience last night, except with different costumes, and in a different time period.

"Like highwaymen and frock coats?" he muttered.

The jacket in the store had spoken to him. He'd felt comfortable wearing it. But that made little sense. And just now he'd had a flash of the woman he'd thought had lured him into the baptistery. But she'd been wearing an elaborate black dress, like something from Louis XIV's court.

"I must have a fascination for history," he muttered. It was the only explanation.

He stepped inside the cathedral, but paused when he heard organ music. The entire front of the sanctuary was seated with…mourners. "A funeral."

Not his scene. A glance to the left spied the baptismal font, secured behind locked iron doors. Truvin returned to Lucy's car.

"No luck?"

"I didn't want to interrupt the mourners. Can we swing down that block at the bottom of the hill? I think that's the direction I came from last night."

They did so, and Lucy found the alleyway where Truvin recognized he'd come to from being knocked out. They drove by the door marked 4D.

"It is behind the seafood restaurant," Lucy said. "Do you want to go in and ask around?"

The ambient beam from a streetlight shone across Lucy's face. The low-cut blouse she wore revealed cleavage that smelled warm and sweet. The closed confines of the car heightened the scent, and there it was again—heartbeats. The beguiling pulse of Lucy.

Truvin shook his head and looked away from the enticing sight. "Go inside? No." He'd lost interest as quickly as he'd vacated the cathedral.

It didn't matter anymore. He was here. Without memory. Yet, he was forming new ones. He may never discover how it had happened, and it was becoming less important that he did. Curiously, the most urgent thought to mind was how to go about getting another kiss from Lucy.

"Probably tomorrow will bring some answers," Lucy offered as they settled in her living room.

Truvin tossed the shopping bags on the floor by the couch. As if it was his little area. How pitiful must that feel? He could very well have a fine home to return to, and here he was, stuck living on some chick's couch with a few bags of clothing to call his own.

"I can't imagine how you feel," she said when he didn't reply, but instead took to pacing the room, as seemed to be his thing. "I'm trying to do what I can."

"You've been more than generous, Lucy. I feel utterly out of control because I don't know if there is anything to control. You know?"

"Control is good. Another difficult thing for me to imagine—loss of control."

He approached her, rubbing his neck in thought. "Is my discontent because normally I would be busy with a grand life right now? I feel as though I'm missing out on something important. Yet at the same time, I can dismiss that feeling with the snap of a finger. I really have no idea what I'm missing. Perhaps that's why I can't summon much emotion over the loss of it?"

Head bowed, he stood there a moment. Lucy wished she could take away his discontent. It was difficult to feel so helpless knowing that she had no right to feel this way when *he* was the helpless one.

So Lucy reacted again. "Truvin?"

The soft cashmere sweater glided under her palms as she drew her hands over his shoulders and embraced him. Her mouth moved onto his as if magnetically attracted. And he kissed her back, but too quickly, so he pulled away and pressed her against the wall.

"Truvin, I'm—"

He pressed two fingers to her mouth. "I know. You're not sorry."

"Why should I be? I like kissing you."

"You think kissing me can solve my problems?"

"No, I—"

"Neither do I." He tilted his nose aside her hair and Lucy distinctly sensed he was sniffing. "You smell good."

"I don't wear perfume. It's…just me you're smelling."

"Well, *you* smell interesting. Like snow."

"But snow doesn't have a scent."

"Oh, yes, it does. It smells like Lucy."

The hand that did not hold hers pinned to the wall had begun to glide over her hip, and up along her waist. He was…moving closer, becoming more interested in her curves.

Lucy's heart pounded. He nudged his nose along her jaw. The touch of his mouth to the corner of her lips shimmied gorgeous sparkles through her being. If she smelled like snow, then his kisses were as exquisite as a crystalline snowflake.

"You're completely unaware of your sensuality, aren't you, Lucy?"

"My sensuality? I've never..." He glided his lips over hers. Not a kiss, but a tease. "Well, I mean...uh..." Her? Sensual? No man had ever called her that before.

"You're far more beautiful than any of the butterflies you've pinned and consigned to hang upon your walls."

"Really? But I'm not..." Oh hell, the old excuses didn't come. And why summon them when it was apparent she didn't need them? This chick didn't need constant reassurance. She'd take a compliment the first time and run with it. "Kiss me, Truvin."

"I don't know what I'm doing," he whispered against her mouth. Vivid eyes flashed open to connect with hers. "I know nothing. Yet I feel everything when I'm this close to you. I don't need to know the who or what of me, because there's something more interesting to distract those thoughts. I want you, Lucy. I want...to taste you. You are winter."

"You think I'm cold and icy?"

"No, I think you're fresh and enticing. I could marvel over you for hours, but I prefer to dive in and experience the pleasure of you."

No tentativeness this time. Truvin's tongue touched the middle of her lower lip, and then slid inside her mouth with all the assurance of one who belonged there.

And he did belong. He felt right. He'd entered her life with a bang, and she had every intention to experience the adventure.

Skating her palms down his arms, Lucy touched the waistband of his velvet pants and hooked her fingers into the belt loops. She wanted to unzip the pants and touch him, feel if he was hard.

Moving too fast again, Lucy.

Right. Just…let this happen. Let him control the pace.

Long fingers pushed up through her hair, commanding her movements and holding her masterfully so that she would not be denied the kiss. Yes, relinquishing control was good. His entire body, strong and powerful, loomed over her, holding her there against the wall. Owning her, as if he owned his life.

"Everything is so new," Truvin said. "Like it's happening for the first time. Except this snowflake kiss. I've had it before from you, and I want it again and again."

Snowflake kiss? Take me now, you sweet talker!

"No two snowflakes are alike."

"I'd like to taste them all."

"Hold me, Truvin. Don't let me go."

"God, you're exquisite."

He bowed his head to kiss the rise of her breasts, where her shirt buttons strained against the buttonholes and revealed cleavage. Hot breath skittered across her flesh, causing her nipples to tighten. If he would kiss her there, lash his tongue across her nipples…

Lucy moaned. "That feels good."

He pulled back suddenly. Was that a wince?

"Is something wrong?"

"I don't know." He pressed a finger to his upper lip. "Might have a bit of a toothache coming on. Will you excuse me?"

He backed away, leaving Lucy clinging to the wall. Her fingers clawed, wanting to dig into the Sheetrock, because she required anchoring before her body literally lifted off and took flight.

Down the hallway, the bathroom door closed. Lucy let out her held breath.

"What an amazing kiss. A snowflake would never survive that heat. My God—" she slid her palm down her stomach and over her groin where every bit of her tingled "—if that would have gone on any longer, I think I might have come."

Closing her eyes, she pounded the back of her head gently against the wall.

"Oh, Lucy, this guy is the one to put all the rest to shame. Truvin Stone," she whispered. "Let Lucy Morgan be the only name you ever want to learn."

Chapter 8

Truvin swallowed the lump rising at the back of his throat.

The reflection in the bathroom mirror wasn't right. A funhouse prank of curved images and distorted truths flashed back a horrific image of the person standing before it. That wasn't him. Where did he—?

How did his teeth—?

Leaning forward, he touched the canine teeth that had seemed to lengthen as he'd rushed down the hallway, away from Lucy and that marvelous kiss. A soft wanting mouth on his, and soft, curvy flesh caressed in his hands. He'd been so hard and had been on the verge of crushing himself against her body to let her feel his want.

What a way to impress the girl. To run from a kiss?

But for good reason.

"Bloody hell," Truvin hissed, but kept his voice low. "This is nuts."

He turned his head, studying the teeth, and then gave each a wiggle. They were fixed firmly in his mouth. Which didn't help his own freak-out level right now.

Pressing his hands to the vanity, he leaned forward, hanging his head. A swipe of his tongue across the teeth felt the sharpened points. Made for piercing, as if *an animal.*

Or a…

I prove the myth a myth. You wouldn't believe the nut jobs I've interviewed. They actually believe they are vampires.

Oh, this was going to go over well with the crazy cat lady and her stack of vampire romance novels. Wouldn't Lucy love to see this?

"No!" Truvin fisted the mirror. It cracked. Silvered shards scattered across the sink. Large pieces shattered on the floor around his feet.

"Everything all right, Truvin?" The door opened. "I thought I heard—oh my God. What happened?"

Shocked that she would enter the bathroom so casually, Truvin realized he stared at her gap-mouthed. He closed his mouth, but the process involved biting his lower lip. A wince and a gaped jaw revealed his new weapons.

"You're…" She pointed at his face. "Oh my God…"

"No, it's not what you think. Don't come any closer. Get out of here, Lucy!"

He stretched his mouth, feeling a strange tingle in his upper teeth, as if a sharp sliver of food stabbed beneath the gums. The damn things were not going to rise back into the sockets, no matter how much he wished they would.

"You'll step on glass," he hissed.

"But Truvin, your—"

The scent of her fear wrapped around Truvin's body like a vise. Smoky and metallic at the back of his tongue. It pressed so hard he had to break free. And yet, a part of him wanted to lunge and grab her, to feed off the fright.

How twisted a thought?

"Your teeth!"

A frightened woman stood in the doorway, staring.

No, now that he really looked at her, not so much frightened, as curious. Behind Lucy, a cat hissed and scampered high-speed down the hallway.

Could he dash by her and rush out the front door to freedom?

A prick to his lip made Truvin jump. "Damn it." Blood swirled over the tip of his tongue. It tasted…not awful, but neither appetizing.

He took a step, but glass crunched beneath his shoe. What a mess—this unidentifiable life of his. "This is not what you think it is, Lucy."

Was it what he thought?

He grabbed a piece of the broken mirror to inspect his mouth. Two vicious white fangs hung from his upper gum line, where once he knew there had only been the rounded canine teeth.

"Vampire," Lucy whispered wondrously from over his shoulder.

He slammed a fist onto the stone vanity. "Don't be ridiculous. It's just…I don't know what it is, but it's not…that."

Pushing past her, he stalked out into the living room. Pacing felt appropriate. He should leave. That's what he did. *Leave. Stalk them, bite them and leave them.*

You remember. It was the blood.

Yes, he must remember. He was a—no. Impossible.

What kind of joke was this? A man gets amnesia, and instead of discovering his family and friends searching for him, he learns he's a creature of the night?

His only influence since he'd lost his memory had

somehow led him to this conclusion. Lucy had told him about her work. Those damn novels he'd been paging through. Possessed of a completely blank mind, he'd filled it with far-reaching fictional notions.

That explained it all. Except the teeth. They were real.

You know it to be truth, as you knew the woman in the cathedral. You are…

A vampire.

"Midge… The witch had no idea," Lucy said, still close behind him. "Of course, she said there's no way to tell a vampire unless you've the Sight. Or the shimmer! Truvin, do you shimmer?"

"Lucy, you're smarter than this."

"How can you attempt such convoluted rationality?"

"Me? I'm not the crazy one."

"Crazy?"

"Sorry, I'm…just a little put out at the moment. Do you see these things?"

"Yes. And how else to explain fangs? Unless they're fakes you stuck in to tease me?" She flicked out a finger and managed to tap one of the fangs before Truvin could pull back.

"Lucy? Stop being so cheeky! They're real, all right? Just don't get too close. I don't know what I'm capable of doing."

"You mean like biting?"

She stepped backward a few paces, and her hand slid up to clutch at her neck. Those wide green eyes twinkled with fascination.

How could she be fascinated when she should be… cowering, or…running?

"This is incredible," Lucy said in a loud whisper. "You're not supposed to exist. I know, I've done the research. I've interviewed all the freaks—"

"I am not a freak," Truvin muttered contemptuously.

"Right. Well, it's just a word. And I've read all the books, and watched all the docudramas. I know vampires don't exist. But I'm not stupid. Those fangs are real."

"Maybe I have a condition," he tried, but knowing it was a futile attempt to waylay her suspicions.

"Condition my ass. How to—? I've some garlic in the kitchen. We could see if it repels you."

"Please, do not—"

"Sorry." She put up placating hands. "That was tacky. But how to know? Coffins? Do you feel the overwhelming urge to close yourself away from the world in a small, contained box?"

"Lucy."

"Or stakes! I should find a stake and we could—no, that's a horrible way to test a vampire."

"Lucy!"

"What?" She stopped, clasped hands to her mouth, and a gleeful glint in her eye.

"You don't believe in vampires, remember?"

"I don't. They're…an impossibility. No living thing can survive on blood alone. And to never age? And to fly—oh! Do you fly?"

"Lucy."

"I know it's fiction, but what other explanation is there for your—ohmygod, now they're gone."

Truvin touched his teeth. Indeed, the canines had receded up into his gums, and now they sat in line with the rest of his teeth. They were even less sharp, it seemed, though they were quite pointy to the touch. More so than usual, but then, he hadn't paid much attention to his teeth the past twenty-four hours, so maybe that was usual for him.

"There's only one way to know." The solid pressure of her hand upon his shoulder prompted Truvin to reach up and place his hand over hers.

"I know what you're thinking, Lucy." Vampires bite people. She wasn't actually suggesting he bite her? "This is…suddenly this isn't funny. It's not a game or a stupid trick. It's…this might be real."

"I know."

Lucy stood so close. To possible danger. She may not think herself crazy, but the institutional are always the last to consider their truths.

No, she was not crazy. Very trusting. Too trusting, but not certifiable.

And he had to admit, her standing next to him, offering a weird kind of accepting support, kept him from a complete freak-out.

Could they possibly go back to making out and forget this ever happened?

Not likely.

She had called him a freak.

"You said you've interviewed people who believe they are…" He couldn't say the word; it got stuck in his throat like a burr poking sharply into a soft sweater. "What about medical anomalies? There must be some medical explanation for this."

"There's porphyria. That's an acute sensitivity to sunlight. The victims are pale and live in the shadows in fear of burns and scarring from the sun. But they don't need to drink blood to survive, nor do they have fangs or fear crosses and garlic, and—wild roses! I just remembered there's something about wild roses repelling vampires, too. I've some out back on the porch hanging to dry. I'm going to get them."

"Lucy, no! Just." He pressed up his palms and stepped back until his shoulders hit the wall. "Back off, all right? Give me some air to breathe here."

"Right. Backing off. Backing away from the vampire."

* * *

Awareness softened Lucy's excitement. She needed to consider this revelation carefully. That one probably shouldn't piss off a vampire.

Blessed Mary, a vampire? A real, bloodsucking vampire?

Just back off, Lucy.

Air. Right, he needed air. And quiet. A moment to consider this surprising development.

Surely, if vampires did exist—and Truvin was one—he would be compelled so desperately to drink blood, he'd have Lucy against the wall and be draining her right now.

Yikes. Lucy took another step back. If she'd been wearing a collar, she would have tugged that up to her chin. The man's threat level just rocketed off the scale.

Truvin dashed down the hallway into the living room.

"No, you can't leave," she pleaded. "You don't know what to do. Do you? Truvin, it's not safe out there. Someone is after you!"

He shucked her off and grabbed the long black coat from the end of the couch. The front door swung open to reveal moon-streaked darkness. "I'm sorry, Lucy. I have to be alone. Please try to understand. I…I don't want to hurt you."

"Oh. But. You would never—" Threat level, Lucy. It's real this time.

He lifted a challenging brow to her unflinching trust. How did she know whether he would hurt her or not? How could *he* know?

"Will you come back?"

He stepped down to the sidewalk and strode off. "Don't wait for me."

The phone rang as soon as Lucy closed the front door. Her mind frantic—she had been hosting a real vampire—made her drop the receiver. She fumbled for it. "Hello?"

"Lucy, it's Midge. There's a hunt tonight."

"What?"

Midge? The witch. Probably a *real* witch. Because certainly vampires did exist. Maybe. It had just been his teeth. There could be a perfectly reasonable explanation for them growing out to long pointed weapons.

Oh hell, what had happened to her carefully controlled and orderly world?

"Ah, er…hunting. Vampires?"

"You betcha. Me and a few other witches. I'd invite you along, but that would so not be cool. But you want to meet tomorrow morning for brunch? I might have some interesting information after the hunt."

"Yes," she answered automatically.

While her stomach churned, and her thoughts followed Truvin, fleeing—she had scared away a vampire?—she knew that what the witch could tell her might be important.

"Café Latte, eleven o'clock?"

"I'll be there."

To help Truvin.

Chapter 9

Y ou are a vampire. Be a vampire. This is what you know.

Know? He still knew nothing about his life, save for an innate acceptance that he was a man who lived on the blood of others to survive. That was enough to freak a man out for a good while.

It mattered little that he could not remember what he'd done for the past decades. Had it been longer? No way to know. Nor did it matter that he vacillated between an utter mental breakdown and a strange calm acceptance. Right now, hunger called.

And he instinctually knew how to answer that call.

Very little reluctance surfaced. In fact, a confidence that fit as if a lost skin arrived and fit into Truvin's being. His flesh tingled, an ache for sustenance. And his heartbeat raced in anticipation.

Stalking down the center of a residential street, he held out his arms, palms up, to catch the cold thick flakes that had begun to fall from the gray sky. The sun had set hours earlier, yet the streetlights were only now beginning to blink on. Snow cover across the yards and the falling flakes illuminated the landscape with a mysteriously haunting light.

The heavy highwayman's coat with the silver skull buttons flapped at his knees as he marched forward. He still wore the black jeans and cashmere sweater, but had donned the Doc Martens as the dress shoes had pinched.

A bit of a ridiculous image for a vampire, Truvin thought, the classic black clothing and menacing look. He knew it wasn't a requirement for his kind; in fact, most blended so seamlessly with the population it was startling to discover who among the mortals really were of *the dark*.

"The dark," he muttered, turning a corner that led into a cul-de-sac. Yet another fact he knew without question.

Witches called vampires *the dark*. And themselves, they labeled *the light*. He felt the terms derogatory and wrong, but he wasn't able to grasp the root of that rejection.

Ahead, a dimly lit garage attracted his attention. A woman stood up from bending inside an SUV, one arm wrapped around a brown paper bag. She was attractive, young and wearing a slim gray wool skirt and fuck-me pumps.

"A butterfly."

A pulse of heat gripped Truvin's chest. The hunger pleaded for answer. Nourishment. And in the form he preferred: pretty, young and female.

And while the surroundings felt so wrong—a neighborhood filled with cozy houses, families and minivans—a necessary craving carried him forward.

The woman startled as Truvin gained on her just inside the garage. "Oh, I didn't see you there. Oh." Wide brown eyes softened and a smile curved her mouth.

Truvin performed the method of calming his victims by using mental persuasion without thought or wonder to its method. He knew how to do it. Nothing startled him about this memory that forced him to feed. The vampire had resumed control over a mind that yet struggled.

The woman relaxed to the stranger standing before her. An initial reluctance shed as her jaw fell slack, and she opened to him. Blood rushing through her veins warmed the surface of her exposed skin and flushed her cheeks.

"Do you need help with that bag?" Truvin asked softly. "Allow me."

She released the bag, and he didn't grab it, so much as make sure it landed on the concrete floor of the garage without breaking open.

"Cold out tonight," he whispered.

Her neck was hot. He slid a palm along it and back to tangle his fingers in her hair. The connection briefly released the sweet rose fragrance of her shampoo before it died in the fumes of gasoline that lingered in the garage. "But you are warm."

"Have to bring in…"

"The groceries will keep, sweet. Such a pretty necklace."

She touched the pink glass beads strung along a silver chain. "My husband…"

"Will be wondering about supper. We must be quick."

She didn't protest, and in fact, tilted her head to the side, as Truvin leaned in to kiss her neck. He had not to even will down his fangs, for it happened at first touch of lips to skin. Biting into the thick jugular vein, he cradled the back of her head. At his intrusion she gave a small cry. But the persuasion slipped deeper, softening her to his command.

Truvin drank. This was what he had hungered for. Not pizza or eggs or apple juice. Blood, the sweetest drink. The only means to his survival.

He squeezed her breast, small, but the nipple rock hard. Had they not been standing outside, half exposed to the neighborhood, he might have considered a quick fuck, but he didn't need that right now. And he didn't have sex with other men's women. That was gauche.

So you know that, too, eh? Yes, the strange morality felt right.

When he was finished, and had kissed the puncture wounds and licked away the last droplet of blood, she slid from his arms. Truvin guided her down so she collapsed on the step before a door that must lead inside her house. A puddle of melting snow began to seep along the hem of her skirt. That weird little thing reminded him of waking in the alleyway surrounded by slush.

Who would mug a vampire? Had his attacker known he was one of *the dark?* How could he have allowed anyone to surprise him like that? It was so wrong. He was strong. The only thing that could overpower him was someone not mortal—but who, or what?

Had it been a wolf?

A wolf. It took but a moment for the knowing to fill his brain. It moved into him as slickly and fluid as the woman's blood had. Yes, werewolves. They existed, as did vampires. But beyond that, knowledge remained evasive.

And now was no time to wonder. Soon enough, the husband would come looking for this sweet snack.

Making a hasty escape, Truvin shoved the open car door shut as he exited the garage. He took the street in a run, and traversed a few snowy yards to put distance between him and the remains of his hunt. A butterfly stalked and pinned.

Reaching the edge of a park, Truvin shoved through a single row of snow-dusted evergreens. Pine permeated the air, crisp and unusual. He plodded into the center of an open area, packed down by the footsteps of children. Stone benches circled a frozen pond. He jumped to a bench and stood tall, pleased with this small accomplishment of memory.

Closing his eyes to the cool kiss of snowflakes, he swallowed the remnants of warm blood at the back of his throat. The vampire remembered. The vampire could again stalk the night for blood. He was...

...a creature without a past.

Mining his memory, he grasped for a flicker of reality, of past activity that would give him clue. Nothing.

And yet, he knew of witches and werewolves, and the very existence of *the dark*. Had it been because of the blood?

Sweet memories encapsulated within the corpuscles and cells and platelets that flowed like jewels down his throat and nourished his very being.

If it had been the blood, then he needed to find more.

Six blocks to the north, Truvin took another victim. A lonely woman sitting before the television watching a show about a vampire slayer. He entered her unlocked door, glided up behind her and tilted back her head before she surfaced from her blurred media haze.

She didn't scream. The persuasion crept easily into her thoughts. She wanted this, had dreamed of such an encounter.

Truvin stumbled to the back door and opened it. He settled onto the threshold and decided to go with the swoon, which was the incredible rush blood-drinking gave him. It warmed him. It seduced.

His victim lay passed out on the couch.

And he closed his eyes and slipped into a blissful state...

Bitter, thick snowflakes raged through the sky, making traverse on foot difficult. The wheel tracks were completely covered over, though he could not have been gone from the carriage for over an hour.

An hour spent in hell.

Ahead sat the damaged ride. Knowing she waited for him

was the only thing that kept him going. Cold enveloped his heart, and his flesh had lost feeling. Yet he could not pry from his mind the vision he had just witnessed.

Horrific. The thing of nightmares, and surely he would forever after envision the sight.

Earlier, their carriage had broken a wheel, and a horse had slid into a ravine. Fortunately, the carriage body had merely shifted, keeping him and his darling Anna safe. Not so for the coachman, who had fallen from his perch and landed on a broken elm stump. A wood shard pierced him through the heart. An evil thing.

He had not told Anna. Instead, he'd left her with explicit directions not to leave the carriage or look out the window. He'd covered the coachman with his cloak, but she would see if she looked.

A lesser horror to witness than what he had looked upon inside the small cottage. Less than half a league away from where the carriage had crashed, he'd seen the small glow of light and had decided to walk for help.

Anna had been upset that he was leaving her, but he had not wanted to take her out into this unforgiving weather. A fur cloak and a fine, wool dress, along with muff and hat, would keep her warm. This deep, loose snow was not fit to be traversed in a lady's delicate shoes, let alone a man's thigh-high boots.

Lifting his leg high, and slowly—for it now seemed a lifetime for every step—he stumbled forward. His gloved palms plunged into the snow, sinking him up to his elbows, and his face collided into the deceptively delicate surface of flakes.

A spot of crimson flowered in the glittering snowflakes. Not his own blood.

There had been so much blood!

He bit out a cry of despair that traveled upward through the

*barren birch stalks spiking the forest and out into the sky. What
he had seen!*

*Initially, he had not gauged the immensity of the situation
when he'd lunged into the great room of the cottage. He'd
thought them merely sleeping. Five of them—three men and two
women.*

*Frantic for Anna's safety, left alone in the cold, he'd
screamed for them to hear his beckon. Please would someone
accompany him to rescue his fiancée? Bring along warm
blankets and a horse so they may return her to the safety of the
cottage.*

*And then he smelled the scent of death. So abundant and
crisp, warmed by the hearth and filling every portion of his
being. And he saw the blood. Spilled upon the table and
dripping over fine clothing. Strewn in splashes across the
rough-hewn wood floors. And trickling down a bare arm to
pool in the creases of a splayed palm.*

*Blood had made the floor slippery. Blood everywhere. Blood
yet dripping from the wounds on their necks. A creature had
bitten them, ravished them and left behind their corpses.*

*Maddened by the horrible sight, he had stumbled backward,
caught himself in the open doorway and clambered out into the
wretched storm. He'd stood there, staring at the blood on his
hand. What had he touched? Everything had been splashed
with the wicked red substance.*

*Was the creature still here? Did it stalk the shadows for
more living prey?*

*He looked about as a rabbit darts its ears for danger.
Feeling alone and vulnerable in the middle of the snow-
blanketed yard.*

Anna.

*He turned to rush away, but the cold had chilled him deeply.
Numb with the freeze, his toes tingled. A lantern, yes, he must*

have one. Warmth to bring Anna, for he could not know how quickly he might find help.

A glance to the stable sighted the open doors. Deep hoof-prints beat a path across the yard. The horses all gone? Something had released them.

A predator would not do such a thing.

Forcing himself to stumble back across the threshold, he let out another cry as the blood scent put him against the wall. There, at his shoulder, hung an oil lantern flickering with flame. He grabbed it, and made haste.

Now, he struggled to hold the lantern high, away from the snow, for he feared snuffing out the light.

"Please be safe, Anna," he muttered through chattering teeth. "I am almost returned to you."

The carriage sat at a tilt above the ravine. He saw now that what kept it from falling into the deep ditch was a series of birch stumps, thick and obviously cut years ago. They supported the carriage at a forty-five-degree tilt. The door was open.

"Open?"

He trudged forward, but no matter his determination, he could not force his body to move faster than a crawl. The snow, so thick and loose, grabbed at his numb legs like quicksand. Perspiration brewed up by his exertion had frozen to his scalp and neck. The cold had fixed to the back of his throat. It made every breath sharp and painful.

A black boot poked out from the carriage door. It twitched, or perhaps dangled. It was not Anna's foot. Had the coachman—?

Landing the carriage, he grasped the side of the door. The glass cracked and crumbled away. Inside he saw his Anna—in the arms of a grinning bastard. Cloaked in black leather, and with eyes as dark as coal, he sat cradling Anna in his arms, his legs stretched before him, as if in repose after a delicious swiving.

Chapter 10

"You say there are dozens of real witches in the Twin Cities area?"

Café Latte was quiet after 8:00 a.m. Only a few tables were occupied with friends and lovers quietly chatting.

Midge smirked behind her cup of Earl Grey. "You say that as if you never believed I was real."

Taking the affront for what it was worth, Lucy held her tongue. Midge wasn't stupid. Though, anyone who pierced their lip five times—well, never mind.

"Belief has very recently become a strong component in my life," Lucy said. "Or rather, the need to question what I've thought to be solid beliefs."

Yeah, because when the guy you think you like sprouts fangs, well, then.

"Good for you. An open mind is a healthy mind. Taste?" Midge offered a generous forkful of her German chocolate cake.

Lucy refused but not because she didn't love chocolate. She didn't have much of an appetite, knowing Truvin was out on his own, so vulnerable, in his state of absent memory.

"So," Lucy said, "you do know the witches who have been hunting vampires with the priest?"

Midge choked on her cake. "I'd like to know how *you* know such a thing."

"You told me."

"About the hunt, but, uffda, I didn't mention a priest when you were at my home the other day."

Right. Because this was a suspicion formed from Truvin's details of his attack. Lucy was used to coming up with excuses off the cuff. "It turned up in one of my other interviews. With a vampire."

"You actually spoke to a real vampire?"

She shrugged. "Who can know? He didn't shimmer. Rather dull and gloomy, if you ask me. Are they that way? Morose and preoccupied with the dark and death?"

Midge shrugged. "I haven't befriended any lately to know."

"I suppose there are all sorts."

Including the ones with amnesia and a surprising penchant for highwayman's wear. It was almost as if Truvin knew what the vampire in him had wanted to wear.

"So, Midge, what does matter is that what this vampire suggested as rumor to me, appears to be truth to you. You know about a priest baptizing vampires?"

"Yes, but I'm not in that particular clique, if you will. We don't use the word *coven*. At least not in these parts. But you're not doing a show on witches, so that doesn't matter. Unless you want to?"

Lucy hadn't picked up on Midge's eagerness to be in the spotlight before, but now she couldn't miss it.

"You never know what the show will be offering in the

future," she said. A severance, she hoped. "Certainly witches would be a good subject, but they aren't myth, so that spoils the interview."

"Vampires aren't myth either. How are you going to report that one?"

"Leave that to me. About the priest—"

"Yes, there is a priest. They've hired him to do what only he can do."

"Why baptism?"

"Holy objects can kill a vamp. Slowly. Agonizingly." Midge drew out the word dramatically. "But they have to be baptized. Most older vampires are not baptized and will knock a cross from your hand as if a child's toy."

"Witches and a priest allying to go after vampires. Who would have thought?"

"That set of witches is very dangerous, Lucy. I suggest you steer clear of asking about or trying to make contact with them."

"But if they could lead me to evidence that vampires really do exist?"

Because now the story had become more than a quirky human-interest feature—it had become Truvin's life.

Midge leaned over her cake and whispered, "You're lying to me, Lucy. And I don't know why. You'll never report on this. No one would believe you. Nor can I figure what you want with a real vampire. Though I can guess." She sat back in her chair. "Immortality is not all it's cracked up to be."

"Are you suggesting I—? Want immortality? I don't think so." Though the princess of forever would have snatched the opportunity before it could flutter away. Lucy wasn't a child anymore. Life had become…controlled.

And yet—immortality? Hmm…

There were too many things to consider with this new

insight she had on Truvin. Should she fear him? Want to stake him? Befriend him as the women in the vampire novels did? Just how awesome would immortality be? But in exchange for drinking blood?

"Lucy?"

"Huh? Oh. I think this chat is over. I appreciate the information you've given me, Midge, and I wish you the best with…whatever it is you do."

As Lucy stood and shuffled into her coat, Midge grabbed her wrist. "I'll send you away with a blessing to be wary and wise when dealing with *the dark*."

"The dark?"

"Vampires. They're called *the dark* for a reason. And we witches? We are *the light*."

"Let me guess, the witches assign those names to both factions? What have the vampires to say about such a derogatory label?"

Midge gestured before Lucy with both hands, drawing them together at the top of Lucy's head and bringing them down to outline her sides.

"What was that about?"

"I'm giving you a protective white light. You can do it yourself, too. It works, Lucy. At least for you mortals. Just imagine a pure white light coating your very being. Start from your head and allow it to pour over your body all the way to your toes."

"Right. I'll leave the hocus-pocus to you and your…kind. *The light*, wasn't it? Thanks for the tea and the chat."

Taking the carpeted stairs down from the dining loft, Lucy glanced up once, but couldn't see Midge from where she stood by the doorway.

A white light for protection?

If anyone needed a white light it was Truvin Stone, recently recalled vampire. Lucy left the restaurant and drove toward home. Switching off the mindless rock 'n' roll station, she dived into her thoughts.

He was out there alone. With witches after him. Witches, and a priest, of all things. And their goal was very obvious. Why else baptize Truvin and send him on his way unless they wanted to deliver the most awful death possible?

What kind of vampire had Truvin been to attract such heinous trouble? Had he done something horrible to the witches? Knowing the little she did about Truvin, Lucy found it hard to believe. But what did she know? *He* didn't even know who he was.

Though he must now. He had accepted the appearance of his teeth as fact. Lucy had felt he'd argued with her only for show. So did he know who he was?

"Come back to me," she muttered as she turned into the driveway. "I want to help you, Truvin. You're vulnerable. And I'm…I'm what—?"

A nut to be thinking she wanted a vampire in her life. Over the centuries they'd been recorded as vicious, murderous creatures. Ugly, undead things that had stalked villages for blood. Bram Stoker had been one of the first to romanticize the vampire. And Anne Rice had really taken it to the extreme.

Was it because she'd studied the vampire so much that now she'd met a real one, she couldn't see beyond the myth? How stupid was that? There was no myth—vampires were real.

"Maybe you should let this go?" She stopped the car in the garage and sat there while the overhead light blinked, as it would for a minute after she'd parked.

"It's risky. And it's not at all what the station wants to see for the story. To come out and claim that vampires really do exist? Although, maybe what *Myth: Confirmed* needs is a shot of reality. Maybe we need to bust a myth every so often. How awesome would it be…"

Lucy sighed and opened her car door.

"No. Don't do that to him. You can't expose him for the world to see. Not like the world would believe anyway. Save the witches trying to find him. I can't draw a line right to Truvin for them to follow, that would be stupid."

Tucking her keys into her wool coat pocket, Lucy scanned the overcast sky as she walked the sidewalk to her front door. "Haven't seen the sun in days." Though why she worried, in the dead of winter, was beyond her.

Must be a boon for a lone vampire wandering the city, without memory of where he lived.

Sticking her key into the door lock, she turned and gave it a jiggle, usual procedure.

"Lucy."

Startled by the hiss from somewhere in the shrubs, she dropped the key. Before she could bend completely to grasp it, another hand claimed the key and pressed it into her palm.

Lucy wobbled, and found herself in the arms of a gorgeous blue-eyed vampire. He held her to his chest to keep her from falling over the edge of the stoop. Warmth from his body touched her everywhere she was cold. A strange thought occurred: Vampires should be cold, shouldn't they?

"Didn't mean to frighten you," Truvin said. "Can I come inside?"

"Truvin," she murmured, a little dazed by the beauty of his presence. His eyes were blue, but had they been so dazzling before? And his face, while she'd thought it a bit gaunt, though not unhealthy, seemed fuller now, robust.

Everything about him was…more.

Lucy shook the bats from her brain and, steadying herself on her feet, she then said, without complete command of her brain, "Yes, you are welcome to cross my threshold."

He smirked. "Thanks, Lucy. Don't mind if I do."

Chapter 11

Truvin shook snow from the shoulders of his coat as he entered the living room. He gave no care for the slush he tracked in on the bottoms of his boots. It hardly mattered to Lucy. It would melt and dry without a trace.

The vampire commanded the entire room, waiting for her to speak, but she was still in taking-him-in mode. His presence seemed fuller now. Stronger. Really here. And the coat went a long way to putting him out there as a larger-than-life figure. Hero stuff.

Only in the romance novels, Lucy. Snap out of it.

Right. She was a smart woman. There had to be a logical explanation for his behavior, and a logical reaction should that behavior prove he really was a creature of the night. Running and screaming wasn't allowed, nor was swooning.

So that left curiosity.

"You're okay?" she asked. She clutched her purse to her

chest, and her eyes wandered frantically up and down him. "You spent the whole evening and day outside? You...got what you...needed?"

"Blood. Yes, Lucy, I'm fine."

Blood. Uh-huh. "So, stop by a blood bank?"

His smile, so knowing, ended in a regretful sigh. "We can't drink soulless blood, Lucy. It does nothing for us, cannot sustain us. Which means, I can only drink from living human beings. No dead people. No blood banks. Not even blood samples taken from a live person. It's got to come directly from the vein."

She nodded once and dropped her purse and keys near the edge of the coffee table, missing, and creating a great clatter.

How awkward to stand in a room with a man she knew— and yet he was completely different now. Changed physically and filling the room with a greater presence than he'd ever had. One of her strays. And yet, a mythical creature stood before her. A vampire. No longer was he the helpless man who had charged into her life out of desperation.

The reality was so large and ominous Lucy didn't know how to react, so instead, she remained quiet. Feeling small beside one so large. And yet his apparent danger did not register as a tangible reaction. She could not begin to feel fear.

Was it so wrong to feel awe?

"I had to return," Truvin said, genuine concern softening his eyes. "Wanted to make sure things were all right between us. I didn't rush out last night to hurt you. I did it because—"

"I know you didn't want to hurt me. I understand. Been there, done that a dozen times before with nervous dates. Not that it was a date. You aren't beholden to me. You could have left anytime you wished."

Truvin bowed his head.

And she was rambling. So she was more nervous than she realized.

"So." Huffing out an exhale, Lucy focused. "Look at you. A vampire. For real."

"In the flesh. Not a myth about me."

"And you drank blood."

"Sustenance."

"Uh-huh. Okay."

There were no visible signs of blood on him. No crimson drooling from the corner of his mouth. Apparently only movie vampires were so careless.

She thought of the bloodstain she'd tried to get out of his shirt. His? Or a victim's?

Don't lose it, Lucy. Be. Calm.

"So, that must mean you have your memory back?"

He sucked in a breath, which lifted his shoulders and grew him even larger in the room. So powerful a man. She had not understood the virile strength in his carriage before when he'd strode about half-naked with a towel around his hips, unknowing. And now that he did know? Wow.

Threat level?

Lucy vacillated between a five and a ten.

"Actually, the memory isn't up to par. I know what I am. But I still can't put a finger to who, exactly, Truvin Stone is," he said. "I have no clue where I live, how I live, or for that matter, how long I have lived. Although…I did have a strange recall."

"Flashes of memory?"

"Yes. After drinking blood I saw bits and pieces of what must have been my life. So I figure if I get a lot more…"

"Your memory would return completely. Makes sense." She blew out an incredulous sigh. "In an alternate universe."

"Lucy, I know this is difficult for you—"

"No, not at all. I am a sensible, logical woman. You don't have to hit me over the head with obvious facts to prove a truth.

Though it will take some time. It's not every day a girl learns the guy she's invited into her home, and—ohmygod—made out with, might be eyeing her up as a snack."

"Lucy."

"I'm sorry, that was absolutely gauche." *She'd made out with a vampire.*

A tilt of his head changed his stare to a nasty accusation. Though he didn't open his mouth, she sensed he held back the need to flash her the deadly weapons. Because she deserved it. How cruel could she get? But she had never done this before.

How did one accept the presence of a vampire?

Lucy pushed aside her hair. *Yes, do something with your hands. Don't stand here like an idiot. Be casual. Chill.*

Right.

"So! Do you…want my blood?"

"I do."

Her heart dropped to her stomach. *Why did you ask?* Fool!

Truvin leaned over the coffee table and picked up a paperback book. "But, Lucy, if there's one thing I do know—" he thrust the florid pink and purple cover toward her "—I'm not this."

She took a step back, surreptitiously reaching behind her for the wall—or a weapon. *The villain struck over the head with a lamp, the heroine makes her quick escape.* "I—I know that."

"Really?" His sigh entered her, literally seeping through her pores and claiming the anticipation of the moment. "You must confess, part of you has this romantic idea of what a vampire should be."

"It was research, Truvin, I don't subscribe to falling in love with a handsome, virile, immortal…" Were any of those three items at all unpleasant? "Well, to be honest, the notion isn't that vulgar. I mean, immortality? Come on, who could ask for anything cooler than that?"

"The princess of forever?"

"That was a pet name from my mother. I've grown up. I don't think like that now. Though—" curiosity just wouldn't let go "—what must immortality be like? Pretty remarkable, I imagine."

"And for that reason I cannot trust your judgment, nor should you."

"I know you, Truvin," she spat out, feeling the argument more necessary than logic. "You're lost. You seek as much as I do."

"You know nothing, Lucy." The air in the room deepened, growing warmer with a sweep of his hand before her. The vampire found her gaze, and would not relent his hold upon her soul.

Yes, he touched her very soul. How else to describe the quickening that focused in every atom of her body? Had he the power to master her blood? Make her feel his presence within?

"Do you know I can smell your blood right now, Lucy?"

The idea of him knowing her so intimately was another of those not-so-vulgar fantasies. Lucy stroked her fingers across her chest. Goose bumps rose in their wake.

"It is innate and sweet and powerful. Cream stirred into cherries." His voice hypnotized, drawing her through a velvet darkness of sound. "I want to taste your blood, Lucy. To become engulfed by your life."

The passion of his words touched her from head to toe. Heat flushed her face. It wasn't a blush; no, this was desire. Every pore on her body tingled, opening for a new experience. Wanting. Wondering. Craving. *Come inside me.*

He wanted to drink her blood. He wanted *her.* And she had wanted him for too long—longer than she had known him.

Lucy stepped closer to the vampire, her hands rising nervously to her neck. She wouldn't meet his gaze, so Truvin tilted up her chin to get her full attention. "Look into my eyes."

"W-why? Can you hypnotize me?"

"I can persuade, but I won't do that to you, Lucy. I want you to know what it's really like. What your fantasies are not."

"I don't have fantasies. I take everything life throws at me with my eyes wide open."

"I want to believe you are being rational."

"Most of me is. Well, maybe half of me. Oh, Truvin, my brain is holding on for dear life, while my body wants to surrender."

Hooked upon his gaze, Lucy swallowed the heaviness she knew to be reluctance. She wanted this to happen. To experience. To know. "I want to help you, Truvin."

"Like another of your strays?"

"No, yes—no, you're not a stray. You're a man who needs connection."

"A connection to my history that you can't possibly offer me."

"Then let me give you something else. My God, I want you, Truvin."

"I believe that you do. But…" He held up his palm, fingers splayed before her face—but not touching—as if to draw out her energy, or perhaps infuse her with his. "I want you to want me because it is what your soul wants."

"Oh my God, yes."

"And what your body needs."

"Since the moment I took you home, Truvin. I've kissed you twice. Both times because it was what I wanted. To take from you." She touched his chest, splaying her fingers across the hard muscle beneath the sweater. "Take me, Truvin."

"And your mind…"

"Yes?"

"My reluctance overwhelms my rationale. I know your mind isn't ready for this, but—Lucy, darling, I need you."

Squeezing a fist—a futile effort to resist her allure—Truvin then let it go and threaded his fingers through Lucy's silky hair. Luxurious, it slid over his hand liquidly.

How many times before had he enjoyed a woman's embrace? Many? Few? Was he monogamous or did he play the field? The answers wouldn't come, so he'd have to begin his own experiments.

The more blood you consume, the more memories you regain.

She matched his kiss. Not gentle. Urgent, fired by a need that must surprise her, for her willingness even startled Truvin.

Yet her overwhelming acceptance, so absent of late, felt real and right and so needed. Were she thinking with her whole brain, and not influenced by the heady thickness of desire that tends to cloud any person's intentions, she might have pushed him away.

Maybe.

Lucy was unique. Everything was black and white. She leaped and then, later, looked back. If she wanted something, she took it. And he did admire that about her.

Truvin swept her closer, taking pleasure in how her breasts curved against his chest. Her hips collided below his own, his erection blatantly obvious. He coaxed her forward to crush her thigh over his wanting ache.

This was good. And, it was just a kiss. A hungry prelude to—

"Truvin?"

Her fingers wandered to his mouth. Nudging them aside, he then noticed the blood. But he didn't see it immediately, no, he smelled it. Fruity and thick. On the tip of her finger. On her lip.

You've cut her. With sharp fangs.

Withdrawing, Truvin couldn't pull away because she gripped at his forearms and held him. And he didn't retreat because the connection of bodies and the heat and the utter hunger for her would not allow him to relent.

"Christ," he muttered. "I…Lucy…" He poked out his tongue, tasting the faintest trace of blood on his lip. Yes, sweet and full-bodied, just like her. "You should get away from me. Right now. Go…I don't know, drive far away. Go to the cathedral."

"I'm not leaving you."

"Then go get that cursed rosary of yours."

"It's in my car, still at the shop. I don't need it, I—"

"You don't know me. You cannot care so much for a man—a blood-hungry vampire—Lucy! Get…" He clutched her shoulder, squeezing the soft hair and wondering how fragile she might be. The lush fruit of her blood coated his sinuses. The back of his throat felt dry, so desperate for liquid. "Run. Please."

She did not.

And he was no longer in the mood to encourage her to flee. He'd given refusal a shot. Now, thirst must be satisfied.

Diving forward, he shoved away the hair from her neck and pierced the vein with both his teeth. A spurt of hot blood felt right, as if he had done this a thousand times before.

And he had. He knew it as a man knows his own breath and heartbeats.

Lucy's cry of pain did little to discourage his actions. It frenzied him more, made him eager to quench a need. Didn't matter if the blood would enhance his memory; right now, he simply wanted. And it was a want far deeper and visceral than that for sexual pleasure.

Drawing out his teeth, he sucked the blood from a vein, supporting her across the back and at the same time coaxing her hips close to his. To be inside him, to flow through his life, to feed and nourish him.

"Yes." The tiniest whisper sounded at his ear. Long fingers clenched his shoulders and back. And a moan, full and vital, vibrated in her throat and against his hand. "Truvin."

"Lucy, darling." Dizzied by the blood and his claiming of the spoils, the swoon encompassed Truvin unawares. He dropped her. She slipped to the floor at his feet.

Straightening, he grasped out for support but didn't need it. He wavered, coiled in a wondrous rush of sexual energy and utter satisfaction, compounded by victorious elation.

How he could have ever forgotten something like this was beyond him. And even as he relished the success of the moment, he dug deep, seeking another flicker of remembrance.

The vampirism fit, but it did not give over completely. He could accept, but still could not understand *how* he was this creature, or who he was in this world.

And as the swoon subsided, he remembered the woman at his feet. Curling down, he lifted Lucy into his arms and carried her over to the sofa. Conscious, she smiled drunkenly as he brushed aside the hair from her face.

So eager she'd been for him to bite her. Not horrified, as he knew his victims usually were, or at least, until he seduced them and persuaded away their fears. Lucy Morgan was a strange beast, herself. What with her romance stories and free-spirited nature. So open to that which lay beyond the normal. So eager to please.

Truvin traced the bite wounds on her neck. The torn flesh allowed blood to still seep. A cruel bit of work, that.

"Does it hurt?" he asked.

"It aches a little, but when you were drinking from me, oh, Truvin, I think…well, no, I know, I, um…"

"It's like sexual release," he filled in for her, knowing it was the one pleasure he allowed his butterflies. There was no sense to stealing nourishment when the favor could be repaid with what amounted to a miniorgasm for the victim.

"For you, too?" she wondered.

"Pretty close. Not so explosive as the real thing."

"No, not at all, but not bad." Flushed with the afterglow, she grinned and sighed. "Not bad at all."

"I'm sorry, Lucy."

"For what? I'm none the worse for wear. Probably only a few cc's short. Can you remember more?"

"I need to concentrate, to see if more memory will return. Be quiet and rest. I'm going to lie down, see what comes to me."

He left her and wandered into the bedroom. Truvin collapsed on Lucy's bed as the visions blurred his reality and showed him a glimpse of a wretched past.

"She was delicious," the man pronounced with sated glee.

Anna lay—lifeless—in the arms of the stranger. Blood pearled from her neck.

"Would you like a taste? She is still warm."

Enraged, Truvin pushed himself up from the snow and lunged into the carriage. He fitted his hands about the man's head. The bastard retaliated by kicking Truvin with such force that Truvin actually flew backward a great distance, landing in the snow like a sack of discarded turnips.

And in the next moment, the creature was upon him. A leap, and he landed in a crouch over Truvin's prone figure. Menace glittering in his eyes, he flashed a fanged and bloody grin.

What means of creature was this? Was that Anna's blood dribbling from his mouth?

Truvin's body hummed with anger. A spill of Anna's white damask skirts pooled over the carriage floor. Blood spattered the pristine white. A glimpse of her void eyes, staring at him, and the blood about her neck, lifted a shout from his gut. "Bastard!"

Where he found the strength, Truvin did not know. But his aching, frozen limbs suddenly warmed and he was able to punch the attacker in the chest. The force made the man cough up blood, which spattered Truvin's face.

Swiping his vision clean, Truvin kicked and landed a solid

*knee to the man's gut. It was difficult to push upright in the
thick snow, but he managed to lever his body to stand.*

*"What are you?" he asked, but not wanting to know. Not
caring. Yet, he required some explanation to the atrocious
nightmare. "Did you kill those people in the cottage?"*

*"I did." The man licked his lips, and without seeming to
have to push up, he brought himself to a stand. As if drawn up
by invisible strings.*

*Otherworldly, came to Truvin's mind. Not right. A demon,
surely.*

*"As I did your ladylove." The intruder bowed, sweeping the
skirt of his coat grandly, and then nodded toward the sky. "It
is the moonlight, you see. Makes me a lunatic. I am not responsible for my actions."*

"You fiend! You should be locked up!"

*"I was." He shrugged up his leather greatcoat, and then
spread out his arms. This revealed the pale blue silk frock coat
beneath, beaded down the center with huge diamond buttons.
"But they set me free!"*

*"Anna, my darling…" Truvin turned to the carriage. But
he was lifted from the ground and landed a tree twenty paces
away. His back hit the solid trunk, and he collapsed upon the
snow. The sections of his spine screamed with a vicious pain.*

*To the side, the oil lamp hissed yet, the flame extinguished
from the wet.*

*"What are you?" Truvin gasped. He closed his eyes to the
cloying smell of blood breathing against his face. "A demon
from hell?"*

"Not so spectacular as that."

*The man straddled Truvin in a curious crouch. Had he toyed
with her before killing her? Please, no.*

*"I—" the man whispered in a tone that conquered the chill
in Truvin's limbs, and made him take a breath "—am a vampire."*

"I believe it," Truvin murmured. Now he opened his eyes. A nightmare grinned upon him. "Finish your murderous rampage. Kill me."

"Now, that is the coward's way out, good man. You don't want to face the truth? That you could have saved her?"

"I should not have left her alone."

"There was not a thing you could have done to protect her. Had you been at her side, I would have tossed you across the ravine and murdered her as quickly while you struggled through the deep snow to return."

"What do you want from me?"

"Do you really want to know?"

It could not be good, whatever twisted notion it was that glimmered in the depths of the lunatic's eyes.

"I wish—" the vampire crept up close so his lips brushed Truvin's cheek "—to share the nightmare."

His body lifted, Truvin was pulled to his feet. It happened so quickly, he only registered the piercing of flesh and the strange rush of surrender as blood flowed from his neck. It lasted a moment.

It lasted a lifetime.

Dropped unceremoniously at the vampire's feet, Truvin felt he could now close his eyes and surrender to death.

But he was not dead. And he could not keep from watching as the vampire stalked to the carriage and dragged Anna's body outside.

"Unhand her. Have respect!" Pulling himself to his feet, Truvin trudged through the now-apparent trail to the carriage. "She is mine!"

The vampire dropped Anna into Truvin's arms. "And so she is." He tilted aside her head to reveal the wound, which still pulsed out reddest blood. "Still warm, as I've said. You must drink now, Truvin. You must!"

Chapter 12

Truvin sat upright on Lucy's bed. He shook. A fine sweat tickled his scalp. A miserable cry stirred at the back of his throat, but he did not allow it to voice.

"I did not protect her."

The horrid realization felt as if it had just happened. He shivered from the cold. And he shivered because Anna was dead. His sweet, darling Anna.

His first love. He *knew* that. But how long he had carried her death in his heart he could not summon. The clothing he had worn in his dream could be hundreds of years old—he wasn't sure of the time period.

Now he knew how he had become a vampire. A bittersweet memory, for Anna's death had been cruel and undeserving. He'd not drunk from her that night under the moon. Instead, he'd carried her over his shoulder for five leagues until he'd reached a small town. There, he'd procured a coffin for his fiancée, and later, a victim for his hunger.

His creator? Mad to the bone. But not a person Truvin had been able to immediately walk away from.

Part of the puzzle had now revealed itself. A wicked memory, but a memory, and that was most important.

Previous disinterest in his past was replaced by a burning desire to know. Because he'd had a glimpse, and now he wanted it all.

He stalked back out to the living room where Lucy sat on the couch, a blanket wrapped around her shoulders. Gorgeous, disheveled and still smiling from the swoon.

Lucy lay nestled on the sofa in the quilts Truvin had slept on the previous night. A dreamy comfort enveloped her. She'd been bitten by a creature she had never imagined could be real, and though her neck did hurt, what followed after the initial bite had been too incredible to argue a little pain.

She fluttered open her eyes and looked up at her lover.

Not your lover. You didn't have sex.

But it felt as if they'd done something sensual and intimate and—ah, hell, it had been a form of sex. Truvin had been inside her, albeit with his teeth.

"Hey," she offered. "What's up?"

A stroke of his hand across her hair sent a ripple of desire to focus in her groin. Lucy purred.

"This is what I know." He paced before the sofa, sleeves pushed up his strong forearms to expose thickly veined arms.

"The whole baptism thing?" He spoke as if he was working out his memory on the fly. "If a vampire is baptized, then the holy can be dangerous to him." Pressing a finger to his temple, he paused, and then nodded. "Yes, that's right. In fact, any holy object that touches the flesh will burn it, and the wound will not heal. It'll eat deep into the vampire and eventually kill him."

"Truvin, that's awful." She wouldn't mention she'd spoken further to Midge. It wasn't important right now.

"Yeah, it's not a pretty thing to witness. But I, apparently, was not baptized. Until the other night. Whoever decided I needed to get some faith, well, I'm not so sure why that happened. Who would know that about me? And why be compelled to make that change? Was it one of *the dark* or *the light?* Or something completely unrelated?"

"It's the witches working with the priest."

He shot her a curious look. "If that be true, why wouldn't they have tried to kill me immediately following that ridiculous ceremony?"

"The sacrament of baptism is not ridiculous."

"I know, I know, I'm sorry. I didn't mean that. You have to understand, religion has probably persecuted me and kept me from seeking any sort of faith."

"Are you sure they wanted you dead?"

Truvin paused in the center of the living room. A splay of his hand. The silver ring on his thumb glinted. "Why would they *merely* want me baptized?"

"So you'd fear the holy?"

"Makes sense, but doesn't explain the trouble. To give me a healthy fear of holy objects? It's a bitch, to be sure, but not the end of the world. They gave me a head start, Lucy."

"Maybe they wanted you to die a slow, painful death." She cringed into the blanket. Just saying such a thing would not make it true, but she hated to know it could become true.

"That makes sense, too. A suffering death for one they fear. Damned witches. They hunt us, you know."

"So you remember more now?"

He winced. "Yes, and no. Some of those things I say are

facts. Like I know them without thinking, but the *why* remains elusive."

"It'll come. It's just amazing you're getting some memories back. Isn't it?"

"Yes. And no. I also know I hate witches. And it frightens me that I can feel such venom for another person."

Truvin remained in the center of the room. Strong and powerful, yes, but he also looked so alone. More alone than when he hadn't a clue about himself.

"A witch can kill me with but a drop of their tainted blood," he continued. "Which begs the question—why the baptism when they could have taken me out with their blood? A witch has merely to spit upon me…"

He toed aside the jacket he'd let fall to the floor sometime during *the biting*. A renewed shiver of desire tickled Lucy's skin to think of their incredible embrace. *You let a vampire bite you.*

Yeah, and I loved it.

"This all still confuses me, Lucy. There's something more, I can feel it, but I can't…grasp it."

"Sit down. We'll think about this."

"No, I've been inactive long enough. It's time to start figuring this all out. To be decisive. I will not be pushed around by witches who've allied themselves to the very Christianity they find revolting, and who think to toy with me as if a cat batting about a mouse."

Drawing up her legs, Lucy wrapped an arm around them and nestled her head against the pillow. He was so handsome. Forceful. Strong. Sexy.

Hers. For now.

Could she really claim him? He could not make a claim to knowing himself, so how dare she?

She glanced over the romance novels on the coffee table. True love never came so easily. At least, not in her world.

And yet, she was now living it. What kind of hero stalked the floor before her? Was he a hero? Or was he a horror-novel vampire, promising a bloody and vengeful denouement?

No matter which of the two, fact remained: Truvin was being hunted. The poor man. What must that feel like?

"In less than a day my beliefs about vampires have changed," she said softly. "They do exist. And witches, too. Who would have thought?"

"Yes. And werewolves and faeries and all those fantastical creatures the novelists write about." He tilted a look down at the books on the table. "We don't do pink, that's for sure. It is ridiculous to sell a deadly creature like the vampire in such a manner."

"Deadly. Right." Lucy choked back a swallow. The wound on her neck tugged, but the sensation of it pleasured more than pained. "You have to tell me everything. I want to know what real vampires are like."

"Shall I wait while you get out your video camera?"

"Truvin, I promise this is all off the record. I can't include any of this in my story. Who would believe me anyway? It's apparent that real vampires survive because the common man would never believe the truth."

"Then why do you believe so easily?"

She gestured toward her neck and the aching bite marks. "Hello."

"I'll give you that." And a smirk lit in his eyes. It was an unguarded moment of mirth that Lucy found irresistibly attractive.

Hell, what was she thinking? Everything about him was irresistible, else she'd not given it up so easily to a man she'd known briefly.

"There's not much more to tell," Truvin began, pacing unmindfully before her. "Truvin Maximilien Stone is my name. Stonewall, actually. I...hmm, I must have changed it, but the facts elude me. Now that I think of it, I couldn't have been mugged. I...don't carry a wallet, or any personal identification. I know that."

"How do you pay for things?"

He rubbed his brow, thinking. "I don't know that yet. Maybe I steal things."

"Doubt it."

"Too trusting."

"Going along for the crazy ride, so don't judge."

"Touché. Anyway, I live on blood, Lucy. It is how I survive. Can you honestly tell me the idea of a man drinking blood from a human being is attractive to you?"

"Not if you look at it mechanically—teeth rip through flesh, blood is extracted, victim passes out at the creature's feet."

Lucy slid to the edge of the couch. Tracing her forefinger lightly over the bite wound, she closed her eyes to the stirrings that signaled growing desire. No, she wasn't horny, but she was warmly open to pleasure.

"Truvin, I felt your power when you embraced me. You made me feel so good. It's your way of life to drink blood. Here's Lucy Morgan, logical skeptic, admitting I can accept that. How else would you survive? And you obviously don't need to kill, so that makes you leaps and bounds morally better than most of the vampires I've read about."

"Fiction, Lucy."

"Right. The line between fiction and reality is a weak one. So what about—"

"—the kill?" He bowed his head and turned his shoulder so she could not see his face.

Lucy's heart sank. *Please, no.*

"It is an innate knowledge to me that the kill is not necessary for survival."

Lucy sighed. *Yes.*

"But I also know it can be—and has been committed—by many of my kind. Have I killed? I don't know. I may have."

He swung a serious gold gaze at her. The blue in his irises was barely visible now. "And how would that make you feel if I have killed?"

She thrust the tip of her thumbnail against her teeth.

"That is the question, isn't it?" He walked around to sit on the coffee table before her. Legs spread and hands dangling between them, he asked, "Do you feel safe with me? This vampire? Beyond the sexual attraction, can you rationally *see* me and know whether I am moral and safe, or a step beyond what you would normally consider acceptable?"

He tilted up her chin so she met his gaze. "What is normal to you, Lucy? I mean, you're accepting this all very well. What would startle you?"

"A serial killer hiding under my bed. A cougar on the loose—which happened last summer, I'll have you know. Mangled a kid before the DNR got to it. Real danger makes me worry and fear. But as for what I believe to be normal? There isn't a norm."

"Why do you have to be so smart about this?"

"Why does my intelligence threaten you?"

"It doesn't. Bloody hell, it attracts me."

"Huh. I've never heard that from a guy before. Being attracted to a woman's brain? Pretty damn refreshing. Come sit next to me," she said, patting the sofa.

"If I sit next to you, Lucy, I'm going to kiss you again. And that's not a vampire thing. It's a man attracted to a sexy, smart woman thing."

"I'm cool with that."

"But a kiss may then lead to another bite."

She shuffled over, clearing a spot for him, and again patted the cushion.

"You never think beyond the moment, do you, Lucy?"

"It's dangerous to have hopes for a future that hasn't yet happened. The now is where I thrive." Thrusting out a hand, she flicked a come-to-me gesture. "I'm attracted to you, Truvin. And it's not because you're the immortal alpha creature I've been reading about in those books. I promise. I've never had such a handsome man interested in me before, and I like the attention."

"That's hard to understand." He sat on the couch and brushed aside her hair from her cheek. "You've had lovers?"

"Of course, but I've never been a serious long-term dater. Men don't look at me and go 'there's a hot one.'"

"I do."

"You don't even know who you are, so you may well wake up one morning and realize I'm not your type. Or do you wake in the evenings?"

He chuckled. "We don't know what I'll be like once the complete truth returns to me, but for now, I know one thing. You are the sexiest woman I have ever laid eyes on."

"Truvin, I'm the *only* woman you've had contact with since you lost your memory."

"It's not a lie. I'm speaking from the gut." He drew her hand over his stomach. Yeah, those abs really did feel like stone, so hard and tight. "Earlier, the scent of your blood drew me. It focused me on the need to fulfill hunger. But now, I scent your life, Lucy, the sweet sexy allure of you. It's different. I've sated the thirst, but now desire demands attention."

As he moved over her, Lucy twisted to lie on her back, her shoulders and head supported by the pillow. Truvin pushed up her shirt.

"No bra," he growled on a deep tone that eddied in her veins. "Love that."

Fingers playing over her nipples, he squeezed and massaged her breasts and leaned in to suckle at them.

Lucy adored it when a man paid attention to her breasts. It felt worshipful, and she the deity. Long, graceful fingers, like that of a musician, danced across her flesh. Could he be a musician?

Working down the front of his shirt, Lucy unbuttoned it and slid her palms over his hot, hard chest. Not cold, like the undead. *Should* he be cold? Some books made the vampire cold and dead, while others styled them alive.

That is fiction. You want the truth? Ask.

"Are you…dead?"

"As in risen from the grave?" He considered it for a moment. "No. Just an extended mortality is what I've come to know. Though, as for how extended, those memories yet allude me."

"All right then." Thankful for his *alive* status, Lucy set her worries aside. "Resume."

"As you command, darling."

The swirl of his tongue tip over her nipples played her the right way. He was going to make love to her, and she would allow it to happen. Right here on her sofa. With the three cats seated across the room, staring at them.

Lucy laughed, and Truvin kissed her. "What?"

"We've an audience."

He noticed the crew of curious felines, and whipped a pillow across the room, which sent them scattering. "I don't like cats."

"A vamp thing?"

"No, a me thing. Oh yeah, Lucy, right there. Feel how desperately I need you. To be inside you."

"I've condoms in the bedroom," she said.

And in the next breath she was airborne. Truvin carried her down the hallway and deposited her on the bed. He went immediately to the nightstand where the crinkle of plastic relieved her immensely.

"Can vampires get mortal women pregnant?"

Tearing off the end and tossing the condom to the pillow, Truvin then lunged in to hover above her. "I think so, but am not sure. So we won't take chances."

"What about—"

Bad, Lucy. For now, she'd curb the discussion of STDs. It wasn't very romantic, and he had been enthusiastic about the condoms. Points for the vampire.

She slipped his shirt down his arms and he balled it up and tossed it over a shoulder. Breaths hushed heavily from his lips, and he groaned an encouraging whimper as she released his trousers and shoved them over his hips.

Every part of his body burned beneath her touch. He felt ten degrees hotter than she, a furnace pulsing with fire. The combination of her cool skin sliding beneath his hot flesh had her tearing her own shirt away to toss with abandon. The skirt, Truvin tore at, and ripped out the delicate hook and eye.

"No panties, either? Lucy, you wanton."

He kicked off his pants, and Lucy felt the heavy fall of his erection against her thigh. It was perfectly hard and she grasped for it, while also finding the slippery circle of condom.

"You want me inside you?" He kissed her jaw and bent to nip at the curve of her breast, but did not use his sharp canines.

"You've already been." She gave a tug to his cock. "But not with this fellow."

Pinching the end of the latex to keep a reservoir, it then slid fluidly over his length. Lucy sucked in a gasp to measure its width. Girth always won over length, in her department. To be filled, oh…

"Show me the way." He spread her legs and then supported himself with his hands to either side of her. "If it's what you want, then take it."

She loved the empowering tone of his words. Permission to

take the lead. She knew he must be a kind man, for surely, though he didn't remember his life, his body reacted instinctively as it had over the years.

Directing him inside of her, Lucy arched her back as his thickness slowly filled her. Exquisite claiming. And she, in turn, hugged him tightly as he began to glide in and out.

He pushed deeper. Jaw tight and eyes closed, he began a pistoning rhythm. Lucy sensed the minute shudders that moved through his body. Coming into her. Wrapping her legs about his back, she spread her arms out to her sides.

She had never had sex with a vampire. This was certainly a night to remark.

Chapter 13

Truvin woke and eased a hand down his abdomen. His entire body was relaxed. Satisfied. Sated. After-sex felt great.

Shifting, his feet rolled on the pillow. Hmm... Feet on pillow? And head at the end of the bed. Now, *that* had been awesome sex. And just thinking about it hardened his cock to semialert mode. He could do with a slow, easy spooning, perhaps.

The sheets next to him were empty. The click of computer keys nearby disturbed the quiet.

Lucy sat in the ambient light of the monitor, tapping away. Her hair fell in loose waves across her shoulders. The changing light from the screen flashed on her profile and touched the side of her neck where the vampire's bite still advertised red and angry.

"You're up," she announced, her attention on the screen. "You nodded off, so I thought to do more research."

Truvin sat up and instinctively reached for his pants. No spooning, then. Apparently, Lucy wasn't a snuggler. The very thing he admired about her—decisive, forward-thinking—also robbed him of much-desired after-sex bonding.

You don't need it. You don't do that.

A glance to the framed picture over the bed captured his attention with a double take. Going up on his knees, he studied the black-and-white etching that, at first, appeared a jumble of lines and shaded shapes, but closer inspection discovered it was really capital letters interwoven within one another into a massive monogram.

"I know this," he said, tapping the glass. "It's a monogram of the entire alphabet."

"Yep. Nineteenth century. Demen—"

"Demengeot," Truvin finished the name of the engraver, marveling that he knew.

"You like monograms?" Lucy prompted.

"Probably. It's just such an amazing piece. How can a person not be utterly floored by it? Huh. So we have a love for ornamental letters in common."

"And interesting sexual positions."

"Indeed." He sat on the bed and began to tug his trousers up a leg. It had been Lucy's idea to try it sideways, and then on all fours, and then…well, he'd lost track of their contortions after that. "What are you doing?"

"This time I tried searching with Google for just your first and last name, without the middle name. Still nothing. It's as if you don't exist."

"Not a bad thing when one is a creature of the night."

"I wonder how long you've been alive." She propped her chin in hand and tilted a look his way. The flimsy pink nightgown she'd pulled on hugged her erect nipples. "Decades? Centuries?"

"Who can say?" Truvin pulled up the pants and buttoned them. Another perusal of the monogram made him wonder if he'd been around when it had been created. "I did feel compelled to the highwayman's coat. Maybe I was a highwayman?"

"You honestly think so?"

He loved the utter astonishment that glittered in her voice. Instant acceptance. Something he felt he'd never quite had before. "I have no idea where or when I actually lived."

On the other hand, those flashbacks he'd had… He'd been dressed in garb that reminded him of—when? To think on it, he couldn't place the clothes to a particular time in history because he wasn't sure what had gone on in the world before his attack.

The notion startled him. "I've lost all history?"

"What?"

"The president…" He searched his memory. "What's his name?"

"Truvin."

"I honestly don't recall, Lucy. And just now, I was trying to place a moment in history, but I cannot. I… Am I so uneducated? I can't begin to conjure a historical event to mind."

"Nine-eleven?" she questioned.

"I don't know what those numbers mean."

"It's when the twin towers were taken down by terrorists in New York. In September 2001. You don't remember that?"

He shrugged. "I've a grasp on the basics of living a life, such as dressing and moving about, and I know I need money to purchase things. And, yes, I am a vampire. But, the world and what it has been, and where I have been?"

"I think I remember reading about that." She keyed in a few strokes. "Yes, it's your semantic memory. The knowledge of the world and facts like you would have learned in school. It's common to lose that with amnesia, and less common to lose the procedural memory, which are basic survival skills, knowing how to do things."

"Like sex?" he gasped, but wasn't thinking about the good things he'd just done, only that he had lost so much more than he'd imagined.

"I'm so sorry, Truvin. I never realized the magnitude of your loss."

"And yet, I had not realized that loss until now."

Tugging on his shirt, he then looked around for his shoes.

"You going somewhere?" she asked.

"I don't stick around after sex. It's not usual. Did you see my other shoe?"

"Truvin, did you just hear yourself?"

He found the culprit wedged under the nightstand and tugged it out. "I said I should probably be leaving."

"You said it wasn't usual, like you knew what usual—for you—was."

"Huh. You're right. So the stuff I do know is an instinctual thing."

"Your procedural memory. Which means, you must do this often. Escape from women's beds?"

Toeing off his shoes, Truvin flung himself back across the bed. "Sorry. I…don't want to leave. And I don't know my history with women, though if I had to wager…"

"A real Casanova, eh?" She glided alongside him, and began to work on his shirt buttons. "Love 'em and leave 'em. So how should I take your lying back down?"

The satin nightgown tickled his abs and tightened his core. "Take it as me wanting to make love to you again. Are there any positions we've yet to try?"

"Plenty."

He stopped her from unbuttoning his shirt. "What else did it say online about my memory? Did it give methods to get it back?"

Lucy climbed upon his legs, straddling his hips. "I looked up amnesia and its various forms. I think you might have dissociative fugue."

"Which means?" He shifted his thigh to snuggle his erection against her warmth.

"It's a sudden-onset amnesia that comes following a trauma. The person loses memory of a certain distressing event, or even major portions of their life, if it was also quite traumatic."

"You're saying I've lived a traumatic life?"

"I'm guessing a vampire's life is pretty disturbing."

"For someone who is not a vampire. But for the vampire, it is all that he knows."

"All right then, maybe you experienced a real doozy right before you lost your memory. You had blood on your shirt. Do you think you attacked someone, but then they fought back? A surprise to a vampire who may be accustomed to easily overcoming his victims?"

Drawing a finger down her forearm, Truvin watched the goose bumps on Lucy's flesh rise in his wake. Her fingers curled over his shoulders, and the tips of her hair tickled his nipples. He was ready for sexual position number seven, or nine, or whatever number they'd left off on.

"You're so casual about all this, Lucy. Knowing what I am. Aren't you the least bit frightened?"

Lowering her body onto his, her breasts snugged against his chest and she placed her knees to either side of his thighs. "Do you need me to be?"

"No. I don't know." The utter softness of her could not be disregarded. And he knew to touch her there, just below her breast, would—yes—draw up a shiver. "Maybe. A healthy fear of anything that can kill you is a good thing, darling."

"Everything can kill me. A bus, a car, a misthrown rock. If I feared everything that could harm me, I'd have to stop eating out, move to a dirt farm and swear off mankind all together."

She was too comfortable. It wasn't right. While he appreciated her easy understanding of what he was, he expected her to react, to stir his desire with the fear.

Truvin sat up on his elbows.

That's what you require, vampire. The fear to stoke your desire. You crave it. You can get it up with a healthy bit of fear.

"Truvin? Was it something I said?"

"Just now, I was hoping you'd show me your fear. Like I needed it. How pitiful is that?" He pushed her aside and slid off the bed. Pacing the room, he paused before the computer screen. "alt.vampires.net?"

"Nothing of help there, unless you want to buy blood wholesale from the black market or hire a werewolf to be your thug."

"They do that," he said. A click of the mouse brought up a screen that featured "known vampire tribes."

"Werewolves? Don't tell me…?"

"They exist right here in your lovely city, though they tend to stick to the suburbs and the countryside. Lucy, I think this might be something." He slid onto the chair and scrolled through the short list of about two-dozen tribe names.

She peered over his shoulder. "No, I think that's role-playing stuff. All those tribal names. It's an elaborate world created for gaming."

"Gaming?"

"Adults assuming roles of their creation, and acting out stories in a virtual world. Vampires against werewolves. Mortals seeking vampires. You know."

"Again, I do not. But vampires *do* run in tribes."

"Now that you say that, Midge did say something about

tribes." She slid onto his lap and read a few of the tribe names. "Zmaj, Veles, Kila."

"I know that one," Truvin said, pointing to Kila. "I…think that's my tribe."

Lucy settled onto his lap, her bottom snuggled teasingly against his rock-hard length. Truvin leaned in to press his cheek against her cleavage.

"You are a member of a tribe?"

"I'm sure of it."

"Then all we have to do is find your tribe, and we find the people who know you. Maybe seeing them could stir your memory?"

"It's a possibility. But not a smart one. The tribes don't put themselves out there. It's not as if you'll find them strolling Hennepin Avenue with the bar crowd or dancing in the Goth clubs. Does it include information for any of them?"

Lucy clicked the mouse. "Nope, just the list. I wonder who created this? Don't you think it would be stupid for a vampire to put out a list of known tribes?"

"Maybe it was a witch?" He leaned forward, giving a nip to her breast. She smelled like sex and winter. "Do you know how to trace the original creator of this site?"

"I can view the source." She clicked again and a screen of text popped up. Scanning through the nonsensical code, she suddenly pointed out a name, or rather, a moniker. "The Priest. Oh my God. It has to be the same Midge mentioned. The priest working with the witches."

"A strange alliance."

It was getting more difficult to concentrate with the blood pounding through his erection, demanding attention. He kissed her, gliding his hand up through her hair. Tilting back her head, Lucy wiggled on his lap. She found his cock through his trousers and rubbed the fabric against the rigid shaft.

"Truvin, aren't you even a bit scared? You've been baptized. That means if you are so much as touched by a cross, you're…"

"A slow and painful pile of ash. I know, Lucy. But right now, what you are doing with your hand is pushing me to the edge. More sex now. Talk later."

"Sounds too good to resist—oh, I just remembered. The appointment I made for you with my doctor is today. In a few hours."

"Vampires don't see doctors."

"Yeah? What about the ones who can't remember where their own home is, if they own a fancy car, or if they run with a crazed vampire tribe?"

"Now you're implying that all vampires are crazy."

"Sorry, that was not nice. Since I don't know anything at all about vampires and witches I'd better bow out on this conversation."

"I'm not going to the doctor," Truvin said. "I'll have to…I don't know. There must be some other way to find my memory. Doesn't a bump to the head bring it back?"

"That's as silly as me assuming all vamps are crazy."

"Right. I think if I can take more blood that might bring back more memories. You donated to a good cause lately?"

"My neck is still sore."

He rubbed the swollen wound. It hadn't begun to heal. It should be scabbed over by now—damn, he'd not licked the wound. Fool. A vampire introduced his saliva to the wound to ensure quicker healing and to keep out the vampire taint. And persuasion was used so the victim would wake thinking it merely a hallucination. Perhaps they fell and struck themselves. A victim usually never put two and two together.

But Truvin didn't want to consider that right now.

He wanted to be inside Lucy. Nothing would sway his focus.

* * *

They met in a warehouse at the edge of the city. Severo didn't like coming into Saint Paul because his territory was the northern suburbs. He and the rest of his pack felt most comfortable treading the countryside and farther up north in the state. Werewolves favored lesser-populated areas. The Boundary Waters Canoe Area was one of the best, but it was far north of the Twin Cities.

But the witches had come to him, seeking a means of retaliation against the vampires—one vampire in particular, and he had liked their idea of taking slow revenge, so here he was.

There were fewer witches in the Twin Cities today than there were a year ago. Thanks to Truvin Stone and his gang of witch hunters, who had reduced their numbers. Abigail Rowan led the witches' council for the Midwestern states. Witches were not normally organized, but they had the council should problems arise that one single witch could not handle on his or her own.

The weres' relationship with witches had always been solid, respectful and never intrusive.

Abigail sat across the expansive mahogany office table from Severo. Stick-straight black hair poked out all over her pixie head, drawing the eye immediately away from her muddy lip color and the dark rouge she used on too-thin cheekbones. Not an ugly woman, but not Severo's voluptuous preference. She was three centuries old to his seventy years, and he respected her opinions.

But that didn't mean he understood.

"Tell me why Stone was allowed escape." Severo prompted as the two of them awaited their third guest. "I thought the idea was to kill the vampire and have done with his entire gang." Calling Stone's conglomeration of killers a tribe was too good even for a vampire.

"Because—" the door creaked open and a priest wearing a solemn black suit and white collar walked inside "—if one dies immediately following the holy rites of baptism, that person then goes straight to heaven. Do you really wish that on one so heartless, Mr. Severo?"

"How can a man who has murdered for centuries even win a glimpse of heaven?" Severo countered.

"Baptism erases a man's sins."

Abigail leaned forward, sliding her bright blue fingernails across the table. "We had to let him loose. Give him a day or two to kill again, then his soul is doomed and we can take him out, knowing he'll go to hell where he belongs."

"We will all go to hell," Severo said. "It's not as though we're upstanding citizens."

"Speak for yourself." Abigail cast him a pixie sneer, which didn't have the impact it should. "I do no harm."

"Nor do I," Severo added, "but often I've not choice in the matter. So, Father, do you still wish to accompany Abigail and her crew on the hunt for Stone? With the baptism completed, your services are no longer required. We will compensate you generously, as discussed—"

"No money shall exchange hands," the priest blurted out. He was pushing fifty, though he was fit. He'd indulged in the sin of vanity, Severo noted from the slicked-back hair and tanned flesh. "It is my right to follow through, to ensure Truvin Stone is punished."

Severo knew the priest had a personal investment in the matter. His daughter was murdered last year. Young and pretty, completing her second year in college. Stone had killed her, or so the priest claimed.

Didn't matter to Severo who participated in stalking Stone's gang, so long as they were discreet, and the job was done efficiently. "We'll make no claims to knowing you."

"To be expected," the priest answered. "I don't require your protection. I've the Lord on my side."

Severo winced as the gold cross strung round the priest's collar glinted. Holy objects had no effect on weres, or witches. But if it were fashioned from silver and wielded as a weapon, then all bets were off. Silver killed weres.

"Good then." Severo stood. "If you require muscle, I and my comrades are at your service, Abigail. Just let me know. Do you have a location for Stone?"

"We lost him, but I believe he's still in the city. We'll pick up his scent. Should have had one of the weres with us that night so we could have tracked him easily."

"We're not keen on the city, but for Stone, I'm sure I can coax one or two out to assist you. Good evening, Abigail. Father."

Chapter 14

"That position was called the wheel of love," Lucy said as she snuggled alongside Truvin, stretching her leg down to twine between his.

"How do you know?"

"I have a book." She kissed his neck and walked her fingers down to trace the cut muscles curving inward to define his hips. Had to be the sexiest part on a man. The lines of muscle all pointed toward his groin and the eye tended to follow. "Tired?"

"Nope."

"Do you sleep during the day?"

"A few hours."

"And the rest of the time you…?"

"Live life, I suppose. Not too sure about my life, remember?"

"Right, sorry." She walked her fingers up the ridges of his abs. It gave her no small relief that he actually had a belly button. No aliens in her bed. Lucy Morgan drew the line at vampires. "But you're up on the vampire stuff. What about garlic? Do you have a coffin?"

"Lucy, that's morbid."

"What about stakes?"

"You're very inquisitive."

"I want to learn everything about you."

"I don't *know* everything."

"You seem to know a lot about sex."

"That—" he gripped her hand and tugged it up to kiss the knuckles "—is a given. On the other hand, I do not have a book."

"So…ask me some questions. About my book. About my life. I'm wide awake and need to talk. Unless you want to go another round?"

He glanced down, beyond where she traced his abs. "Soon enough."

"So ask me."

"Very well. Questions about Lucy." Truvin teased his fingers through her hair, moist from exertion. It occurred to him that he had no questions. Sex had been great. He knew Lucy was kind, and maybe a bit needy. But that only resulted in an insatiable appetite for connection.

Had he ever spent an entire day in bed with a woman? Kissing and making love and exploring one another, not afraid to try new things, or maybe they weren't new, but they were to a man without a past.

His history was slowly coming to him. He just wished there was a way to get it all at once, and to be done with the wondering.

"Truvin," she singsonged. Her fingers began a search lower on his abdomen, twirling into the hairs that began just below his belly button.

"I guess my first question would be, what's the name of that book you have, and does it have pictures?"

"It does," she answered eagerly. "Want me to get it?"

"Quickly." His penis bobbed in anticipation.

Eight hours of lovemaking had come to a bittersweet end. Lucy had fallen asleep in Truvin's arms, with his cock still inside her. It had been a delicious moment to feel himself soften within her and slowly slip away. And she had not stirred as he'd dressed and set aside the book on sexual positions before it slid from the bed with a crash.

He'd decided to go out for a walk in the brisk winter night, and now stood before Saint Paul's Cathedral. The building was lit around the ground and high on the dome with low beams, giving it a solemn, peaceful air. It was the only place, other than Lucy's home, where he felt a connection. And connection to anything right now was hard to come by.

He'd thought to come here for answers to those questions he'd not been able to respond to as Lucy had fired them at him. And yet, knowledge would come at a price.

He could not risk entering the cathedral. One brush against a holy object, a mere picture of a cross or Jesus, and he would take on a wound.

If he were to die, he preferred a spray of witch's blood. A few seconds of sizzling flesh as the crimson poison worked into his bloodstream, and then the inner burn as his veins fried, and, ultimately, an explosion of vampire bits and flesh. Not pretty, but quicker than a holy wound.

One touch from a cross—no matter it a large gold artifact or a small tin souvenir dangling from a cheap rosary—and the vampire's flesh would be irrevocably wounded. Initially, it could be shallow, a mere scrape. But a holy wound never healed. It ate into the vampire, spreading, widening and fixing itself into flesh and bone and organs until it literally ate the vampire alive. The entire process could occur over days, weeks or even months.

Truvin knew the consequences because he had—

Falling to his knees on the snow-covered lawn before the cathedral, Truvin was hit with the immensity of memory. A bold and merciless memory…

The vampire Gabriel stared at the gold cross around Truvin's neck. A small cross Truvin wore in defiance to others of his kind. He was not vulnerable like most of them.

Dare you any, it spoke, to step forward and challenge me.

Gabriel had issued a secretive challenge, one he'd thought Truvin would never discover. He'd taken up with one of Truvin's former lovers. More a weekend fling than anything. But Truvin had marked her as his own. No other vampire should have gone sniffing around her, let alone taken her.

It was a small affront, perhaps worthy of a fight, but never death.

But Gabriel was allied with Nikolaus Drake, a vampire who'd had the audacity to survive a witch's blood attack. He remained on this earth a phoenix, the most powerful of all vampires because they literally survived ash and returned to form. And now, Drake would forever be immune to the blood of all witches. He'd once led tribe Kila.

Truvin had stepped into Drake's place while he'd abandoned the tribe to mend. But now, Drake was back, healed against all odds, and defiant in his bold new power.

"I need to send Nikolaus Drake a message," Truvin said, and then pressed the gold cross to Gabriel's chest…

"I've killed my own kind?"

Truvin gouged his fingers into the snow.

It didn't feel possible, but he knew it to be true. The memory became a part of him, his past, it moved through his very blood.

Witness your past indiscretions. Know them to be your truth.

The cross high atop the cathedral gleamed with the glow of spotlights from below.

"What am I?" Truvin asked. "We are not…"

The vampire was *not* a monster. He knew that much. They were a different kind of human who merely answered to a unique hunger. Strengths and powers were beyond that of mortal humans, but he was not a monster. Monsters had no compassion for their fellow man. Monsters…killed others.

"And I have?"

Standing and stepping off the lawn to the sidewalk, Truvin turned his back to the cathedral.

"Could the memories be false? Am I seeing someone else's life with the blood? The only blood I've had is from a few suburban housewives and Lucy. Lucy hasn't killed anyone. Not with a cross. Not like I've seen. Hell, do I *want* to remember?"

Placing a palm over his heart, Truvin closed his eyes.

Could a man simply walk away? Straight off from his past and into a future of his own creation? Because, what if that past was not something the man could be proud of?

What kind of man had been Truvin Stone? Or more troubling…what sort of vampire had he been?

He knew to survive he must drink blood. Warm mortal blood, not anything dead or stored in plastic bags. The blood must have the soul in it. Yet, the kill wasn't necessary.

"But it is not forbidden." He walked absently down the sidewalk, toward the city and the huge Xcel concert hall on the corner of a triangle of streets.

"The vampire is a creature who feeds on the blood of mortals. If we must, the kill is—" Not accepted, but rather… "—allowed. We do not judge our fellow brothers for such an act. We cannot."

Pausing on the corner for a red light, Truvin shoved his hands in his pockets. He knew he was not one who blindly accepted faith, and in fact, had flaunted his immunity to the holy by wearing a cross. To show other vampires who may have been baptized that he was more powerful than they. To lift himself above others.

A cruel mien.

"You've been a bastard."

And now what would he do with that knowledge? Could he change? Did he want to? Did the real Truvin Stone desire a change? Did he, without full knowledge of his past, have a right to *attempt* a change?

"I must." Because it felt right. He did not want to be cruel.

He wanted…to show Lucy she could trust him.

Without full knowledge of who he was, Truvin was not safe alone out in the world. Oh sure, he was probably strong enough to fend off a physical attack. Maybe. There were witches and crazed priests after him. He could not have the proper judgment to know who was an enemy and who was not.

He needed protection.

"And you think you can give him that protection?" Lucy said to her reflection. She lifted her arms to examine in the mirror. Still a long purple bruise on the underside of each from the air bag. "Some protection."

Her shoes had been knocked under the bed and it was difficult to bend in the tight pencil skirt, so she performed a sliding-lean move.

Tony scampered out from under the dust ruffle, swishing his tail across her forehead.

The black cat was the first stray she'd brought home three years ago. She remembered that evening well because a boy-friend of eighteen months had broken up with her at the

Cheesecake Factory, of all places. Of course, she wouldn't have made a scene over Chocolate Turtle Supreme. The jerk had been counting on that.

Toast, the mottled brown-and-gold mongrel, had followed after an argument when a new lover had made her realize how needy she really was. Yes, she liked to call the shots in her relationships. And, yes, it was difficult to take things slow when the rush of new love always pressed her to plunge in for the deep dive. Yet that dive often scared away most of her dates.

Life felt easier with a man in her life. It was good to know there was someone to talk to, to unwind around, to fall into bed with.

And when there weren't men, there were cats.

So what was she going to do about her sudden lack of a vampire?

"You don't need a vampire, Lucy. You would like one, but you don't *need* one. Besides, he's not your boyfriend. You have no hold over him. And if vampire doesn't scream 'so wrong' to you, then you need to pack it in for good."

Slipping on her shoes, three-inch-high black heels that were inappropriate for this weather, she then dragged herself upright, using the bed and a splayed camel walk.

"What made me think this skirt was sexy?"

She studied her reflection again. The skirt, snug from waist to knee and ending in a tease of flirty ruffles, made her long legs longer and emphasized her curvy hips. She was proud of her narrow ankles and had to admit she had perfect high-arched feet for heels.

"Right. Because it *is* sexy. And so am I."

Smoky eyeshadow granted her eyes a mysterious, sultry look and the bright red lipstick called attention to her mouth, which still felt swollen after making love to Truvin all day. She'd read about bruised lips in romance novels, and had scoffed. But now, she knew differently.

Tracing her tongue along the inner side of her lower lip, she winked at her reflection. Her lips had touched his mouth, his chest, his penis, his—well, every inch of skin, she felt sure. And she wanted more.

But did she really intend to go out tonight?

"Yes. I have to look for him."

If Midge was right, the witches wanted to see Truvin suffer before he died an excruciating death.

Lucy sighed and wandered out to the kitchen. "Should I care about a man who may have harmed others? Yes. No. But."

Sprinkling a cup of Kitty Nummies into a bowl attracted all three cats into the kitchen.

There was always a but, and if it could be argued well enough, Lucy could get behind that indefinite answer.

The fantastical world of vampires and witches was entirely out of her realm of understanding. Surely vampires were not deathless creatures.

But what about witches? After getting an earful from Midge, obviously witches were not the benevolent Samantha Stevens type Lucy had once imagined them to be.

Both sides did what they had to survive.

"Truvin has forgotten all history and his life. Maybe this is his chance to start over. If I can get to him before the witches do."

Decided, Lucy grabbed her car keys and headed out.

As he drew the blood into his mouth and languished in the glide of it down his throat, he was very aware of what he held in his arms. A living being. A gorgeous butterfly who had followed him into the darkness of the dance club, shimmying her red silk hips and gliding up to him with a dangerous invitation.

He'd accepted her invite, kissing her passionately and thumbing her hard nipples through the silk. But the real treat was in the blood.

And there were horrors in the blood.

Memory.

Carnivale. The icy depths of winter made bright and winsome with fabulous costumes and colors and ceremony the Italians celebrated in their waterlogged city of Venice.

He'd purchased a black domino mask edged in paste jewels that resembled rubies. The festivities had begun in the morning, when he had not been conscious, but rather hidden away in the spacious chest he traveled with.

Now, the sun had set upon the frozen lagoon and Truvin insinuated himself into the spectacle of the masque at the Piazza San Marco.

They smelled delicious, the bodies. Humanity. But it was the female of the species, the helpless mortal women, he sought. Bold or quiet, tall or short, audacious or seductive. He sought all varieties of the fluttering beauties. Butterflies, each and every one of them, clad in colors to attract, intrigue and seduce.

They moved toward him with a glitter to their eye and a pursed sigh of lemon-breath. He would not dance with them. A dance held too much promise. But he would entwine them into his dark embrace...

He had stalked them in Venice. Had taken what he'd needed to survive. Butterflies, he had begun to call them. Brightly colored beauties who fluttered about him as if a flower. He'd perfected his stalking techniques then. The early nineteenth century.

Which meant—yes, he grasped the memory—he had been born late eighteenth century. England was his birthplace, though his mother had been...Irish. Yes.

Stonewall. That had been his surname.

The name on the roster Lucy had found online—yet had dismissed because it was centuries old—had read Truvin Stonewall.

"Huh. So there is a record of my existence."

That knowledge turned a certain key in Truvin's brain. Yes, he *existed*. He had walked this earth over two centuries. That small knowledge felt so immense.

He had done what he must to survive. And as he let the girl in red silk slide to the floor of the dance club to sleep off the swoon, he stepped away from her and back into the crowd.

Everything was blue. The walls, painted white, reflected the bouncing blue spotlights and erratic blinking blue beams. Faces took on a pale blue pallor, and bright red lips pursed darkly violet. Life beat around him in a frenzy of techno sounds and jumping, moving bodies. It electrified his blood.

Yes, he'd done what was necessary to survive. And the witches?

His memory still wasn't clear on them.

Crowded dance clubs had never been her thing. And though she'd been here a few weeks earlier to get the vibe, see if she could scope out any wannabe vamps, Lucy was as uncomfortable now as she had been then.

The Blue Room was so called because it was all blue. From the neon-blue bar to the blue spotlights and the electric-blue drinks. The initial effect was disconcerting, especially the flesh that appeared gray, almost dead, but it was probably better than red. The place attracted a huge Goth crowd, so perhaps red would have been a more interesting choice.

The white Rachel Ray ruffled dress shirt sucked up the color, and her skinny gray skirt darkened to black under the lights. There were a few dashes of red and white and more flesh than should be legal.

So why had she come here? This seemed like a spot that would attract a vampire. Or, if the vampire had an ounce of self-respect, repel him.

"This was a mistake," she muttered.

Truvin Stone was not the kind of vampire who would be caught dead in a place like this.

"Why am I being such the ditz lately? It's almost as if I'm compelled to follow him like some kind of zombie girl. Did his bite do that?"

She clasped her neck. The wounds were still there. Though no longer swollen, but they had yet begun to heal. The ruffles around her neck hid them well enough, but they could not hide her sudden anxiety.

Did a vampire bite make the victim his slave? Someone who no longer thought rationally and became a sort of Renfield-esque follower?

"You're being irrational," she murmured as she cringed to avoid a man whose leather jacket sported four-inch-long spikes darting up and down the sleeves.

Lucy had learned that while the Goth culture wasn't as doom and gloom and death-frenzied as outsiders liked to believe, there was a certain cluster that lived as if they were immortal bloodsuckers. They even exchanged small amounts of blood with one another.

A stupid practice, Lucy had thought. But when she'd questioned them about the risk of contracting HIV, they'd merely shrugged. Vampires are immortal, you know. They really believed. Which was the tragic part.

On the other hand, was it all that different from sharing a common cup during Communion practice?

Faith, no matter in what form, was a curious thing.

Lucy had faith when it suited her. And while she knew it was supposed to be a constant and not an as-needed kind of thing, she hadn't come to grips with her religious beliefs. Raised Catholic, she'd strayed after high school, straying so far from the flock to test a Universal Unitarian. They hadn't been structured enough, so she'd given a Lutheran and a

Baptist church a try. Turns out, group worship just wasn't her thing.

If yoga could be considered a religion, then ten points for her. She was in no rush, and there were many more religions out there to explore.

Dodging a waitress who swerved toward her with a tray of blue drinks held high, Lucy decided one turn around the edges of the dance floor, and then she was out of here.

The rock band Evanescence caterwauled from the speakers, and a frenetic flash of strobe crossed the far wall, creating eerie shadowed effects against the silver-and-black-striped wall. Above the dance floor a huge, blue iron candelabra burned what looked like real candles, but they had to be electric. How very eighteenth century.

I can't place history.

She assumed that many people didn't know a lot about history, but most were able to place a few simple events or at least recognize significant people and happenings such as George Washington or the terrorist attacks.

"Poor Truvin."

She was feeling sorry for a vampire?

Rubbing her palms up her arms alleviated the sudden rise of goose bumps. It wasn't a dreadful feeling, but instead a sensual return to their earlier lovemaking. So she had feelings for a vampire. Life could get more surreal. Really, it could.

Thinking a trip to the dance floor would be just the thing, Lucy bounced in rhythm to the beat. She wasn't a solo dancer, and had never invited a stranger to boogie with her, but the music compelled. Sliding her hands up through her hair, she shifted her hips and tested the rhythm.

An arm slipped around her waist and splayed fingers curled against her breast. Tugged back against the solid form of a man a little taller than she, Lucy began to struggle.

"No, I'm sorry, I don't—"

Prepared to kick backward and land one of her spike heels in his calf, Lucy calmed when her aggressor spoke next to her cheek, "What are you doing here, darling?"

Chapter 15

Smiling more with relief than recognition, Lucy answered, "I could ask you the same. Not exactly subtle, would you say?"

"Were you looking for me? Please say you were, and this isn't one of your usual hangouts."

"I had hoped the milieu might attract you." She turned in his arms, again finding the beat and swaying her hips. He still wore the highwayman's coat and a white shirt beneath. A possible eighteenth-century rogue? She could place him in the costumes of the time.

Heck, she'd initially thought Truvin an old-fashioned kind of guy. Maybe he was much more old-fashioned than either of them could guess at. But imagining he'd actually lived that long ago still pressed the boundaries of her sanity.

A spot on his shirt, small but noticeable, drew her attention. It was dark, and the blue light obviously changed it from…red? Blood?

"Truvin, I'm sorry, I shouldn't have been so forward earlier. Asking all those questions. But I don't think you're safe out here on your own, not knowing the whole picture."

"The memories are rushing back with—"

"Each victim?" She pointed to the spot and he merely tugged the lapel of his coat over it.

The vampire darted his attention from her, to a constant surveillance of the room, his eyes predatory yet protective. And in this light, the blue irises grew otherworldly in intensity.

A new song began. Lucy recognized the band: Bullet For My Valentine. She loved this group. The DJ had dubbed a great techno beat into the original. "Come with me."

"Oh, no, I don't dance."

"How do you know?" She snagged her fingers in the opening of his shirt and shimmied up to him. "I want to dance, Truvin. I'll go by myself…?"

Turning, she danced to the main floor, not looking to see if he would follow, but holding back a hand for him to grab. Tilting her head and thrusting up her other hand, she succumbed to the intoxicating beat. She hadn't danced for months, and it always put her in a great mood.

Probably it was the all-day sex, too, that heightened her sensory freedom. Alive and full of vigor, she wanted to breathe it all in, touch the blue and dance all night.

A man's hand slapped into hers and tugged her roughly to his chest. Truvin fit himself to her body, barely moving to the beat.

Lucy shimmied down before him, and swung her hips. Pushing her fingers through her hair, she fluffed it out and gave him a catty snarl. "I dare you," she called, and slipped deeper into the dancing masses.

To his credit, he followed. The music began to work at his limbs. Still a little restrained, he did have a deadly hip shake that Lucy approached to meet with a syncopated grind.

"This is great, isn't it?" she shouted above the music, but it was too loud. A jump, and she spun around, fitting her thighs against Truvin's and sliding her palms down his hips.

"Lucy, you tempt me."

"Glad to know my efforts aren't going to waste—whoa!"

"Come." He tugged her from the dance floor and toward the darkness at the back of the club. "Step up."

She hadn't known there was a step, and who could see in this awful light? A vampire, that's who.

Giddy with the high of her body's exhilaration, Lucy blindly followed the vampire into the unknown.

Truvin navigated the shadows of the club with catlike ease. The entire back section featured a series of hallways and grottoes and small, open rooms. Lovers occupied the blue-and-gray crannies, and drunken revelers sang to the music, lifting their arms and spilling more than they consumed. A disturbing few were actually cutting themselves, and then sharing their blood. Humans, not vampires. The idiots.

But the scent carried to him, musty and bright, some of it tainted with alcohol, all of it so loudly cloying it was all Truvin could do not to veer in their direction.

He'd been on the verge of selecting another victim. It wasn't because he hungered, but because taking blood seemed to be stoking his memory.

What a dream to see an angel standing amidst the dancing demons and devils. Lucy had shone brightly beneath a blue spotlight, her gorgeous chestnut hair shimmering like gilded bronze. The white shirt, stitched in ruches up and down the front so that it caressed her breasts, drew his eye to her curves. All eyes.

Truvin didn't want to share her, so he would not. She

shuffled along behind him now, her hand warm in his. So alive, yet unaware of the peril.

Because she was in danger. He didn't want to hurt her, but he knew the vampire's nature.

But you now know you don't need to feed for survival. You're doing this for mental clarity. And really, it doesn't hurt them all that much.

"Truvin, slower," she called, and gripped his hand tighter.

Unique amongst a flock of orange-and-brown monarchs, Lucy was one of those azure-blue specimens that could only be found in the canopies of a rare rain forest. A breed that should not be pinned, but rather allowed to flourish and flutter freely.

Could he have a relationship with this butterfly?

You can certainly have sex with her. But an emotional connection?

An idiot notion. Any relationship between a vampire and a mortal was doomed. Yet how could he be sure? Had he relationships with mortals before?

Stupid memory loss. It was becoming more a nuisance than anything. Initially he'd not been curious, but a few sips of blood had introduced intrigue. Yet it also put up his ire and made him want to punch things.

The scent of this butterfly—*his butterfly*—pressed him farther into the dark depths of the club until he found a quiet corner. Truvin drew Lucy into his arms. He plunged his nose into her hair and slid his hands up the back of her hips. A tilt of his hands urged her forward. She moved into him, fitting her mons against his hard-on. It was a position of memory. One both knew very well—yes, even the amnesiac vampire.

"This is exciting," she gasped into his mouth as he kissed her hard. "The club. The darkness. Being here in your arms."

"You want to have sex?"

The Reader Service — Here's how it works:

Accepting your 2 free books and 2 free mystery gifts places you under no obligation to buy anything. You may keep the books and gifts and return the shipping statement marked "cancel". If you do not cancel, about a month later we'll send you 4 additional books and bill you just $4.47 each in the U.S. or $4.99 each in Canada, plus 25¢ shipping & handling per book and applicable taxes if any. * That's the complete price and at a savings of at least 15% off the cover price, it's quite a bargain! You may cancel at any time, but if you choose to continue, every other month we'll send you 4 more books which you may either purchase at the discount price or return to us and cancel your subscription.

*Terms and prices subject to change without notice. Sales tax applicable in N.Y. Canadian residents will be charged applicable provincial taxes and GST. Offer not valid in Quebec. Credit or debit balances in a customer's account(s) may be offset by any other outstanding balance owed by or to the customer. Please allow 4 to 6 weeks for delivery. Offer available while quantities last.

If offer card is missing write to: The Silhouette Reader Service, 3010 Walden Ave., P.O. Box 1867, Buffalo, NY 14240-1867

NO POSTAGE
NECESSARY
IF MAILED
IN THE
UNITED STATES

BUSINESS REPLY MAIL
FIRST-CLASS MAIL   PERMIT NO. 717   BUFFALO, NY

POSTAGE WILL BE PAID BY ADDRESSEE

SILHOUETTE READER SERVICE
3010 WALDEN AVE
PO BOX 1867
BUFFALO NY 14240-9952

Play the Lucky Hearts Game

and get...
2 FREE BOOKS and
2 FREE MYSTERY GIFTS...
yes! YOURS to KEEP!

I have scratched off the silver card. Please send me my *2 FREE BOOKS* and *2 FREE mystery GIFTS* (gifts are worth about $10). I understand that I am under no obligation to purchase any books as explained on the back of this card.

Scratch Here!

then look below to see what your cards get you... 2 Free Books & 2 Free Mystery Gifts!

▲ **DETACH AND MAIL CARD TODAY!** ▲

338 SDL ESUM   238 SDL ESXX

FIRST NAME

LAST NAME

ADDRESS

APT.#

CITY

STATE/PROV.

ZIP/POSTAL CODE

(S-N-07/08)

Twenty-one gets you
2 FREE BOOKS and
2 FREE MYSTERY GIFTS!

Twenty gets you
2 FREE BOOKS!

Nineteen gets you
1 FREE BOOK!

TRY AGAIN!

"Here? Right where…everyone can see us?"

He tracked the worry that blossomed in her gaze, which quickly became a glint of excitement.

"Maybe," she offered, though it was an unsure decision.

He would not press. Nor did he feel he'd be comfortable with public sex. "I need more blood for the memories." He revealed his true desire.

"Yes. Take me now. Push your teeth into me."

Overwhelmed by her unquestioning suppliance, Truvin ignored the disturbing urge to pull away. He did not want her to be a slave to him.

Already breathing heavily with desire, her breasts rose to nudge his palms. The sound of her cry as he pinched her nipple pleased him.

She kissed the corner of his mouth. Dashing out his tongue, he tickled it inside her upper lip, knowing how the pressure rocketed up her libido. The urgency of their touches, the heat of their breaths, made him push her against a wall and pin her wrists above her head.

The darkness surrounding them murmured with gasps and cries of pleasure while the music thumping in the background worked its way into Truvin's veins.

But there was room inside yet for Lucy. So he kissed down her chin and nuzzled in the shallow at the base of her neck. There she smelled salty and lush. Wanting.

He bit into Lucy's breast, high on the exposed curve of it where the ruffled shirt curled back. When aroused, blood swelled in the breast and flushed to the surface arteries. Delicious crimson ichor trickled and filled his mouth. A wicked sacrament offered to the vampire; her body and her blood.

"You belong to me, Lucy."

"Yes, I want that. To be yours."

While he sated his cravings for the elixir of life, Lucy

stroked her hand up and down his cock through his pants. He ground himself against her touch, urging her on. And when her hand slackened and he knew she was drifting into the orgasm of release, he also tipped into the swoon.

Heartbeats palpitating in his chest, he licked across the wound and then pressed his fingers to the open punctures. Engulfed in darkness and erratic sound, the gush of blood through his system frenzied it all to a heightened noise of ecstasy.

Lucy shuddered in his embrace and sighed against his throat. "Truvin…"

And the blood gave up another secret from his past.

He stood on the steps before a warehouse, which blazed behind him. Werewolves stalked the sidewalk in human form, though their skeletal structure had begun to stretch across the shoulders, a threat to beware their transformation.

The wolves stood down his tribe, Kila. He was the leader. Or not. Nikolaus Drake challenged his recently acquired authority, and now the wolves had joined the mix.

He did not want to lead, but he was no longer content to sit by and do nothing while the witches annihilated his fellow vampires. Somehow, the witches had gotten the wolves to take their side.

A bloody battle ensued, which left Truvin defeated. The tribe would not follow him. They would not get behind his incessant desire to destroy all witches. To take away anything that could harm them all.

He and his gang of witch hunters had regrouped and had only been stalking the city for months since the tribe had dumped him. Vengeance fueled him.

Vengeance tasted so sublime.

But not so rich as Lucy Morgan.

Korn's "Coming Undone" blasted from the speakers and

filled the atmosphere, the heavy bass beat thundering in Truvin's chest.

Lifting Lucy up to stand, her body slack against his and her hands lazily stroking up his forearms, Truvin bent to kiss the blood from her breast.

So long he had walked this earth. So long… And where was he going? He squeezed her breast and more blood crept over the flesh.

Minneapolis. It flashed with the blood. *You live in the Carlyle penthouse. You've a Porsche in the garage and a bank account in Switzerland that oozes gold and silver. You're a loner. You take what you wish and damn those who protest.*

You are a vampire.

"Lucy."

"Truvin, I've never felt like this before. Owned. But in a good way."

The heat of her breath hushed upon his mouth. He eased a hand over her arse, wanting to pull her up onto his rock-hard cock, but sensing the presence of a couple not far down the hallway. No public sex. It was so gauche.

"Let's go back to my place," she said. "Finish this there."

"How about my place?"

"You remember where you live?"

"Yes, across the river in Minneapolis."

"Let's go."

He led her forward, toward a stained-glass window set at the end of the hallway, and as they were passing, both noticed the strange occurrence below in the parking lot.

A priest held a cross high above a man who was held immobile by three women.

"Witches," Truvin hissed.

Chapter 16

Truvin ran, but Lucy clung to one of his wide coat sleeves. They stepped outside behind the club. The alleyway was neatly swept, with stacks of empty pallets against the wall. A parking lot paralleled the back lot.

The cold air prickled Lucy's skin to goose bumps. Yet her breast, where Truvin had bitten her, pulsed warm and ached for his mouth again.

The priest was nowhere in sight. Two witches dragged the moaning vampire behind a green Dumpster.

"Murderers!" Truvin spat as he approached the Dumpster.

Lucy's heels squished through slush.

One of the witches emerged, pushing up a sweater sleeve. Recognition shone on her face. "It's Stone!"

"You've got to get out of here." Lucy grabbed his arm.

Truvin stood his ground. "I never run from anything."

"Yeah? Well, I'm thinking now would be a good time to alter that firm stance. Just a touch?"

The witch spat, landing but a foot from Truvin's boots.

Behind the Dumpster a spray of…flesh and blood announced a dead vampire.

"Truvin, let's go!" She gave his shoulder another shove, and Truvin grabbed her hand and took off running.

Lucy glanced over her shoulder. The witches followed, but slowly. Their attention had been diverted by the exploding vampire.

"Let's take this." Truvin straddled a motorcycle parked at the end of the lot.

"It's not yours!"

He held out a hand to her. "It's either theft or death, Lucy." The bike rumbled to a start. The keys had been left in it? Must have belonged to the dead vampire. "Your choice."

"Why does it have to be my—"

One of the witches shouted what sounded like a curse, and not a swearword curse, but a get-you-gone-to-hell-or-we'll-do-it-for-you kind of chanting curse.

Threat level? Off the scale.

"Oh hell." Climbing onto the bike behind Truvin, Lucy felt her skirt slide up to her crotch, but modesty didn't apply right now. Before she got a firm clutch around his chest, the bike kicked, and took off down the tarmac. They picked up speed, veering off the main drag. A residential neighborhood surrounded them. Not the easiest milieu in which to be discreet, but she trusted Truvin.

"You know how to drive one of these things?" she shouted.

"Isn't it obvious? Just like riding a horse!"

"Christ." Lucy clutched Truvin tightly. And she tossed in a "Holy Mary, pray for us sinners, now and at the hour of our death," for good measure.

Maybe the Catholic church would take her back. A stray returned to the flock?

No, she wasn't afraid, so much as venturing into the unknown. Of which she had done quite a bit lately.

It was easy for Truvin to be cavalier about the whole thing. He was immortal. It was possible he was incapable of becoming roadkill. She, on the other hand…

Tucking her face against the back of Truvin's shoulder, she closed her eyes as the cold winter wind rushed over her forehead. *He'll protect me. Trust him.*

Every part of her crushed to every part of his warmth. Maybe it was the blood that kept him warm. Her blood. To think of him biting her breast earlier in the club filled her with giddy shock, and a shuddering remnant of orgasm tickled her groin.

She could do this. Have a relationship with a vampire. Because the blood-taking part was really hot. What was so horrible about that? The pain? Minute, compared to the pleasure.

Oh, Lucy, what are you thinking? Only Goth chicks in shredded clothing and black lipstick dream of shacking up with a vampire.

Because Truvin was right, he was nothing like the vampires in the romance novels. His life was not all pink-and-purple flourishes. And her life would never be happily ever after with a vampire. How could it? Sooner or later she'd run out of blood. *And die.*

Truvin slid a hand back and along her thigh. It wasn't to make sure she was firmly astride, but more to touch. And maybe reassure.

"We've lost them," he called back.

Hail Mary for that. So why wasn't he stopping?

Why stop? Lucy realized her fear had fled. Let him drive across the entire city. It felt too damn good clinging to his body and abandoning her cares.

The motorcycle veered from the street and rolled down a sloping stretch that led to a riverside warehouse. Lucy wasn't sure where they were. Bright streetlights pocked the vast grounds, but it was apparent no one was around. Not a night guard to stop them from riding past the entrance posts and through the courtyard. Beyond the main warehouse stretched a dock littered with moorings and snow shoveled into mounds up near the building.

"I think this is private property."

"Then they should have put up a fence." Truvin stopped the motorcycle and tilted his head back to nuzzle his cheek against hers. "You okay?"

"My first motorcycle ride. It was good."

The melting warmth of him seeping into her pores chased her fears into the shadows. A sexual tingle stirred her veins and Lucy hugged him, riding the last remnants of the motorcycle's vibrations.

"You've never been on a motorbike before? Lucy, you need to get out more often."

"I know! It felt like freedom. I want a change, Truvin. It's like I can feel it brewing within me, waiting for release."

Hooking a leg up over his thigh, she scooted closer and lifted the other leg up to wrap about him. He caught her under the knees and held on tight. Skirt hiked high, she snuggled her crotch against his ass.

"I've been working since I was sixteen. Work is, well…work. And my job is probably not going to be there for much longer. Which is fine by me. It's not what I need to be doing with my life."

"Let me guess. Taking in strays is just the beginning of your goals. You want to help others?"

"Yes, philanthropy."

"I was thinking more on the lines of an animal shelter."

"Too small of a dream. I want to help people. Do you know I'm on the Red Cross charity-ball committee?"

"That is some fine irony."

"No kidding. Begging for blood donations while shacking up with a vampire. But you know what I'd really like to do?"

Dare she say it? She'd been thinking it, but maybe it was too selfish.

"I'd love to take off a few years, not have to work at all, and travel. Do things for myself. Sounds selfish, doesn't it?"

"Sounds like a smart woman taking care of herself. Why don't you? Do you have savings?"

"I do." *Did.* "But probably no more than a few months' worth of freedom. I suppose that should be enough. But then it's back to the grindstone. I don't know where to begin, you know? How to get the things I really want, and to start to give to others in a meaningful way."

"Don't you have to be rich to be a philanthropist?"

"It would help." A few thick snowflakes dropped onto Lucy's face. She shivered and wrapped her arms around Truvin's chest. "Charity can start small. But I'm not an idea person. I want to raise funds and leave the real work to someone else."

"I think it's a noble pursuit. But it could take a lifetime, and even then, you might not be satisfied with the little you've accomplished."

"I need two lifetimes, perhaps. Oh, Truvin, don't you love your life? I can't imagine having so much time. What do you do with yourself? Have you worked since you became a vampire? How do you survive? Do you remember?"

"My darling, inquisitive Lucy. I've never worked in the traditional sense, but I do know the stock market up, down and inside out. That's how I survive. Couldn't imagine doing the nine-to-five thing."

She slid a hand around and tugged his shirt out from his pants, then slid her fingers up over his abs. "You're so warm."

"And you are like ice. What am I doing?" He leaned forward and shrugged off his coat, then wrapped it around her shoulders. "Better?"

She nodded and then tilted back her head. Thrusting out her tongue, she waited to capture a snowflake. The chilled morsels were thick as goose down and melted instantly on her tongue.

"You ever taste snowflakes?" she asked. A lash of her tongue caught a particularly thick specimen. "Mmm, raspberry."

"Raspberry? Is that so?" He tilted back his head, and landed it on her shoulder. A teasing smirk preceded a dash of his tongue. "That one tastes like water. That one, too."

"You've no imagination, Truvin." She closed her eyes. A few flakes lit upon her eyelids and melted cool tears down her cheeks. Another landed her top lip and she licked it off. "That one tastes like eight."

"Eight?"

"Yep. Me, eight years old, playing in the backyard in the middle of February, all bundled up in my purple Arctic Cat snowsuit and homemade crocheted mittens and cap. I'd dig myself an igloo and crawl inside and just lie there, talking to myself, carving pictures on the snow walls. I used to love playing in the snow. My mother would have to come looking for me after a few hours for fear I'd freeze."

"But you never did."

"I'm Minnesota born and bred. I've snowflakes in my veins."

"All that from one snowflake? I must be eating the wrong ones."

She leaned in and again circled his chest with her arms. "Do you have any memories of your childhood?"

"Not at the moment. Though, I'm sure they're in the old noggin somewhere. Perhaps nothing so sweet as yours. You said your parents have passed?"

"Yeah."

"Then you'd better keep eating snowflakes. What a great way to remember the good times."

It was, and would continue to be. Lucy hadn't thought of her parents for a while. The memory of her childhood, while bittersweet, also felt rich, valuable. Because she'd learned, through Truvin, how awful it could be not to remember. To never know if he had been loved.

She hugged him tightly. This man would not stand alone, she wouldn't think of it.

"I suppose we should be heading back."

"We were headed to your house before we saw the witches and the priest."

"Lucy, they were the people who did this to me. I'll never have answers until I face them."

"But is death worth the risk?"

"There must be some way to take precautions. I've done enough running."

"I'm glad you ran tonight. For me."

"I like doing things for you."

"I could think of a few things I could do for you right now." She tugged at the waistband of his pants.

"You didn't want to have sex in the club, but you're willing out here in the middle of nowhere? It's snowing, Lucy."

"Yes, but can you imagine the flavor of those snowflake memories?"

He twisted to lean in for a kiss. "I think I can taste them already."

And a huge snowflake *plonked* between their close faces, landing his mouth.

* * *

Truvin insisted they return the motorcycle to the nightclub parking lot. He was no thief. From there, they took a cab to his home in Minneapolis.

Far from a simple apartment, he owned a penthouse near the top of the Carlyle, one of the most elite buildings in the city. The walls were ninety percent windows. Hanging plants were the only color in the white-and-black space. Upon arrival, Lucy rushed about the vast living room, checking the skyline.

"You can see the whole city from up here," Truvin commented as he strode into his home for the first time in almost a week. "Not that the city is all that large, but on a clear night you can see Saint Paul, as well."

He smoothed a palm over the back of the leather couch.

It felt good to be home. And to know it was *his* home. To know that it was he who had tended to the design of the layout. The black marble countertops in the kitchen. The sleek black leather furniture in the living room. The silver sculpture that separated the living area from the bedroom and bath.

To simply…know.

He felt he'd gotten about forty percent of his memory back. He knew the who and the what, but not the why or when. The why was all his history, and that was still in fragments that meant little more than flashes of indiscernible scenes.

There were still things that eluded him. Like why the witches were after him. What had he done? And to bring in the priest, and want to destroy him in such a manner that would see him suffering a miserable holy wound?

Lucy's high heels clicked across the floor and she spun into his arms. "This place is amazing. You really live large. Oh, look at the crystal in your kitchen cupboards. Truvin, I wouldn't expect you'd have dishes. Do you eat real food?"

"All for appearance," he said. Lucy went to the glass-fronted cupboards and studied his collection of china and stemware. "Now that I'm here, and I look at things, it's as if the world is returning. Or at least the part of the world that is my home. I have a maid who comes to dust once a week. She always seems to miss the light fixtures, though." He glanced to the modern white glass globes that hung over the kitchen bar. The dust was thick up there. "How about a glass of wine? That's something I enjoy indulging in."

He poured them goblets of wine, while Lucy excused herself to the bathroom. Probably to snoop. Females liked to do that. But he had nothing to hide. At least, that he could remember.

As he sipped the wine, its heady body filled his mouth and tickled the back of his throat. He knew this label. It was a late-eighteenth-century burgundy. A time of remarkable memories…

The gelding simply would not allow him to approach it. It kicked up onto its hind legs and snapped out its front legs. Truvin almost took a hoof to the skull, but he'd mastered the finesse of moving quickly.

He'd been a vampire for a month now, and had, reluctantly, followed his blood master to the city of Paris. Damien Desrues was the name of the haunted soul who had transformed him. Haunted and *mad* were the only words to describe that vampire.*

But he had no one else to lean on as he learned this new and peculiar life, so Truvin followed.

"You need to get that one bewitched," Damien commented as he mounted his own horse in a stable behind his sister's house. "Beasts of fur and feather do not favor our kind." He slapped the horse's withers. "Vixen adores me, don't you, girl?"

"Bewitched?"

"Yes, a witch must put a spell to the horse so it will not recognize you as a vampire. Simple enough. The spell, that is. It's getting a witch to do the task, without first murdering you, that's the tough part."

"I thought your sister a witch?"

"Yes, and she and the vicomte have left for the Americas on a sightseeing excursion. Won't be back for months. I can direct you toward a particularly pretty witch who lives on Saint-Honoré. Fancy part of the city."

"What if she spits on me?"

"Then you, my friend, are no more."

The witch in question would not know Truvin was a vampire unless she actually saw him drink blood, or do something vampire-like, such as taking large leaps from building to building. Yet Truvin formed a plan. Seduction. He'd seduced many a woman before settling down to ask for Anna's hand.

He found the witch, Mademoiselle Rowan, at a narrow home stuck between two grand estates. A little wine and lots of foreplay, and she became putty upon the tattered damask divan. She fell into his arms, and their clothes shed as quickly about their feet. It was difficult to hold back the blood hunger, for Truvin found that the desire to take blood always accompanied sex.

Caution remained paramount. The moment the witch spied his fangs, he was dead.

"Now, my love…"

"You're a vampire, aren't you?" Wide, wondering blue eyes beseeched from under a scatter of black bangs.

How did she know? Did he wear a sign of advertisement such as what hung above a butchery?

"Don't worry, Truvin. I love you."

Love? He had known her for all of two hours. Besides being pretty, she must be as mad as his blood master.

"I could never harm you. I'll bespell the horse right now, to prove it."

The sudden uneasy shiver that had crossed Truvin's scalp the moment she'd revealed she knew what he was just as quickly dissipated. She seemed true. And right now, she stood before the horse, chanting a rhyme and making strange signs upon its forehead with her finger.

"Done." She gestured he join her.

Truvin joined the witch's side. She slid her hand into his, clasping it possessively. The horse did not rear back at him.

"You've done it. The beast is docile and accepting. Thank you, Abigail." He leaned in to kiss her, yet paused before tasting salty flesh.

As new to vampirism as he was, he was not a fool. In fact, it could only be so much time before she turned on him. A witch would always hold the power over a vampire.

"What is it, Truvin?"

"Abigail." He traced her collarbone and slid a hand along her neck. "You've been very kind, but you know this can never be."

The tip of her pointed chin began to quiver. "Oh, but it can. I would be very careful, Truvin. I promise you. And no one would ever have to know."

"I would know." He kissed her forehead, while bracketing his hands about her neck.

And then he squeezed.

And he turned her around so she faced away from him, so her scrambling hands could not reach up and claw at him. It took but a minute, and she collapsed at his feet. Strangled.

"Had to be done."

No longer was he the man who had been engaged a month earlier, set on a quiet life with his one true love. He had been irrevocably changed. And there was nothing he could do about it.

Truvin mounted the horse, and sped out of the stable.

Chapter 17

He had only done what he must to survive. No regrets. Not a one.

And if any mortal sought to point a morality gauge his way, they should point it back at themselves. The world he occupied was leaps and bounds different from that of mortals.

Truvin Stone was a good vampire. But not necessarily a good mortal.

Though, now he'd had a taste of the mortal life and its sweet rewards, he desperately wanted to remain as good as he had been since Lucy had rescued him.

"I wonder…"

The baptism. Such a ritual was supposed to erase a man's sins. Could it possibly be that the sins of his past had been erased? The idea overwhelmed. It was just too incredible to imagine. But maybe?

"S'pose drinking blood knocked me off the sinless list, though."

Ah, well. For a brief moment, he had been without sin.

Hooking the goblet of burgundy between two fingers, Truvin strode into the bedroom. Lucy lay on the black Matelasse spread, looking up at herself.

"This is so cliché," she commented on the mirrors tiling the ceiling.

"Would you believe me if I said they were there when I moved in?"

"Sure. But you kept them." She reached for a goblet, but missed it. Instead, she rolled into a coil, pressing her face into a pillow.

"Lucy, what's wrong?"

She grimaced and eased a hand over her stomach. "Just a little hungry. We should have stopped for something to eat. I'm guessing you don't stock real food here."

"I might have some Asiago bread around here somewhere." He wandered the periphery of the room, taking in the shape of it, reacquainting himself to the room. "Though when the maid last shopped, I'm not sure."

"I'll pass. Hand me the wine. Oh, this smells good."

"Burgundy. Appellation 1799. Grown in earth that was once a raspberry field. It's from my private collection."

"A good year?"

"If I recall correctly, it was certainly very interesting."

He wandered to the opposite side of the room to inspect the large picture framed on the wall.

"And do you recall correctly?"

"I do. Lucy, will you look at this? I'll be bloody damned, it's the Demengeot. The very same monogram you have above your bed. Isn't that a lark?"

She turned on the bed to inspect. "It looks very old. Don't tell me—is that—?"

"The original." He turned with a satisfied grin to his face. "I remember now. I knew Demengeot. In fact, I had fancied having my own sort of monogram and engraving shop when I was younger. Before all this happened."

"Wow. You're a creative man?"

"I've my moments."

"How much do you remember now, Truvin?"

"A lot of my past, but still nothing from my recent present."

He sipped the wine and twirled the goblet stem between his fingers, sloshing the deep liquid around the globe. "I moved to Venice the year this was created."

"What a romantic city."

"Have you been?"

"Only in my dreams." She patted the bed beside her.

Truvin slid onto the bed and sat with one leg stretched before him. Lucy snuggled into the many pillows. He never could figure why it was necessary to have so many, or how he acquired them. Did they multiply?

Setting back all the wine, he then put the goblet on the vanity and leaned in to nestle aside Lucy. "I had just arrived in Venice after fleeing Paris."

"Who was after you?"

"Well…"

Trusting green eyes waited with anticipation behind the rim of the wineglass.

Maybe this sharing thing wasn't the smartest idea. He didn't want to hurt her with evidence of the real vampire he had been. *Racking up more sins for that list?* Right. Yet, not telling the truth could be far more dangerous.

"A witch," he finally said. "I'd tricked her to bespell my

horse, and, well, let's say that was the beginning of my education in the vast divide between vampires and witches."

"Why would you need to put a spell on a horse?"

"Because." He leaned in and kissed her stomach. "Horses—as most beasts—fear my kind. They innately sense we are not completely mortal. And it was difficult to get around at the end of the eighteenth century without a horse, so…"

"You needed a spell. Huh. My cats didn't fear you."

"Cats are strange creatures. Not completely of this realm. I don't like them because they are so independent and yet, it always appears as if they know you better than you do yourself."

"In your case, that would be true, Mr. Amnesiac Vampire. That sounds like the title of a romance. Ha!"

"I'm all for romance. And sex."

Tugging Lucy's shirt buttons free from their tiny slots, Truvin pushed back the silk, exposing a pink lacy bra. Beneath the lace waited two tasty confections all wrapped up for his pleasure.

Kissing beneath her breasts to trail down to her belly button, he remarked she tasted like the outdoors. A hint of motorbike exhaust clung to her clothing—to both of them—and beyond that, the fresh taste of winter.

Landing the monarch-butterfly tattoo down and to the left of her belly button, he traced the pad of his thumb over the delicate artwork. He remembered that first night at Carnivale when he had taken the girl in the butterfly mask.

It had been a beginning to a carefully mastered life. And now here he stood at a crossroad. To step back into that which he found comfortable, or to step forward into the new and the unknown?

Rolling to his back, Truvin let out a sigh and said, "I call them butterflies, you know."

"Who? The witches?"

"No, my victims. The gorgeous butterflies who fluttered about at social events, and in and about me like winged insects hoping to capture my attention. I stalked them. Each victim was a butterfly, trapped in my net. Pinned, like those you pin for your pleasure. I pinned them for my pleasure."

"Sounds decadent."

"It was." He marveled at her greedy interest. Perhaps the wine had begun to take hold of her senses. "But I never killed them. I simply left them in the swoon, under the spell of persuasion."

Twining her fingers within his, she tapped the silver ring he wore on his thumb. "Have you used persuasion on me?"

"No, and I don't intend to. You are too exquisite to control, darling."

She rolled onto him, straddling his hips with her knees. Loose, wavy hair dusted his chin and face. "Am I a butterfly? Do you want to stalk me?"

She kissed the underside of his chin, nipping teasingly at his neck. Right there, where he always pinned them. He'd never been bitten himself, save by his blood master. Nor had he created a blood child. So he did not know the sensation of giving blood.

"I want to be the only butterfly in your net."

"Lucy—"

"Do you need to drink blood often? I could survive. During my research I learned it takes the human body about a day to regenerate small blood loss. And we've got five quarts in our bodies. Something like that, anyway."

Flipping her onto her back landed her in a nest of pillows. Truvin pulled down the pink lace bra and the plastic center clasp snapped open.

"Lucy, you ask too much. It wouldn't work. Should I make you my sort of…blood slave, you'd be dead within the month."

He bent to lick her nipple. Her moans stabbed him deeply with the sweetest kind of torture. Her hands clung to him, clutching, pleading for acceptance.

He tore off his shirt, dropping it on the floor by the bed. Finding the zipper on Lucy's skirt at the side of her hip, he made quick work of it, but—she suddenly cringed into a ball beneath him, her head snapping to her chest.

"Those can't be hunger pangs, Lucy. Are you sure you're feeling all right?" He smoothed the hair from her face. Her eyes watered and she shook her head.

"Not sure. Oh, it's getting stronger."

"Your forehead is hot."

"Maybe I've picked up a touch of flu. Or maybe I'm just horny again." A small chuckle did little to convince. "I feel…I don't know…I want comfort, closeness. I need you to touch me, Truvin. To take blood from me again. Yes, and then I'll be fine."

If she wanted to be bitten something was wrong. All his victims could walk away from a bite, never remembering, and not once pining. It generally took many bites over a short period for the blood slave to actually crave the bite.

Sliding her skirt down her thighs, Truvin kissed her mouth. "I think we'll take it slow tonight. It's only been a few hours since I drank from you in the club. Let's just make love."

"You can do that without taking blood?"

"Of course. I'm not ruled by my hunger. Unless it's for flesh." He licked her nipple. "You taste like cinnamon."

"Must be from the pancakes I made after sex. They were good. You should have tried them."

"This is the only sustenance I require. Yes, Lucy."

She directed his cock inside her, and the gorgeous hug of her drew a gasp from him. Lucy wrapped around him. Lucy caressing him. The blood could wait. He'd taken from her earlier. And the previous night when he'd been a little out of his head, and should have been more careful.

Bloody hell. Had he—he'd not licked the wound that first

night when memory of his vampirism had been so new. No wonder the bite marks hadn't begun to heal.

"Oh hell, Lucy." He pulled out from her, even as she greedily grasped at him to remain. "No, I did not. I couldn't have."

Sliding off the bed, Truvin stalked to the end of it and began to pace before the large monogram on the wall, pounding at his forehead with the heel of his palm.

He remembered now. And this memory was not a boon to own.

"Truvin, I was so close to coming. Did I do something wrong?"

"Your hunger pangs. I've been such an irresponsible fool!"

She climbed to the end of the bed and knelt there. Loose curls spilled across her shoulders, and ended at each nipple. Her taut stomach glistened with a few dots of perspiration.

That tattoo, it screamed at Truvin for what he had done. An innocent butterfly…caught in his net…*until otherwise inclined.* The priest had been all too knowing.

"I think I've changed you, Lucy."

Chapter 18

Lucy sat up in the center of the bed, unmindful of her nudity. Chestnut hair tickled her breast. Legs spread and bent, she leaned forward between them and tapped the soft white velvet comforter crushed at the end of the bed. Though the furnishings were spare, the materials used were rich and lush.

What Truvin said made sense. She didn't have to question him. Didn't feel the need to blurt out protests or random pleas for it to be untrue.

A vampire had bitten her. And now he'd told her that she was changing.

She was becoming a vampire.

Which explained the weird ache in her gut. It didn't feel as if she needed food, but it was an insistent moan for...something. Fulfillment. Satisfaction. Life?

It must be the way Truvin had felt after she'd found him and he couldn't know what he was craving, while his body had insisted. He'd thought he'd wanted food; a man with amnesia could never imagine that craving would actually be for blood.

Lucy reached out for Truvin, who paced beside the bed. "Sit down with me. Let's talk about this."

"Talk? Lucy, do you realize what I've done to you?"

"Yes, but it won't help me to rant about it. Or to cry."

She sat back against the stack of pillows, wondering where the tears were. A girl should have a good ole cryfest if she's learned she's to become a creature of the night.

She didn't feel anything right now. Except the hunger. And a hankering for more Truvin. The man was naked, and his erection had not gone down.

"I can accept this," she said. "I have to. I have no choice, right? It's not as if you can take it back, make me unbitten."

"You do have a choice." Truvin gripped her by the shoulders and knelt before her. Sex scent and a sharp aggression coated his aura—it smelled great to Lucy. He was in control; he had power over her.

"Let's make love again. I want to come the same time as you do."

"Listen to me, Lucy. I remember something my blood master taught me. If you don't drink blood before the full moon, the vampire taint will pass through you," he explained.

She listened, but it was difficult to hear beyond her body's insistence for more sex. He smelled so sexy. It was as if she could scent his blood. And the desire to taste it was as strong as a craving for chocolate.

"But if you do drink blood," he continued, oblivious to Lucy's distraction, "then the transformation occurs. So you must wait. The full moon is—" he glanced out the window to find the three-quarter moon peeking in on them "—less than a week away. And those rumors of madness, well…"

"Madness?"

"I won't allow it to happen. With support, you can resist the call to the hunger. I don't want this for you."

Madness? She wasn't sure what that was about. It certainly didn't sound as appealing as chocolate and Truvin's making love to her.

"Lucy, the ache you feel is the blood hunger." Truvin smoothed a hand down her stomach, pulling back as if stung when he touched the tattoo. "It was a horrible mistake, biting you, without then ensuring the wound was sealed. So now I must take responsibility. Don't hate me for wanting you to have a normal life," he whispered in her ear.

His scent frenzied her desire. She wanted him, needed him. "I'm cool with that."

"Are you?"

Bowing her head against his shoulder, she sighed. "What's this madness you mentioned? I think that's something I should know about. Sounds ominous."

"It's a risk should you decide to wait for the moon. If you can resist drinking blood before the full moon, you will not become vampire. But the blood hunger can become so strong, so persistent, madness may set in should you try to fight it."

"Peachy. A good reason not to avoid my destiny."

"This is not your destiny, Lucy."

"How do you know? How do you know I haven't been walking toward this my entire life? My fascination with vampire novels? Maybe that's been a strange sort of preparation for this moment."

"They are research, Lucy. You have no more fascination for the vampire than I do for your cats."

"Oh yeah? Well, how about my job? Seeking out myths and people who claim to be paranormal? Don't you see? If not fascinated, then at the very least, I'm ready for this. It's been waiting for me. Now I simply need to accept the offer."

She smiled an easy smile. A resolute smile. "Truvin, I'm not a little girl. I can think for myself. I can deal with this."

"*This* is a dangerous life. It's not glamorous, nor is it only for the beautiful people. Vampires are monst—er, they drink the blood of mortals. And…you'll never again have sunshine."

"I've always burned horribly anyway. Attribute that to my Scandinavian heritage. We made good Vikings but horrible suntan models."

"Lucy! What about the butterflies? They don't come out at night. You'll never again experience the joy of watching them like you do now."

"Then it's a good thing I've got a few pinned. I can look at them whenever I want. Besides, there are some gorgeous night-flying moths to be had."

Lucy slid off the bed. The sex had been brief, and she'd not come before Truvin had freaked. Unfulfilled. Empty in her belly. And he was just prolonging that quest for satisfaction. "What if I want it?"

"Want—Lucy, you don't know what you're talking about."

"Since when did you become my master? You can't tell me what to do." She retrieved her shirt and skirt and began to dress. "Or can you? Is that it? You're my blood master now. I have to bow to you and do as you command?"

Clasping his arms high across his chest, Truvin paced the floor, head down. The muscle in his jaw pulsed.

"Listen, Truvin, I know there are things I'd have to give up. My job, for one. But I wasn't happy at KSNW5, nor was I appreciated. That's no biggie. I think I'll have to learn to invest though, because I don't know how a person sustains themselves over the decades without a job."

"It is as simple as hiring an investor—what am I saying? Lucy—"

"And I know I'll have to develop a taste for blood, and maybe even kill."

"You don't have to kill to survive."

"Really?" She exhaled. "Good, 'cause that's the one thing I'm not too keen on. And you know, I'm not really into black and brooding, but I'll give anything a try once."

"Do you think I brood?"

"No, but you do have an irresistible old-world atmosphere to you."

"But don't you see? I cannot simply walk the street as if a mortal. I must always consider my moves before I make them. I live in the shadows."

"You're starting to sound like a certain Goth I interviewed a few nights ago."

"Lucy, you're not listening to me. Do you want to end up like those butterflies you've pinned to hang on your wall? Forever captured, trapped in time."

"Never aging."

"Never free, Lucy. Never free."

"You're being dramatic. You're completely free. So you have to avoid the sunlight—"

Truvin caught her about the waist and pushed her against the wall. "You will not do this, Lucy. Look at me. I won't allow it."

The touch of his influence crept around the edges of her thoughts. *Do as I wish*, it said.

"You're trying to persuade me, I can feel it."

Much as she wanted to do whatever this handsome man should ask of her, she would not allow him to direct her life. "I want this, Truvin. This is the freedom I've been looking for."

"To take on a lifestyle that forces you to stalk innocent humans and drink their blood so that you may survive? Lucy, that is not freedom."

"It's seemed to work well enough for you. For how many centuries? Two or three?"

"Two, but—"

"Don't you see? If I am immortal think of all the time I'll have to devote to helping others."

"Helping—? Taking blood from innocent mortals does not help them."

"But that's only to survive. Who says a vampire has to be a creepy shadow-stalking creature? Why not be a philanthropist? You dress in thousand-dollar suits. You're not a grave creeper. You must be very affluent."

He shook his head. "I still don't have those recent memories. And that's not a reason for you to consider this."

"Oh, I get it. I suppose a man who's been around a few centuries doesn't do the relationship thing. Well, don't worry, I won't bother you. I'm leaving."

She zipped up her skirt, hooked the high heels on her fingers and marched out to the kitchen. "Glad you got your memory back. Good knowing you."

Truvin was at the front door before she could finish buttoning her shirt. Lucy cocked a hand at her hip and worked her best glare on him. He had no right to tell her what to do.

"Why are you being this way, Lucy? I don't want you to be angry with me."

"I'm not angry. In fact, I should offer my thanks. When I most needed it, you've stepped in and changed my life. For the better. But if you think you can order me around and tell me how to live my life, I'd rather not be involved with you. I'm not big on clingy men. Or control freaks."

She coached herself to stop eyeing his erection. Snapping her head up to meet him face-to-face, Lucy steeled her resolve.

"Pity, because it would have been great to have you show

me the ropes," she said calmly. "Guess I'll have to dig through my romance novels to figure it all out."

"Those stories are not going to teach you a thing."

"It's all I have."

"Will they guide you through the first bite? That first time you know you need something, but how on earth to get it when you haven't fangs yet?"

"Maybe."

"Can a novel show you how to live in the shadows, to stalk your prey, and to drink so that you don't have bloodstains all over your clothing? It's not easy, Lucy. You can't become a vampire like an actress takes on a new role."

"Let me go."

"No."

Dropping her shoes at her feet, Lucy stepped into them. He still blocked the door, and, no, that erection had not gone down. The world through the wraparound windows was a dull white thanks to the inner-glass shading system he used. She wasn't even sure if it was day or night.

She didn't want it to be this way. She wanted Truvin in her life. "Will you help me?"

The tension in his face pulsed a jaw muscle. Lucy wanted to touch it. To feel his strength. Because she knew he was stronger than her and more powerful, and probably even wiser. Hell, she wanted to plunge into his arms and feel safe, to know he loved her, and to make the world stop while she sorted through her feelings.

Love? No, it was too fast. But caring, she could use a little compassion.

Was she pleased about becoming a vampire?

It was too soon to know.

Maybe she should wait out the full moon. What the hell did madness have to do with it all?

"Truvin—" her body shivered and Lucy dropped her pretense "—I'm scared."

And he embraced her. The tears came easily and abundantly. And though he didn't say a word, standing in his arms made the world easier to live in for the moment.

Abigail Rowan stalked before Midge in the tiny porch that reeked of peppermint and rosemary. The elder witch had not paid a visit since childhood. Midge recalled the morning of her tenth birthday when Abigail had stood in the doorway, dressed all in white, talking to her mother.

It was that day Mother had explained to Midge that she was a witch. And finally Midge had answers to why she could sense the feelings of her friends before they felt them, and why it was so easy to move objects across the table, like the cereal box and milk.

"Miguel tells me you've been talking to the media." Abigail's voice was as cool as her sleek white suit.

Damn that pseudovamp. Sure, Midge had a Goth friend who thought he was a vampire—but he wasn't. Miguel was a normal human with a tendency for piercings and spider tattoos. He did hang with real witches, though, because most witches were female, and they had nothing against mortal friends and companions.

"It's some stupid show that's trying to prove vampires don't exist," Midge said. "I didn't tell them anything that would actually make them believe. Trust me, the woman who interviewed me seemed to be holding back laughter the whole time. You know the scene."

"Did she mention the vampire Truvin Stone?"

Midge made to pour tea so she wouldn't expose her shock to Abigail. "T-Truvin? Weird name. Uffda, no, she didn't mention him. I certainly would have remembered that name if she had."

She'd had a vampire in her home? Curses!

"What was the reporter's name?"

Midge swallowed. Much as she hated vampires, if there was one allied with Lucy Morgan, she wasn't keen on turning Lucy over for the witches to interrogate. She liked Lucy. And since when have Abigail and her clan ever even given Midge the time of day?

The hunts she'd told Lucy she went on? Only in her dreams. The vamp slayers were an elusive crew of witches who did not like outsiders begging for admittance.

"Her name? Not sure."

"Not sure, or not willing?"

"I just know her as Lucy." Midge tugged on the row of earrings queuing along her earlobe. "She didn't give me a last name."

"Business card?"

Midge shrugged.

"What television station?"

"I don't recall. It was a local one, but not one of the big ones. The station with the snowflake in their banner."

Abigail's pale blue eyes held Midge for but a second before releasing her from the intrusion of a fix. A witch could fix another in her gaze and touch her soul if she were powerful enough. Abigail was that powerful, so it surprised Midge when the witch turned and stalked away.

"We never spoke," Abigail said as she closed the front door behind her.

Midge sank against the wall and clasped her arms across her stomach as she hung her head. "I'm getting in over my head."

And so was Lucy. When Abigail's crew went after a mortal, it wasn't for a picnic and girl chat.

"I've got to warn her."

"It's so gorgeous."

The sun had not yet risen. Standing at the top of the world, looking over the city from Truvin's bedroom window, Lucy felt like stretching her arms wide. Heavy, thick snowflakes seasoned the buildings with whiteness.

"It's like a pillow fight gone bad," she said and then did set out her arms and leaned back.

Truvin slid up behind her and kissed the side of her neck. "This part of the world is a good place for vampires. Not a lot of sun during the winter months, and those months tend to drag out for a long time. But spring should be on its way soon."

"Do you go into hiding in the summer?"

"Nope. Just stalk the night. I don't sleep much, if you've noticed. Need less than a few hours a day." He moved around to caress her jaw and what Lucy saw in the depths of his gaze tickled her insides like a grin.

"You talk of it as if it is a dream. Yet you won't allow me to change?"

"Lucy, you will have regrets—"

"Regrets are boring."

They had settled their earlier argument with sex. Wonderful, needy, makeup sex. But sex wasn't going to change Lucy's mind.

"I'm looking forward to a new life. And traveling! I could so travel. I won't miss my job, you know that. Proving vampires a myth? Ha!"

"It's better that way, Lucy. Keep perpetuating the myth, and the mortals will never believe."

"I believe." She turned and drew a fingernail up his stomach. "All right, I'll play it your way. For a while. I want this. You do not. But it's not your choice. We'll see who wins."

"This is not a competition. How can I convince you this is not what you want?"

He strode to the closet and opened the doors to reveal dozens of gray Zegna suits. Safer to have all the same, Lucy figured. Easier. At least where a man was concerned.

"All the same?" she asked. "I never imagined you'd be so…"

"Unimaginative?"

"Right. What's that one?"

"Doesn't look like a suit." Truvin drew out the black set of clothing that Lucy pointed out. He didn't recognize it, that was obvious from his surprise. A set of amber-glassed eye goggles was hung about the neck of the wooden hanger. "It's like heavy-duty protection stuff."

"Do you have a secret life as a spy I don't know about?" She bent to retrieve her clothes from the floor. "Truvin?"

Lucy spun around to find Truvin standing before the closet, the outfit clutched to his chest. Lost in a trance. His fingers dug into the sleeve of the black jacket. A huff of breath preceded his gasp.

No trance, but a memory.

"Bloody hell, Lucy." He thrust the clothing to the floor as if it were on fire. "I know why they're after me. I was after them!"

Chapter 19

"I've a crew of fellow vamps," Truvin explained, a trifle astonished. "They—*we*—go after the witches. We wear these suits of DragonSkin and masks to protect ourselves from their scratches and from witch blood. Then we..."

Slamming his shoulder against the closet door, he searched Lucy's face.

She could guess what he did not say. Then we *kill them*.

"The witches sent you to the cathedral," she tried. Despite Truvin's obvious shock, she couldn't help speculate. "They were after you. Maybe one of their scouts had a scuffle with you in the alley, knocked you out—"

"Lucy, it doesn't matter! Don't you see? I've killed them. I am responsible for many deaths. And I have no remorse for it. It is what I do. I have been running from witches all my life. And only recently have I been able to turn around and run after them."

He held up a pair of amber-lensed goggles. "This is me."

She took a step back as he approached. His eyes blazed boldly, determination squaring his jaw.

"I am a witch killer, Lucy. And—now that I remember—I have no intention of stopping this war with them." He looked down and to the side. "I must contact Gear and Nathaniel. They'll be wondering where I've been."

"So it's as easy as that?" Hurt that her lover calmly took claim to something so cruel, Lucy couldn't meet his gaze.

"Yes, it's so easy." He pushed back his shoulders and assumed the stance that always made her aware of his strength. "How do you like me now?"

Feeling the need to put some distance between the two of them, Lucy backed toward the door. "So much has happened. You are…you're just being honest with me."

"I am."

"I can't begin to comprehend your world."

"No, you cannot. And let's hope it changes your mind about seeking vampirism yourself."

"Yes, I…should go."

"Shall I have my driver take you home?"

"You've a driver?"

"Of course. And now it's mentioned, that explains why I hadn't ID or cash on me when I was attacked behind the building. Jeeves carries all that stuff for me."

Truvin had pulled on a costume of privilege, that of wealth and power. And murder. It wasn't him. Not anymore. Lucy felt it was only a costume, a protection against the real man beneath. The man she knew.

Please, don't let it be what he really is.

He took her by the shoulders. "This life—vampirism—is—"

"I know. It's not like fiction. I'm a big girl, Truvin. And I'm not stupid. I've got all the facts, and I'll examine them carefully. I'm going now. Thanks for…"

Making me fall for a creature that has no remorse over killing others. For beginning my path to vampirism. For making me want something I shouldn't have. For allowing me to fall in love and to finally think only of myself.

And look where that had gotten her. "Bye."

Shutting the door behind her, Lucy stumbled as she made for the elevator at the end of the hallway. Clutching the wall for support, she pressed her forehead to it and told herself she would not cry. Not until she was home and alone.

This home. This life. He was a loner. It was not something he had asked for, but instead, the path he knew he had taken to ensure his survival.

Rare was the vampire who had a family, or mortal lover. Too risky. And even if he could make a go of it, what would come of him when his family died? Left alone again. Truvin had decided, early on, to avoid that risk.

Yet, for nearly a week of lacking memory, he'd allowed another into his life. And he liked it. In a short time Lucy had managed to imprint herself upon him. He didn't want to rub off that mark.

Yet now that he remembered, could he push her away to resume the lifestyle he'd carefully constructed?

Or, could he embrace her and try something new? It had taken a mere bump to the head to change two centuries of thinking. And he still held on to that new mind-set. Was there a possibility?

Could she love him?

"Do you love her, you crazy vampire?"

Stretching his arms out, he swung them back and forth before his chest, flexing out the anxiety.

He'd hurt her with his truth. Lucy hadn't been able to hide her shock. She had needed to know. It wasn't fair to her any other way. Much as it pained him to see the fear in her eyes. To feel her tremble because she did not understand him.

He wasn't sure he understood himself.

But he remembered now. All of it.

Vampires had literally run from the witches over the centuries. Truvin had thought it high time he dug in his heels and turned to face the enemy head-on. He would no longer fear. He would fight back. This was a war. Someone had to step up and lead.

"It's Lucy or the call to arms," he muttered. "I don't believe I can have them both."

Which called to him louder? To wander the world, seeking and killing witches so that his kind would not have to walk with one eye constantly looking over their shoulder?

Or to surrender to the inevitable—that this war was an impossible quest—and to love Lucy?

He had not loved since Anna. Not real, heart-squeezing, soul-baring love. And he wasn't stupid. He'd known Lucy but a week. Love didn't come so quickly. And yet, he did feel differently about her, as compared to any other woman he'd ever had in his long lifetime. The sex was amazing, but he knew the difference between lust and love.

Could he be falling in love?

"I would only hurt her. She wants to transform because she thinks I love her. I can't let her believe that. I…can't. For her own safety."

Truvin nodded. Decided. It felt the wrong decision, in his heart. But sometimes a man had to do things he didn't like, to make it right for others.

He picked up the phone and searched for Gear's number. Gear headed the crew of witch hunters.

Chapter 20

Instead of directing the driver to her home, Lucy had him drop her off at Café Latte. She was a mess, her hair tangled and her clothing rumpled, but she needed some caffeine. And maybe, not to be alone. Sitting amongst strangers tended to tamp down her anxiety; the restaurant was a frequent rest stop after a long day at work.

No sun today. It was up there somewhere, blanketed by white clouds. The Minnesota sun, ever teasing, was always cold in its promise.

Perhaps Truvin had been right.

"I would miss the sun," she murmured. She'd come to terms with the freckles that bloomed on her nose and shoulders each summer.

But seriously, there were things to consider, reasons against becoming a vampire.

"So I've one con. Missing the sun. Never aging? Pro."

"We've arrived, ma'am," the driver announced as he pulled alongside the cars parked before the restaurant.

Forgoing an admonishment for being called ma'am, Lucy nodded her thanks and slipped out the back door. The snow had stopped, but the sidewalks were slick and slushy. Deftly avoiding the wet mess, she scampered inside.

Passing over the rich desserts the café was famous for—and flaunted in the display case as you immediately entered the restaurant—Lucy ordered a cup of Japanese cherry tea and situated herself upstairs in the corner where the windows looked out over the intersection of Victoria and Grand Avenue. The Aveda store below was closed on Sundays, unfortunately.

The church crowd had begun to filter in. Lucy could smell the old-lady perfume and the starch used to press the men's Sunday best.

She took a long draft from her tea to divert her senses. Normally she would never pick up on scents like that. Not this far away.

I am becoming a vampire.

Really. I am.

How strange was that? She didn't feel different. Save, the aching craving that assaulted her in the chest. The vampire within wanted to become whole. Before the full moon.

And if she did make it to the full moon without drinking blood, then she risked madness, for the hunger could be relentless and push her over the edge.

"Great. Such choices. Madness or vampirism."

A couple walked by her table in search of a place to sit. Both wore neat, wool Sunday coats.

"Black clothing? Con. Designer clothes because I'm a rich vampire? Pro."

Inside, Lucy knew she had already decided. She could become the woman she wanted to be with the gift of vampirism. But she did owe Truvin the time to think on it. Hell, this was a major life change. Why was she taking it so lightly?

"Maybe you still don't buy any of this," she murmured as she blew over the rim of her teacup and curled her legs onto the bench to stare outside. "If I didn't have a bite mark on my neck, I'd probably look into a stay on the mental ward."

But she did have a bite mark. And it wasn't going to improve matters to freak about it. The unbelievable had happened to her. Now, to deal with it.

Con: no sunlight.

Pro: less money spent on sunscreen.

Lucy smirked. "Get serious, girl."

Con: drinking blood.

Pro: grocery bill virtually nonexistent.

When she did become a vampire, could she pass herself off among the mortals without sidelong glances and curious stares? Or would she stand out like a morose Goth kid with desperately pale skin and a constant jitter for blood akin to a drug addict's fetish for the needle?

Not that Truvin looked different from any Tom, Dick or Harry he passed on the streets. He wasn't. Breathtakingly handsome was a given. That alone would elicit stares. But there was nothing whatsoever vampirish about his appearance.

"A good thing," she muttered as she scanned the sidewalk below.

Of course, there were his fangs.

"Sexy." Lucy sighed and cast a look around the restaurant. No one was concerned about the daydreaming woman swooning over her tea. And, yeah, she was swooning. This felt good. Love.

Love with a completely different kind of man. It had been but a few days, but it felt like the love-at-first-sight myth she'd heard women talk about.

"It's not a myth. It feels real."

The coal-black hair of someone she recognized passed below on the sidewalk. "Midge." Lucy tapped the window, but realized she was too high up to be heard or seen. The witch turned into the café.

Lucy rushed to the top of the stairs and Midge noticed her right away. She bypassed the line and followed Lucy to the booth.

"I've been looking for you," the witch said in low tones. "You're in trouble, Lucy. I think they're going to try to follow you to get to Truvin."

"They? Follow—you know about Truvin?"

Midge slid close to Lucy on the booth seat so she could speak quietly. Both of them kept their eyes on the nearby diners. The witch was wrapped in a long black cape today, with calf-fitted black leather granny boots. The only color on her was the purple shadow she'd teased to curlicues at the corner of each dark eye.

"His name was brought up in a, er…*meeting* last night. Seems he witnessed a crossing."

"A crossing?"

"Laying of the cross to the vampire's flesh. It's what we call it. I know, weird. But, Lucy, you were there, too."

"Yes, it was outside the Blue Room. Were you there?"

"No, I…don't hang with that particular crowd."

"Good for you, Midge. They chased us, but we got away."

"Yeah, well, they got a good look at you. And earlier I went to your house to warn you. Oh, Lucy, I'm so sorry. I shouldn't have done that."

"Don't get upset. Oh, Midge. You didn't do anything wrong. You were trying to protect me, and I appreciate that. But how did you find out where I live?"

"The receptionist at the station gave me your address. I said I had flowers to deliver and couldn't read the address. You should so kick her ass for giving out your address." Midge grabbed Lucy's teacup and slugged back a swallow. "Uffda, but I think I was followed. It's not safe for you to go home, Lucy."

"Shoot. What about now? Were you followed here?"

"I don't think so. I took a cab and had them let me off in an alley. Where's Truvin?"

"Not telling."

"Fine. Don't. Then I won't be able to give him up if they torture me."

"They'd torture you?" The girl actually shivered. Lucy touched her hand. It was cold. "What kind of people are these witches? And a priest?"

"They're cool, Lucy. They're…my kind. They're just trying to protect their own. You don't understand the war between witches and vampires."

She thought of the armored suit Truvin kept in his closet. "I understand it's deadly."

"You got that right. And not something a mortal should get involved in. Do you think you could get out of town? Until they've found Truvin and taken care of him, I mean."

"I'm not going to let anyone hurt him."

"Lucy, please, he's a vamp—oh, no, you didn't." Midge swept the room with her violet eyes. Then she leaned in to whisper, "Are you in love? Uffda, Lucy, don't tell me you fell in love with a vampire. They are so bad news. You just don't know. They've been romanticized by the media, but you have to understand they are bloodthirsty killers."

"If they choose to be. They don't need to kill to survive."

"Whatever." Midge tugged up a black-and-red crocheted scarf around her neck. "They are deadly and not just to mortals. Truvin Stone and his gang started this war and now they've gotten what they can't stop. The witches are not going to step back and be subservient to vampires. Never again. Don't say I didn't warn you. Watch your back every step you take. I'm out of here."

"Midge." Lucy stood and slipped her hand into the witch's. "Thank you for telling me what you just did. It helps. And...know that I consider you my friend. No matter my alliances, I would never harm you."

"There's only one way to kill a witch," Midge said, her eyes tracing the floor.

"Don't tell me. I don't want to know."

The witch nodded and smiled. "Good."

The black Mercedes pulled up to the curb as Lucy stepped outside the restaurant. Truvin's driver. Had he been told to wait for her? The passenger window rolled down.

"I'm okay, Jeeves," she said. "I can walk."

"Absolutely not." He pointed toward the sky. "The clouds are receding."

The sky was dismal and pocked with thick gray clouds. Receding to reveal more clouds, no doubt.

The driver came around the trunk of the car and held open the back door for Lucy. "I'm not allowed to refuse your safety, ma'am. Please get inside."

"If you stop calling me ma'am."

"All right, Miss Morgan."

Lucy slid inside and settled onto the butter-soft leather seats. Jeeves—how much did she love that corny name?—tilted the rearview mirror to look at her. "Home?"

"I..." Not after what Midge told her. "I don't think it's safe. I spoke to a witch."

Jeeves arched a disturbed brow.

"She said I'm being followed by the witches who are after Truvin." The dude worked for a vampire; it should be safe to tell him this stuff. "I shouldn't risk going home, because they've been there once already."

"Just so. Very well, then back to Mr. Stone's."

"No." That came out entirely too forceful. "I just…I think I need to be alone for a while. With my thoughts, you know?"

"I've just the place." Jeeves pulled away from the curb. "Not far from here in the city."

"Great. Being escorted by my lover's driver. I should so be loving this."

Instead, Lucy felt lost. Carried through the world while it wavered in slo-mo around her. And she was lost somewhere at the center of a rushing tornado—unable to escape.

Gliding a hand along the leather seat, she sighed. "Does Truvin do this for all his girlfriends?"

"Send them off with me?"

"No. Bite them, make them possible vampires and then send them off with you."

"You're the first, Miss Morgan."

"Really?"

Jeeves nodded wisely.

"Huh. Well, the first that you know of. How long have you been working for Mr. Stone?"

"Since 1952, miss."

"Wow." Okay, so maybe he did know.

Lucy settled back as they pulled before the Chambers hotel. One of the most elite in Minneapolis. Even the bellhops had chauffeurs, she bet.

"Oh, I can't, Jeeves. This is out of my price range. Even if for a day or two."

"It's taken care of, Miss Morgan."

"Truvin?"

The door opened and Jeeves bowed as she stepped out. He produced a black Centurion card from his inner pocket. "Actually, I have an expense account."

"Jeeves, you dog. Oh, but I should do some shopping if I'm going to stay for a while. Essentials, you know."

The driver shuffled her a little too quickly toward the door, and when Lucy turned to say something she saw the flash of rare winter sunlight across the hood of the Mercedes.

"Best get you inside," he said. "I'll pick up a few things for you, if you'll allow it. What size are you, miss?"

"Er…" Still staring at the sunlight, Lucy said absently, "An eight in some places, a ten in others. Tall."

"Right. Anne Klein?"

"No, er…Rachel Ray. Jeeves?"

"Yes, Miss Morgan?"

"The sun can't hurt me yet, can it?"

"I shouldn't think so, but there's no sense in testing it, is there."

He left her in the lobby and walked to the registration desk. The whole process took about two minutes. Lucy felt shivers grow stronger at the back of her neck as she stood in the center of the marble floor, staring out the window.

Never again would she be able to set foot in the sunlight. "There goes my vitamin D. 'Course, my bones probably won't break so easily now. Now there's a pro—no osteoporosis. Oh!"

She jumped at the touch of Jeeves's hand to her shoulder.

"Sorry, Miss Morgan. Here's your key. I've secured the penthouse for you."

"The pent—"

"You stay as long as you like, or as long as is required. Everything is taken care of. I'll send clothes and essentials up this afternoon. Rest well."

And he lifted her hand to kiss the back of it in the most chivalric display. Had he been fifty years younger Lucy might have swooned. Hell, so she swooned a little anyway. Impeccable man. Truvin had a valued friend in Jeeves.

Truvin sorted through the suits in his closet. Each one was the same as the next. Plain dull gray silk. Zegna, all of them.

Diamond cuff links hung in the sleeves of each. There must be hundreds of thousands of dollars hanging in here.

Millions actually. He always purchased the finest jewels, cars and suits.

Always.

So why didn't it please him to get dressed now? To slide on the trousers and shirt felt wrong. He buttoned up the dress shirt, stopping at the collar. The material was crisp, yet soft, yet it felt like a stranger's clothing. He should be wearing…

The velvet jeans still lay crumpled in a heap on the floor near the bed. And the soft silk shirt that didn't fit his figure with a tailored hug but instead slid loosely over his body. Now, *that* was comfort.

Gliding his fingers down the sleeve of the suit coat, he knew he'd worn these clothes with pride for decades. It was all about image. He needed to present himself to the world as capable, wealthy and somehow…a part of this mortal realm. As well, one set apart.

Don't get too close. You're not allowed to touch unless I will it.

The suits had become a costume that no longer fit now that he'd spent a few days walking in a completely different world.

A world of his own making. A world he'd been allowed to create thanks to a hit on the head. Odd that he had the witches to thank for that accident of fate.

And Lucy, completely oblivious to the vampire's self-imposed boundaries, had walked right up to touch him. How great was that?

Leaving the suit coat in the closet, Truvin strode into the bathroom and turned on the water to run tepid. Staring at his reflection, he mused that it hadn't changed in two centuries. Not even a line. What did they call them? Lines of wisdom.

Did that mean he'd not gained the emotional maturity associated with wisdom?

"You've always looked out for number one," he said to himself. "It was necessary for survival."

Yet for days he had survived alone and without knowledge of his lifestyle—and with the added bane of baptism—and he'd come through rather well.

"Not alone. It's not good to completely close oneself off from the world." And he never would. "Should I have let her leave like that?"

He searched the medicine cabinet and found the thumb-size bottle of scent he liked to wear. Named after the historical elixir, Laudanum, it was only available at an exclusive online perfumery, and the deep rooty flavor combined with a touch of myrrh always proved initially heady and intoxicating.

His cell phone rang, and Truvin wandered into the bedroom to answer.

"I've settled her in at the Chambers. She said something about a witch named Midge?"

"Yes, what of it, Jeeves?"

"Seems the witches are tracking her, Mr. Stone. I didn't feel she'd be safe alone at her home, and...she asked not to be returned to you just yet."

"Thank you for taking care of her. I wouldn't want to imagine her out there on her own."

"Yes, well, she is rather special." Said without pretense.

"That she is. Do keep a close eye on her for me. I shouldn't wish to step in if she is uncomfortable with my presence."

He hung up and the doorbell rang immediately following. Time to get up to speed.

The vampire who preferred the moniker Gear clapped Truvin across the shoulder as he entered the penthouse and strode into the living room. The electrochromic shades protected the room from the sun's feeble winter rays, though it was evening now. Thick silver chains, wrapped about biker's boots, jingled as he walked. The black leather duster that went to his knees was torn at the back and taped up with black electrician's tape.

He wore a tattoo on his bald scalp. Must have just been inked. It would be completely gone within forty-eight hours, Truvin knew, for the vampire's rapid healing process pushed out the tattoo ink as the wounds healed. No vampire could keep a tattoo, unless he'd had it before being turned. Gear enjoyed the pain. And Truvin knew he dated a tattoo artist at the moment. Her shelf life would last only a little longer than the artwork on Gear's head.

Nathaniel, another former Kila tribe member, was Gear's opposite in every way. Tall, thin and keen on tight denims and a vintage biker's jacket, he wore a black cowboy hat pulled down over his eyes. Strapped around the brim of the hat were a set of the amber-lensed protective goggles.

They were two of a band of six vampires Truvin had gathered five months earlier to take action against the witches. While most witches kept to themselves and did not purposefully seek vampires, there were a few slayers in the city. They were Truvin's target.

Ravin Crosse being such a slayer. Crosse had slipped through Truvin's hands last year. As had his relationship with a good friend and colleague, because the idiot had actually become involved with Crosse. Truvin still could not figure that one.

"Haven't heard from you in a week," Gear spat. He hooked his thumbs in his belt loops. "Thought you'd gone AWOL."

"I had a last-minute trip. I was out of the country." Truvin conjured the lie easily.

"So you haven't heard?" Nathaniel said in his soft voice.

Soft, like his demeanor, he approached his victims, but his bite was vicious and final. "Drake and that witch had a baby."

"They're being real protective of it," Gear chimed in. "Kila stands guard day and night. They're calling the bastard the strongest vampire ever."

"A mere baby?" Truvin hadn't known Nikolaus Drake was quite so enamored of Ravin Crosse that he would have a child with her. The idea of a vampire and a witch creating a child…well, it made him ill. "How can they know what a baby will become? It is tainted with the witch's blood."

"It'll be immune to witches' blood," Nathaniel said. "And its father is a phoenix. Powerful blood to join together."

"Yes, I suppose." Nathaniel's reverence for the tribe leader was apparent. "But enough of that bother. I'm back, and I need to get up to speed on anything I've missed that pertains to our war."

"The priest and the witches have taken out three vampires in the past week," Gear reported. "We also know the prize they're trying to bag is you. We're here to protect you, man."

"Yeah?" Truvin paced to the windows and turned, the pale luminescence backlighting him brightly. "Well, you're a little late for that."

Chapter 21

Lucy lay on the bed in the hotel room, staring up at the white pebbled ceiling. She must have fallen asleep, because it seemed as if the door buzzer rang as she was drifting to Nod. A bellman dropped off a garment bag, and when she checked the time with him, she realized she had slept three hours.

Tossing the bag over the back of the thick, modern white sofa—the grand piano was a snazzy touch; talk about a spendy room—Lucy then eyed her purse. Still without a cell phone. She hadn't checked in with KSNW5 for days.

"I'll give Rich a call." She picked up the receiver from the phone on the coffee table. The cameraman wasn't home, so she left a message. "I've had to go out of town for the weekend. Will check back with you in a few days. I'm, ah…going to leave KSNW5, just to let you know. This vampire story is my last assignment. Thanks for everything."

Hanging up, she stood and shuffled her palms up her

opposite arms and headed toward the bathroom for a shower. Yes, it felt right. The job at the station didn't fulfill her anymore. And there was no way she could now report a story as myth when she knew otherwise.

Once beneath the hot rain stream, and having soaped up with the entire sample of vanilla-bean shampoo, she surrendered thoughts to considering her situation.

Do you really want to be a vampire? Was it the best change for a woman who was used to a simple Midwestern life, who enjoyed drinks with friends after work, chasing butterflies and rescuing cats?

But seriously. Could a vampire do charity work? Fictional vampires always lived for centuries. And for reasons she knew only because the heroes appealed to the readers, they were always rich.

But how did real vampires acquire their wealth? It wasn't as if they could hold a nine-to-five job. And did the night shift pay all that well?

Truvin had mentioned he played the stock market. Was that it? All rich vampires were market and investment wizards? Sounded too coincidental. What about those who hadn't a mind for business or numbers? Did they crawl into their coffins for eternity?

And what about the coffin thing? The idea of checking out each morning, sandwiched between the satin ruches of a tiny box, made her shudder.

What would Tabitha, Tony and Toast think of her? Heck, it had been twenty-four hours since she'd been home. They must be starving.

Soon as she finished showering, she had to go home. Just because she'd taken a reckless turn in life didn't mean she could ditch her responsibility to those she loved.

He's not ditching you. It was you who needed to get away.

Right. Because he had that suit of armored clothing in his closet. The guy kills witches.

And that's so much better than merely being a vampire who doesn't kill witches?

Pressing her palm to the slick bathtub tiles, Lucy tilted her head under the massaging stream that emulated a fresh rain shower.

Now that he'd gotten his memory back, would Truvin revert to the vampire he once was? It seemed so. He had stated his intent to go after the witches.

And why should that bother her? As he'd said, she couldn't begin to understand the war between the witches and the vampires. She fully supported the soldiers who went to war overseas, and knew they were expected to kill in their role of protecting their country.

So maybe the vampires felt they were protecting their rights, and the witches the same.

How could she judge when she had no framework to fit this information into? It was like when she'd first found Truvin, and he'd expressed no concern over learning his past. He hadn't the memories, so he could not even imagine what he was missing. Therefore, no curiosity over it.

She had no knowledge of the vampire and witches, so she couldn't begin to grasp their struggle and its meaning to both sides, but that didn't mean she wasn't curious.

Truvin was like a warrior captain, sending his troops to the battlefront. A handsome warrior. Yet, a warrior who could bend and be gentle. A man who'd once dreamed of opening an engraving shop. A man who liked to page through a sex manual and try new things. A man…

"Oh my God, I do love him," she muttered.

A simple smile felt so wondrous. Love? "Yes."

Shutting off the water, Lucy stepped out, dripping and unsure where the towels were, for the steam fogged the room.

"You silly woman, you've fallen in love with a vampire. And I don't regret it for a moment."

Posing before the mirror, she looked over her naked, wet body. In all the books the vampires usually took on a firm, younger, fit body after they'd been changed. She still had all the same curves, and the same generous breasts that defied gravity, thank you very much. The scar she'd gotten on the edge of the merry-go-round when she was six dashed a white streak across her left knee.

"So this is how I'm going to look forever?" Or *could* look. If she did the deed. She was no size six, but that had never concerned her. She shrugged. "I'll take it."

Forever. That was a long time. She could not expect Truvin to accept her into his life that long. And hell, maybe she'd grow tired of the same man after a few centuries? Did love last so long?

Oh, what was she doing? The Minnesota nice thing did go too far sometimes. Always stepping aside because she didn't want to impose or cause another discomfort.

Always thinking of the other person, and never yourself. When are you going to take what you need for yourself, Lucy?

As a vampire she could have any man she wanted. She could lure them to her with persuasion and seduce them into being her love slave. She could have minions! Men at her beck and call, offering up sexual treats to suit her whims.

Lucy nodded at her reflection. "Oh yeah, this could be very good."

Except, the idea of having men, as in more than one, didn't appeal at all. There was only one man she desired. Truvin Stone.

"I want him," she said. "And I'm going to have him."

Gear had called around midnight. They'd captured a witch, and held her in the warehouse off Washington Avenue. Truvin suited up in the DragonSkin, which included trousers made of the same material, only thinner and very flexible. The Kevlar-like material was much stronger and layered for maximum protection and ease of movement. It was a controversial product, one the military continued to deny their soldiers, even though it had been proven far safer than Kevlar. Only the best for Truvin and his men.

As a vampire, Truvin was worried about protecting his flesh from witch's blood, which could be inflicted through a cut, scratch, by spitting, or even sprinkled from a vial. No part of him was safe; the blood would eat into flesh and bone, and within minutes, begin to travel the vampire's bloodstream. Result? Exploding vampire less than five minutes after contact with witch's blood. There was no way to reverse the action once a vampire was hit, unless he immediately wiped all residue away. An impossibility.

An eye shot had to be the worst.

Securing the goggles to his head, Truvin then had Jeeves drive him to the warehouse. It was a small building at the edge of the river, sitting on property Truvin had purchased just last year. It gave them privacy, and a place to dispose of their prey.

They had taken out two witches since the protective gear had been developed last year. Two notches Truvin was proud of. By removing the witches from this world, they had likely saved dozens of vampires.

Though he had not witnessed their deaths. That was Gear's specialty. Because there was only one way to kill a witch, and enemy or not, no sane vampire stuck around to witness the death.

Lucy's shock, after he'd told her what the outfit was for, troubled him. She didn't understand. Lucy was a compassionate woman. Hell, she'd invited a complete stranger into her home when he couldn't remember if he was good, bad or an ax murderer. Too trusting, Lucy. As a vampire, she would be an easy target to a witch.

"What have I done?" Truvin muttered as the car pulled onto a gravel frontage road. "She's innocent. I've set her up for so much."

She was probably baptized as well, now he thought on it. Yet another chink in her already thin armor against those who would see any vampire destroyed.

A vulnerability to holy objects was a new chink for Truvin. For centuries he had flaunted his immunity to the holy by wearing a small gold cross about his neck.

He wondered now what had happened to that cross the night of his attack. He hadn't been wearing it when he'd come to. Whoever had knocked him out must have taken it, knowing later Truvin would be forcibly baptized.

Strange that he remembered everything now, except that night immediately before the attack. Those few moments when he'd been taken down and knocked out, clobbered him aside the head.

Why did that small portion of time elude him? Had something so terrible occurred, beyond his attack, that his brain simply did not want him to recall it?

Who had knocked him out? A witch? One of the weres, whom Truvin knew allied themselves with the witches? Severo, the leader of the northern pack, had it in for Truvin since he'd stumbled onto the wolves' territory. One time. A vamp just couldn't get a break.

Who was this priest working alongside the witches? Was he really a priest? Could anyone baptize a person? And if not, was Truvin really as vulnerable to the holy as he had been led to believe?

It wasn't a risk he was willing to take to find out. For now, he must avoid all holy objects.

Fully outfitted in protective clothing, Gear and Nathaniel waited inside the warehouse. Nathaniel nodded over his shoulder toward the woman standing in the center of the room. Dangling, actually. Her wrists had been lashed together and the rope strung up over the old square air ducts overhead. The tips of her bare toes touched the floor. She wore black clothing, thick violet eyeshadow and black lipstick.

As he approached the witch he scented her fear. The black mask he wore stretched over his head, while resistant to cuts and liquids, was permeable to the atmosphere. Fear smelled sharp and salty.

A leather strap had been bound across her mouth, to prevent her from biting herself and spitting on them. It was an initial precaution when wrangling the witch. That, and binding her feet and pulling mitten-like leather gloves over her hands to prevent her from scratching herself.

Truvin unsnapped the leather mouth strap and tossed it aside. Though they were completely protected, Gear and Nathaniel both took steps backward.

The defiance in standing so close to one who could kill him with such ease stirred in Truvin's blood. Made him feel powerful and potent, yet he could only conjure pity for the witch.

Stroking a gloved hand along her cheek, he pushed aside her thick dyed black hair. Tears had dried on her reddened cheeks. Her lower lip was swollen, obviously from biting it in a defensive move. She did not react to his touch. She was exhausted, surely. And frightened.

And now Truvin recognized her. Midge. The witch who had offered an interview to Lucy.

Damn. He had no reason to harm this woman. And yet, he could not stand down before his men.

"I need information on the priest," Truvin said. "The one working with the witches."

"I'm…" She sniffled and moaned. The pull of the ropes to her shoulder sockets must be torturous. "…not with the ones who are after the vampires. I'm a lone practitioner. You have to believe me."

"I do believe you, Midge."

She looked up at his use of her name. It was impossible to determine who her captors were behind the black masks. "Who are you?"

"Truvin Stone," he offered, and Gear smacked a fist into his palm. Truvin glanced to his cohort. "Doesn't matter if she knows."

"Because you're going to kill me?" She began to sob. "Please, I don't want to be a part of this. I tried to help Lucy. She's being followed by them."

They'd involved Lucy?

"Who are *them*, exactly," Truvin insisted, "and where can I find them. Come on, Midge, you know where they gather. Is the priest real?"

"He's ordained. He's real, trust me. He…lost his daughter to a vampire bite last year. Said it was you. Truvin."

"That's ridiculous. My victims never learn my name, witch. For the very fact it's not wise to leave a trail for crazed priests to come following. Where do they meet?" He pressed his palm on her right shoulder, forcing pressure against the ropes at her wrists.

"Let's toast her," Gear said. "Then maybe she'll loosen her lips."

By the wall, a gas can waited. A nasty but sure death.

The wobble in Midge's moans seeped into Truvin's mind. She was telling the truth. He could easily persuade her to be more generous with the information, and he began by focusing on her thoughts, sending his own to her through the gathered consciousness of the world. He tapped her fear and slipped through it.

"Abigail leads them," Midge said in a drowsy slur. She was going faint.

Truvin grabbed her head with both palms and focused. "Abigail Rowan?"

"Yes. That's her…"

Bloody…bloody…fuck! That witch again?

"They meet…?" *Location,* he thought forcefully. *And you shall go free.*

It was a promise he would not renege on. For right now, the idea of taking another's life merely to clear the earth of an innocent witch didn't sit well with Truvin. And she was innocent. She did not slay vampires, much as she had wanted to convince Lucy she did.

And knowing Abigail was involved did not surprise him the least. Though it did piss him off. Would he never shuck her from his wake?

"The old chapel on Lark Avenue. It's being torn down this summer. It's abandoned right now. They meet every evening at nine, and then go out hunting vampires. Their goal is you, Truvin." She sighed and her head dropped.

"I'll get the gas," Gear said.

"No! I'll do it," Truvin said. "You two…find the chapel. Go!"

Initially reluctant, when his men saw Truvin begin to walk toward the gas can, they finally left. Truvin waited until he heard a car start and drive away. Then he kicked over the gas can. The volatile liquid leaked across the concrete floor, quickly soaking into the wooden wall and trailing a wobbly stream toward the witch.

Truvin untied Midge and slung her inert body over his shoulder. Out in the car, he found a lighter in the glove compartment and set the warehouse ablaze. All evidence of his indiscretions would be put to ash.

Now to approach his future in a new frame of mind. He didn't want to be a killer in Lucy's eyes.

"What are we going to do with her?" Jeeves asked as Truvin shoved Midge inside the backseat.

"She lives off Grand. We're taking her home and packing her things. She's moving to Europe."

"Top-notch plan," Jeeves said, and backed the Mercedes away from the burning building.

Chapter 22

It took but a few escorts to decide she could grow accustomed to limousine service at her beck and call. Jeeves delivered Lucy to Truvin's building, and she was able to let herself in, thanks to the code the driver provided her.

"Good ole Jeeves," she said as the door opened and she entered the elite thirty-seventh-floor penthouse.

Tossing her purse to the couch and kicking off her heels, she padded across the marble living-room floor, not sure what to do while she waited for Truvin to return home. There were no magazines, and not a single book in sight. Not even an oversize coffee-table book featuring classy nudes, which she assumed should be on every bachelor's table.

Tickling the fronds of a large fern mastering a blocky marble base, she sighed, and then decided, "Time to snoop."

Bottled water and cheese were the only things in the fridge. The cheese surprised her. Must nibble it with wine. The wine fridge was stocked with dozens of fancy bottles. Lucy had no clue what was a good year or vintage, so she didn't bother to act as if she did by looking at the labels.

To imagine never eating again was, well, it would fall into the con category, but Lucy could only consider the cash she'd be saving and the never-having-to-diet-again aspect.

She traced a finger down the brushed-steel surface of the fridge. Everything was so pristine and white on gray. Like a futuristic home featured in a sci-fi adventure movie.

"He needs color," she said as she wandered into the bedroom and glided her fingers across the militant row of suits in the open closet.

The dresser drawers were ordered neatly, the same gray Calvin Klein boxer briefs folded and lined inside one drawer and dozens of pairs of the same dark gray socks in the next.

"How dull, to never change your clothes. And all gray? No wonder he took to the highwayman's coat. And that cashmere sweater looked great. The man needs a woman's touch. He needs a little pink."

And no matter the situation, Lucy fell into what every single woman always did when they were in love. Designing the perfect man and fixing him up and taking care of him.

But what had she that was pink? Hmm… Her undies were black, but her bra was pink.

Landing the bed, she rolled to the edge and tugged open the drawer on a streamlined steel-and-lacquered-wood nightstand. The perfect place to accidentally leave a little present for him.

Inside the top drawer, nestled within the folds of a white handkerchief, a small metal frame slid free. Lucy carefully plucked it out, and flipped open the pewter cover. The frame was as large as an egg sliced lengthwise. Inside, a woman's face stared up at her. A woman wearing pink.

Dark eyes beamed up at her, and dark hair in tight curls

bounced to her shoulders. A pink striped dress ran along the bottom of the portrait, and a gossamer white scarf was tucked about her décolletage. The painted colors were cracked and flaking.

"He keeps this close to his bed." Lucy's heart thudded. "He must love her very much. Or *have* loved her?"

To judge from the dress, it had to be an old portrait. She couldn't guess at a century. Or could she be a vampire lover who still lived, yet he preferred this old picture of her?

Lucy dutifully rewrapped and placed the miniature back in the drawer.

Sighing, she dismissed the abandoned-bra idea. "He already has something pink."

Rolling to her back, she stared up at the multiple reflections on the ceiling.

"He has loved, and maybe still does. Do I have any right to expect him to love me?"

There was a terrace on the east side of his flat. Truvin sensed Lucy was in his home; he smelled her blood, but he also heard light snoring. So he entered the outside air as the sky flashed coral and the glint of brilliant gold shimmered across the metal buildings lining the cityscape. The sunrise. It had been a while.

Having gotten a glimpse of the colors, Truvin lowered the goggles over his eyes. The amber lens, of course, gave everything a golden cast, but that didn't lessen the magnitude of the moment.

He stood outside, defiant of the sun, enclosed within protective clothing. And he almost thought to feel the heat against his face, though he knew even the mortals could not sense heat until the sun rose higher in the sky.

"I've missed this," he said as he leaned over the steel railing. "And she will miss it, too."

Lucy of the chestnut hair and pale complexion. Sure, she

must burn easily, but to give up that pleasurable burn for a life without sun?

He had to think of a way to convince her to wait out the moon.

Maybe if he promised her they could continue their relationship?

But could he really do that? Because the only way it could happen was if he didn't drink from her. Else she'd be dead within a month.

Truvin had held back his desire to sate the hunger before, with women, and instead had merely had sex with them. But he'd never had a prolonged relationship with a woman and denied himself the blood.

Was it even possible?

Closing his eyes, he bowed his head and listened. Below, the city had woken. Cars and buses and garbage trucks trundled by on streets still shadowed by tall buildings. Baked bread tendriled up to tickle his nostrils, but he didn't feel hunger for food.

Though he had once adored a feast.

"What would my life have been like?"

Had Anna not been attacked. Had he never encountered Damien Desrues.

"I would have never met Lucy," he decided.

And a world without Lucy Morgan probably wouldn't be worth living. She gave him something he'd not realized he was missing. A new perspective.

Lucy shrugged a hand through her sleep-tousled hair. Gorgeous. Her cheeks blushed with the lingering warmth of sleep and there was still a crease on her left cheek.

"All that talk about wanting to be free," she murmured. "I was, well…missing you."

"In your dreams?"

"Sorry, I fell asleep."

Truvin hugged her. "Don't worry. You're welcome to sleep in my bed anytime you wish. I'm pleased you returned to me."

"You mean it? Because that's, well, kind of commitment-like. Like…I might be the only woman you'd want in your bed?"

"You are."

"Does that make me your…"

"Girlfriend?" Nuzzling against her neck, he whispered at her ear, "Do you want me to call you that, darling?"

"Not unless it's what you want to use."

"I will, though I prefer mistress. It's more appealing and implies we have sex often."

"I can work with that. You're wearing your witch-hunting gear," she noted with some disdain.

"The guys caught a witch."

"Oh." Lucy turned and went into the living room. She collapsed more than sat on one of the wide black leather sofas. "I don't think I want to know."

Truvin tossed aside the mask and unzipped the jacket and pulled it off. He wore a thin T-shirt underneath, but the whole getup made him sweat, so off came the shirt, too. Unbuttoning the pants, he didn't drop trou to stand in but his boxer briefs. Though he considered it.

Not now. Lucy was upset.

He knelt before her. "It was Midge."

"The witch? Oh my God, you didn't—"

"Don't worry, she's alive. But she's not safe anymore, from vampires or witches. Jeeves put her on a flight to Germany. She's enough money to tide her over a few years—"

"You did that for her?" She pulled him onto the couch and as he sat, she climbed onto his lap. "That's so generous. But I thought you killed witches?"

"I thought so, too."

And that was all he wanted to say on the matter right now. It was a strange turn in his life, but it felt right. It was who he had become in the few short days he had no clue what his past held. Still didn't know it all—*that one elusive moment before the attack.*

"Did you really worry about me?"

"The sun."

"This protective clothing keeps out the sun's rays. I watched it rise from the terrace," he said, feeling a tug at the back of his throat. His last sunrise had been in France, but days before his twenty-fifth birthday. And he'd not opportunity to share it with Anna. "It was discolored through my goggles, but I haven't seen such a wondrous thing for centuries. Unless I include you on my list of wonders—which I do."

She laid her head on his chest and fit her body to his. Their connection sizzled as if a chemical reaction. Flesh to flesh, breath to breath, heartbeat to heartbeat. Made for one another. Truvin had never before felt so comfortable around another person. Comfortable, that is, without then wanting to control that person, or prove himself the better of the two.

What kind of bastard have you been? To suggest you know what is best for Lucy? You don't need to control her.

But what did he need? To give up the hunt entirely? That would be obsequious to the witches. And if he did not go after them, no one else would. The vampires needed someone to watch their backs.

But fore, he wanted to do what was best for Lucy.

How to decide?

"So did you look around?" he wondered. "Snoop?"

"I am a woman. We don't know how to not look."

"Find anything interesting?"

"You live a spartan life, Mr. Stone. You don't have a lot of personal mementos." She traced her finger under the swell of his pectoral. A flick of her fingernail across his nipple made him hiss out a breath. All systems fired to "go." He was ready for sex. "Though I did see the miniature."

"Ah." A portrait he'd carried with him since before he'd become vampire. He'd kept it wrapped and close to him for centuries. Snoop, indeed. His heart speeded up. A flickering image of the cottage, spattered with blood, tightened his jaw. "She was my fiancée."

"She was very pretty."

"Anna Lee. I was to marry her in springtime when the lavender coated the French countryside. I traveled from my hometown in England to marry her. I had met her the summer previous during a holiday my family took to Paris. We were marrying because we loved one another, not because our parents had made a bargain. She was murdered before we could say our vows. By a vampire."

"I'm so sorry."

"The vampire was mad. Literally. The moon had stolen his soul. That same night as Anna's murder, he transformed me."

"The memory must be awful."

"It is. But it is a memory I am thankful to have." He kissed Lucy's forehead. Sweet there. She was too incredible to lose to moonlight and madness. "I couldn't imagine not having my memories now. But when I couldn't remember, it didn't matter."

"Because you had no concept of what you were missing."

"Yes. God, Lucy, I'm so glad it came back to me. And I'm even more grateful for the new memories I'll make with you."

"You mean that?" Lucy trailed a few more lingering kisses up under his chin and finally landed his mouth.

It was like diving into the familiar, she entwined about him. Every bit of her connected to him. Familiar, yet so new. Trusting.

Her lazy kiss allowed him to trace her lips with his tongue.

Matching the slow exploration, he circled her nipple with his fingers. He squeezed the hard round nub. Lucy sighed into his mouth and bit his upper lip, tugging gently. The motion worked as if she tugged at his cock.

He'd meant it when she said she could sleep here anytime. Intrude upon his privacy all she liked. For Lucy Morgan was all that he wanted, all that he needed.

Lucy stood over Truvin, legs to either side of his knees, and slipped off her shirt.

"Pink," he breathed.

She drew the side of her hand down the inner curve of her bra. The feeling of strength and utter femininity so strong. "You don't like it?"

"I love me a little pink every now and then. Let me touch. Devour. Remove."

She remained standing. Truvin's arousal enlarged his pupils. His mouth, she wanted at her nipple. But she pressed two fingers to his pursed lips. "How many girlfriends have you had? In the past two centuries. Should I be jealous?"

"You don't strike me as the jealous type, Lucy." He managed to tug down her skirt so she stood in but her black spike heels and black lace panties and bra. "But truth? Three."

"In over two hundred years? That's not very many. I was thinking maybe a couple dozen."

"It's not easy to suffer heartbreak." He slid to the edge of the couch and kissed the black ribbon at the center of her panties. A hush of warm breath permeated the lace. Lucy's desire shot over the top. Heat flushed her groin and hummed at her breasts. Her cheeks grew hot and her mouth achy for his attention.

One curl of his finger tugged the lace down her thigh. "I've been a loner for so long," he said. "Safer that way." Elastic snapped. Lace tore. "Only in the past few years have I felt the pining desperation for family. That's why I joined Kila."

"Kila?" Lucy's voice wavered. His slow attentions were exactly what she craved. Yes, touch me there. Touch boldly and as if it was his right, as no man had before.

"A vampire tribe."

"That's right, you said you run in tribes."

"Some of us. But they were not for me. I'll tell you about it later. I don't think I can talk vampire politics and eat lace at the same time. Unless you wish me to tell you now?"

"No," she rushed out, running her fingers through his short, silky hair. "You can stop talking." His breath hushed over her mons. The hot intrusion of his tongue at the peak of her sex made her gasp. "Politics...bad," Lucy uttered. "This..."

Her fingers clenched upon his scalp and Lucy curled down her body as the hum of pleasure singed through her.

"Good?" he wondered.

She could but shake her head and mumble a nonsense noise. It was all good. Just. Right.

Pressing her hands to the backs of his shoulders, Lucy cried out his name as the climax swept her into oblivion. She didn't even mind when his teeth pierced her high upon her thigh.

Truvin heard the door to the stable creak open. His bedroom window looked over the small stable, fit out for three or four horses and one carriage. He'd procured a modest home at the edge of Paris on the Left Bank, and thanks to his blood master's connections, had now a wardrobe and a few pieces of furniture. And a horse.

His vampiric hearing was keen, which he appreciated. Peering out the curtainless window, he spied the stable door ajar.

A thief attempting to steal his horse?

The fool had no idea what curse that decision would put upon them.

Dashing downstairs, Truvin hooked up a damask night coat and pulled it over his arms. He'd been lounging in but breeches, contemplating the evening ahead of him. Where to find the best and prettiest necks? And not a cheap whore who reeked of ale and had gone without washing for weeks.

Slipping out the door, he quite delighted at his newly gained stealth. A vampire less than a year, and already he'd accepted it completely. There was no going back, so why mourn the lost mortality?

Stopping outside the stable door, he closed his eyes and listened. A thief would be quick about it. Buckle a lead about the horse's head and be off. Or even ride it bareback away from here. But he didn't hear anything, save footsteps upon the straw-strewn floor. Careful, cautious not to alert his mount, whom he'd named Fury.

It was—he heard a soft, whispered voice, not words, but a cooing reassurance—a woman?

Well, it did not surprise him. With all the taxes Louis XVI pressed upon his subjects it was no wonder the people had resorted to stealing to feed their families. The women had taken to stalking the bridges, hoping to sell a few tattered shoes or even their bodies to purchase bread for their starving families. But how bold to sneak into a man's stable and attempt to lead away his horse.

Bold, and yet, Truvin could sympathize. Who was he to prevent a family from eating?

Had it been anything other than this horse, he would have stepped back inside and allowed the theft. But this horse had been bespelled, and he wasn't sure he could again find a willing witch.

Stepping into the doorway, Truvin made himself known by clearing his throat.

The woman, her palm smoothing along the horse's nose, turned to him and smiled. She didn't show fright. In fact, it was as if she had expected him.

Mon Dieu, *it was her.* "Abigail?"

"I've never stopped thinking about you, Truvin."

Hadn't he…strangled her? This was not possible. He'd thought… Hell, whatever he had thought, it wasn't true. The witch was alive, and approached him with hands extended.

"I know you did it because you were scared," *she said. Moonlight shone through the stable door, highlighting her alabaster skin.* "I forgave you the moment I woke from what should have been my death. Your blood master never taught you how to kill a witch properly."

"Abigail, I—" *Did not want to be standing here right now. One spot of her blood could be his undoing. And for her to have forgiven him for attempting to murder her? Truly, she was touched in the head, as he'd originally guessed.* "How do you kill a witch?"

"Ah, ah." *She waggled an admonishing finger at him.* "The horse is well. You take very good care of it."

"It is my only possession." *And friend.*

Truvin took a cautious step backward, which placed him on the threshold. "You didn't remove the spell, did you?"

"Of course not. Will you invite me inside? It's cold this evening."

"I'm not sure that would be proper, Mademoiselle Rowan."

"Nonsense. I've not the reputation of a* precieuse, *though I am certainly no fishwife. Don't you miss me, Truvin?"*

She drew a finger across her breasts, pushed high by tight stays and revealed at the neckline of her dress. Truvin noticed the glint of steel. A dagger thrust out from her corset laces, positioned between her breasts. The blade pointed upward, instead of down.

Abigail noticed his dismay. "I love you, Truvin. I never want to harm you."

"Abigail," he cautioned, but decided he was in no position to command. "We only ever spent that one evening together."

"Doesn't take me long to fall in love. I knew it the first time I gazed into your changing eyes. Like heaven and stars, they are."

"Yes, well, I guarantee there is no promise of heaven from this vampire."

"Such a daring venture." She stepped up close and fitted herself to him, wide pale eyes staring up into his. "A vampire and a witch."

"Most daring for the vampire, not so much for the—watch how you move, Abigail. Will you let me have a look over that dagger? I shouldn't wish you to hurt yourself."

Her tongue dashed out to wet her lower lip. "Does it frighten you, Truvin?"

"Yes, a little. I've only just become vampire. I should like to enjoy the experience a while longer."

"But you can, my love. I promise I'll never draw blood near you. Now kiss me, Truvin. Show me how much you love me."

Truvin woke with a start. Lucy lay beside him, nestled on the sofa between a scatter of pillows, dreaming. Pray she did not know the nightmares that haunted him.

His life had been a nightmare after Abigail returned. The woman had developed a ridiculous fixation to him. And he hadn't been able to shake her. Nor had he wanted to react violently toward her or suggest he didn't love her. At the time, he'd been too new, unsure how, exactly, to deal with the threat of a witch.

Always, she carried a knife on her person, visible as a warning, should he even think to push her away. What to do? He'd allowed her to stay that night, and had made love to her.

He'd made love to a madwoman to save his own life.

She had stayed for a fortnight before Truvin had finally the opportunity to escape. He'd left one evening while she'd been to a friend's home. Saddled up Fury and rode east toward Italy. It was all he could think to do. Damien was nowhere to be found, and he knew of no other vampires to ask how one did kill a witch.

"With fire," he said, for he knew now. And never again would he allow a witch to hold him a virtual prisoner because of his weaknesses.

"Abigail Rowan."

Now he knew who he was dealing with, he'd take precautions. This wasn't going to be easy. The witch had haunted him for centuries. She just would not be put off.

"I'm ready for you now, Abigail."

Chapter 23

His cell phone rang, and Truvin fumbled through his pants, which were piled on the floor before the couch. "Hello?"

It was Gear. "The warehouse is ash, man."

"Yeah, I...the fire got out of control. I had to let it burn."

"That's cool. The witch is fried. Mission accomplished."

And when did he think he would tell his men he no longer had the stomach for murder? He'd set aside making the decision in favor of sex with Lucy. But his morals were not about to sit and wait for him to come around. He had to be as honest with his crew as he'd been with Lucy.

On the other hand, he no longer vacillated on the whole witch-killing thing. Someone had to do it.

"Did you find the priest?"

"The location the witch gave us is an abandoned chapel, like she said. Nathaniel and I will return after sunset."

"I'll meet you there. When does the sun set?"

"Six. See you, man."

Closing the phone, Truvin lay back and landed his fingers in the softness of Lucy's hair. She slept, but fitfully. It was the blood hunger. Her body would only become more relentless in its demands. He'd have to keep close watch on her now if she were to make it to the moon.

And even so, if he watched over her, would that help? The madness could take her, and probably not in some grand and bombastic manner, but perhaps more subtle. Her mind would be altered, but she might appear normal on the surface. There was nothing he could physically do to hold it off. Save, give her his blood, and complete the change.

And what would that bring her but a whole new race of enemies with blood in their eyes?

Stroking Lucy's hair away from her face revealed her soft pink lips. Pale lashes formed a fringe above her cheek. Barest freckles sprinkled her nose. "Sun kisses, those freckles. You should always have the sun, Lucy. I want to do this for you."

Fact remained, he couldn't step back from the situation to hand. The witches would always stalk him. And he couldn't live a life always looking over his shoulder. Nor did he particularly like knowing that his inaction might bring about the death of other vampires at the witches' hands.

Lucy crawled upon Truvin and fit herself onto his erection. He was hard, and glided into her with little resistance. The solid firmness of him sent a tingle up to her throat. So much of him, and all hers.

"Yes, slow," he murmured. His eyes closed and arms splayed across the couch, he let her ride him while he simply enjoyed. He smelled dark and unlike any man she'd ever been close to. It was that same root-beer and nutmeg fragrance that she'd noticed on his shirt. So good. She inhaled deeply.

"Sassafras," she murmured.

"A special blend."

"I love it. It's deep and delicious. Like you."

Sliding forward, Lucy bowed over her lover's chest. The change in position pistoned him along her clitoris. She measured her pace, forcing herself to go slow, to build up the climax that she could leap into right now. But a few more minutes would increase the high.

Licking the underside of his chin, she glided over to the thick vein on his neck. It pulsed hot. Lucy bit.

"What—?" He didn't stop their pace, but did lift her chin up to kiss her. "No biting, Lucy."

"Why not? You bit me." The climax was right there. She wanted to touch it, but even more, she wanted to taste Truvin's blood. "Just a taste?"

"Never."

"You would deny your mistress?"

"Lucy, please, we're so close." He took her hips in hand and Lucy felt a protest dissolve as they both came at the same time.

It was nightfall when they stepped out from the shower and decided to get dressed. Sex had worn Lucy out, Truvin could sense, for her eyelids were heavy and she now lay on his bed, clothed and dreamy.

"I've got to go home," she said as he sorted through the closet. "Tabitha and Toast and…" *Yawn.*

"I'll send Jeeves to feed your cats, how about that? I still don't think it's wise to go home, darling."

"Thoughtful of you. I thought you were going to call me mistress?"

He crawled onto the bed and hovered over her. "Mistress. Darling. The Amazing Sex Goddess."

"Says the Incredible Long-Lasting Super-Virile Vampire."

"Cheeky wench."

"Nummy lover. Mmm…" She sighed.

The flutter of her lids fanned her thick lashes. Truvin traced the line of them with a fingertip.

"What are you doing?"

"Remembering you."

"You plan to forget anytime soon?"

"You never know what life will bring." He kissed her eyelids, then brushed his cheek over a row of soft lash. "You sleep. I've an errand to run."

"I don't want to know." She turned to her side and fell asleep like that.

"No, you don't want to know," Truvin said as he hooked the goggles on a finger and started out of the bedroom. "And that is why you can't handle vampirism either, my dear."

He clicked off the light switch and left the penthouse, knowing Lucy would be safe.

Truvin didn't dress in the protective gear. Purposefully. Though he had brought along the goggles. He was going to the chapel that Gear and Nathaniel had checked out, in hopes of finding the witches or the priest.

And he wanted to show them he had changed.

It was a fine goal to remain the man he had become, and to turn away from the callous hunter he had been. He felt that, yet a small part of him laughed and turned up its nose at such a ridiculous endeavor.

You are who you are. You have lived for centuries. The years have molded you. Your habits, your lifestyle, your requirements for blood; they have all shaped you into Truvin Stone.

It wasn't as if he couldn't remember now. He could not claim lack of memory to starting a new life. He did know. And how dare he shuck off his very nature?

"I will," he said as he approached the chapel. "I can."

I want to.

For Lucy, of the snowflake memories and eyelash kisses. She deserved the best he could be. And while he didn't deserve her, if she wanted him, he was a lucky man for it.

Of course, it wouldn't be easy. It wouldn't be worth it if it were.

A wistful gulp of air centered in his chest. What would life have offered had he not been changed? Had he married Anna?

He would be dead now. He may have had generations of family to carry on his name. Perhaps he may have even opened the engraving shop he'd oft dreamed to own. The monogram on his and Lucy's bedroom wall might have been one of his own creations.

He was not the man he should have been. Irreversible events had changed that.

Yet if he had changed once, he could again change.

True, the chapel was not in a condition to hold services, though the outside structure was solid. Overgrown yew shrubs brushed across the front steps as Truvin took them, one, two, three. A kneeling stone angel, with head bowed, ignored his entrance.

He had no fear to enter a holy place; He welcomed all into His house. It was only in physically touching the symbols of the sacred that a baptized vampire could be wounded.

Truvin pushed open the front door. There was no furniture, and some of the walls had been stripped to reveal the open framework. Through the open doors to the chapel, he saw there were pews forming uneven rows, and beyond them, up in the empty altar, a single candle flame flickered.

Someone inside? But he knew that already for he could smell the human blood. Not a witch, for their kind had a particular scent that put up the hairs on the back of his neck.

The priest?

Feeling a weird urge to call out, "I come in peace," Truvin held off the declaration. It was a surprise to him to feel his heartbeat increase and to know it was because uncertainty gripped him. The playing grounds had been evened. He no longer held the board.

Taking in his peripherals, he slowly walked along the scattered row of pews. Faint moonlight spilled from above, and stained glass colored the light in azure and crimson. A humid, earthy odor filled the air, making it heavy to breathe.

Why anyone would want to tear down this church was beyond him, because the windows and the basic structure were gorgeous. Urban sprawl, it killed so many beautiful relics.

When he'd walked halfway to the altar, a white-robed man, who had been lying prostrate on the floor, lifted his head. Must be the first moment he realized he was not alone. Quickly, he scrambled to kneel, but did not turn to face Truvin.

With the man facing away from him, and clad in a robe, Truvin could not know if he concealed a weapon, so he stopped where he stood, halfway between the altar and the front door.

Glancing a few fingers over the back of a pew, he cleared his throat.

"Are you the priest?" Truvin called, again shifting his eyes and taking in the surroundings, both high and low. No one else inside the church. For now. "The one who works with the witches?"

Now the man stood completely and turned. He remained on the step before the altar. Candlelight flickered and flashed across a seemingly young face. He was tall, broad-shouldered, and wore his blond hair military short. It was apparent he worked out, for the robe stretched across his pectorals. Truvin recognized him as the man he'd seen in the lot behind the Blue Room.

"You are Truvin Stone," the priest called. "How dare you enter this sacred place?"

"I've come looking for you," Truvin replied. "And I know you seek me, so let's set aside the religious babble and put our cards on the table, shall we?"

"No cards to play. I don't gamble," the priest said, coming down the step. He spread his arms wide, displaying the dusty marks that marred the front of his robe. "Have you come to kill me, too, vampire? I've not the witches to protect me now. You must have lain in wait."

"I don't suspect you fear me all that much, Priest. You've the greater power in this establishment."

"You concede your weakness?"

"Only because you know I have one. I wager the church frowns upon forced baptisms. But I'm sure you've a Bible verse ready to toss out that claims your right to such violence. Your kind always does like to twist that book to fit your needs."

"Repent and be baptized, every one of you, in the name of Jesus Christ for the forgiveness of your sins."

"Ah. Well, there you go. What of 'thou shalt not kill'? Did that one slip below your moral compass?"

"Thou shalt not kill man." The priest tilted down his head, and when he looked up, the shadows from the candle flame danced wickedly in his narrow eyes. "How much more severely do you think a man deserves to be punished who has trampled the Son of God underfoot, who has treated as an unholy thing the blood of the covenant that sanctified him, and who has insulted the Spirit of grace?"

"Well, you're full of justification in the name of God."

"Do not use the Lord's name, vampire."

"All right, all right." Truvin put up his hands to placate. They both held their positions, but Truvin had already marked the quickest escape.

"I'm not here to match Bible wisdom, I want to learn what makes you tick. I know the witches have a good reason to go after vampires. We've been at odds for centuries. But what's a wayward priest like you doing allying himself with witches? Got a Bible verse for that one?"

The priest inclined his head and muttered ominously, "The righteous shall rejoice when he seeth the vengeance, he shall wash his feet in the blood of the wicked."

"All right then." No arguing a well-recited Bible verse.

"Do you even remember Melissa Banks, you lump of demonic trash?"

"Ah, so it *is* about a woman. Love does trump all those Ten Commandments. Except maybe the ones about adultery."

The priest lunged. The glint of a silver cross appeared in his hand.

Truvin leaped, and landed the choir balcony behind and above the foyer. Its wooden floorboards creaked and shook a hail of dust from the rafters above.

"I'm all for a fair fight," he called down, "but you're not playing fair, Priest. Not very godly of you."

"She was my daughter!" the priest cried, brandishing the cross above his head, as if to shake it at Truvin would serve the violence he desired. "You murdered her."

To search his memory, and sort things logically, Truvin determined the man's daughter couldn't be much older than early twenties. Probably blond. He usually did go for blondes. But he did not kill them. He left them in a dreamy state of swoon, their minds persuaded to forget. And he hadn't had an accident in decades.

But have you all your memory back? Could there be one you forgot? One...mistake?

"You've got the wrong vampire." Truvin leaped to the banister and balanced there, crouched, one finger touching the wood for support. "I don't kill my victims."

"She was not a victim." The priest sank to sit on the edge

of a pew. His sigh hung in the air. "She wanted to be like you. A vampire. And you gave her what she asked for."

Talk about rebelling against the father.

"I don't do that. Haven't transformed a human—" Since two days ago. Fool vampire. "What makes you think it was me?"

"She mentioned your name once. After she'd been changed. When she lay dying in the bed her mother and I had given her as a child. Dying, because when you made her vampire, you neglected to tell her holy objects would bring her death."

"I didn't do it. But whoever did should have noticed if she wore a cross for jewelry."

"She had a tattoo of a cross on her back. It…ate into her body. For weeks we watched her die! Finally, I was forced to stake her. To end her suffering. You will never know what it is like to have to take your own child's life. And in such a manner!"

Truvin swallowed. The man was wounded, body and soul. He would have never wished any such horror on the innocent.

"All I want," the man hissed, "is an eye for an eye."

"Wrong eye, Priest. It wasn't me."

"Come down here and face me like a man!"

"Put your cross away, and I'll do that."

The heavy silver cross hit the wall above the altar with a crash.

Truvin jumped and landed but five feet from where the priest stood. He could feel the pain, the grief emanating from the priest. It hurt. He could sympathize. And that struck him deeply.

Because you have not before taken a moment to put yourself in another man's shoes. Huh.

"If it'll help you to get some kind of closure, I'll ask around, see if I can find out who really did that to your daughter."

"Your lies only dig you deeper into hell."

"Already there, Priest. It's part of the deal. Didn't ask for what I've become, but I can accept. But just because one vampire did this to you, doesn't mean it's right to go killing us all."

"You've your own band of murderers. You go after the witches. You are no better than I."

"I'm much lesser than you, I'm sure. And I have committed some grave sins in the name of war between my kind and the witches. But I don't want to do that anymore. I've changed."

"Who can bring what is pure from the impure? No one!"

The priest lunged and fit his hands about Truvin's neck. A futile attempt, but for the moment Truvin allowed the man's anger, to let him believe and perhaps offer some solace to what was surely a raging vengeance that could never be fulfilled.

The man's eyes were wide with an anger Truvin felt sure no church would ever condone. He looked more in need of exorcism; and in truth, he was in need of such—an exorcism of grief.

When Truvin noticed the glint of a gold chain around the man's thick red neck, he pushed off the priest, who landed the floor.

"It's apparent I'll get no forgiveness here." Truvin stepped over the fallen man and marched out of the chapel.

"I will defend my life if forced," he called back. "There's not a man—or vampire—who would not, when confronted by violence. Be warned, Priest. And tell your witches the same."

Lucy breathed deeply. Every part of her craved. A hollow bellow echoed within her rib cage. It coiled her forward until her forehead touched her knees. She knew it was the blood hunger. It was both exciting and scary. She had asked for this.

When could she have it?

Not sure when Truvin would return home, she decided to

go out for a walk. Some exercise might alleviate the wanting ache. Maybe pick up some more clothes. Truvin was adamant she not return home, and Jeeves had let her know the cats were fine.

Would witches harm the cats? No, they might make them familiars, if that were true. Dare she call Midge for some advice?

"No, she's on her way to Germany. Oh, Lucy, there's so much you still don't know."

She touched her teeth, wondering what it would feel like to have real fangs.

"You've got to think on this some more. Truvin is right. You shouldn't jump into anything so life changing without a good long think about it."

The door opened and Lucy jumped.

Truvin smirked at her edginess, then gestured she come to him.

Nestling into his embrace felt the safest and most welcome place on this earth. His breaths owned her as they became kisses and kisses became gropes and then she was standing with her shirt slipping down her arms, and Truvin bending to lick her breasts.

"You ground me, Lucy. I needed to come back to the reality I desire."

He lifted her and carried her to the couch. In two breaths, he was inside her. Lucy wrapped her legs around his back.

"You don't like your reality?" she wondered. Gripping the edge of the couch, she grit her jaw with pleasure.

"My new reality," he said as he strained above her. "I'm not going back to the old one. I can't. I won't. Ah!"

They came together. Digging her fingernails into Truvin's arms, Lucy drew them down his flesh. He made her feel powerful. Like she was the only woman he wanted. Like she could be his.

Forever?

"You've got to change me," she gasped. "I've been achy and wanting all evening. Please, Truvin."

He stood and abruptly pulled up his pants. Running his fingers through his sweat-beaded hair he shook his head and paced to the windows that looked over the dark city. The moon was nearly full.

"No." Quick. Final. "I regret biting you without then making sure the vampire taint was removed. I can't change my actions, but I can make sure you don't become something you're not meant to be. You can do it, Lucy. You can wait out the moon."

"And who are you to decide what I should be?"

Flushed with the high of sex, but feeling an even hotter warmth of anger ride her cheeks, Lucy shoved down her skirt and retrieved her shirt from before the door.

So maybe he wasn't so all-about-Lucy. She was a big girl. No one was going to tell her what she could and couldn't do.

Finishing off the last button, Lucy opened the door.

"Where you going?"

"To the hotel. I need to get away from you when you're like this."

"Like what?"

"Domineering and self-righteous."

"Self-right—oh, Lucy, if you only knew."

"Yeah, well, maybe I know more than you know about yourself. I'll have Jeeves drive me. Thanks for the fuck."

She slammed the door and marched to the elevator.

That's right, thanks a lot, buddy. If he wasn't going to support her choices, then to heck with Truvin Stone. She could do this on her own.

Chapter 24

Jeeves lived in an apartment on the first floor of the Carlyle. Lucy didn't bother to look in and ask for a ride. The hotel where she was staying downtown, not far from the Orpheum, was less than ten blocks away. She stomped down the sidewalk, aware it was well after midnight, and the only women out in high heels and skirts were probably shilling for their suppers.

This part of town was nice, though she wasn't sure if that meant safe. There were plenty of quaint shops mixed in with the high-end storefronts.

She paused as the scent of something incredibly delicious caught her attention. Peering through the window to her right, she realized it was a butcher shop. Choice cuts of beef, pork and lamb hung in the freezer window. Signs detailed price and the local farm the meat had come from.

"Fresh blood."

Something her grandma had once said returned to her.

"Sometimes you gotta snap a few necks if you want to eat." And then her grandma had broken a chicken's neck and handed the limp bird to ten-year-old Lucy. A fine roast chicken they'd had that evening.

Easing a palm over her throat, she whispered, "Never thought I'd have to snap a few to actually survive."

Stomping onward, she did look back once—drew in the alluring smell through her nostrils—then turned and scampered quick as she could in her heels to the Chambers hotel.

Once there, she ordered room service, because while she knew she wasn't hungry, there was a specific craving she needed to answer.

A quick shower turned into a long soak. It managed to settle most of Lucy's tension over the words she'd had with Truvin and put her in a new frame of mind.

Changing into one of the dresses Jeeves had bought for her, Lucy just zipped up the back and rushed out to catch the room-service tray. The valet seemed miffed when she stiffed him a tip, but she said she'd put it on the tab. She hadn't any cash in her purse, it was all plastic.

Not terribly disturbed over the valet's displeasure, Lucy rolled the tray before the couch and settled in. Drawing in an anticipatory sniff, she lifted the silver dome to reveal a thick, rare prime rib. A slab of pink meat as thick as her little finger and rimmed in gelatinous fat. Unappealing.

And yet…

Lucy cut into the meat and swished a thick piece around the bloody juices that pooled on the plate. First touch of the meat to her lips nauseated, but first suck…divine.

The warm, watery juices went down like a dream. She didn't chew. The texture of meat never did it for her. In fact, she cut up a few more pieces and used them to sop the juices. Not an ounce of beef went to her gullet; that remained on the plate.

"I'm going to need more. Oh my God, this is so good."

Then she wondered if this was enough blood to start the transformation. "Doubt it."

And she guessed it might have to be human blood, since Truvin had said something about even vampire blood not being enough to sustain—though it could change.

"He's being selfish," she muttered and rested an elbow on the cart. "I can do this. I could live off rare prime rib the rest of my life. I'd make a gorgeous vampire. And I want the endless future. A life spent living and learning. Traveling. Making a difference." She lifted another fork of prime rib. "I need this."

Only a small part of her questioned her rationality. The rest of her was ready.

The door buzzer rang. Who would be calling this late? No one knew she was staying here. Could the witches have tracked her? She hadn't been paying attention when walking home.

"Damn." Searching the room for a possible weapon, Lucy focused on the fork, and then decided it would look more ridiculous than threatening. "They can't hurt me with their blood," she said as she approached the door. "Yet."

But to be safe, she remembered what Midge had taught her about drawing a white light over her.

Closing her eyes, Lucy imagined a white veil falling over her body from head to toe. With no clue whether it would work, she decided it felt empowering, and that would have to serve.

Blue eyes hit her like a beacon in a foggy night. An intense tenderness lived in the depths of azure that hid the danger of what he really was. Truvin wore a black silk shirt rolled up to his elbows. Muscled forearms flexed as he extended a hand.

"Truvin. I—" she glanced to the tray of food "—wanted to be alone." *With my rare steak.*

"I couldn't let things go the way they did between us. I don't want to fight with you, Lucy."

He stepped inside, finding position right before her. So close she could feel her body tremble for his, and wondered if he could, too. To be controlled and mastered as only he could.

"I'm not angry. I walked it off. But I was busy…"

He walked over to the room-service tray. "What are you doing?"

Guilt crept up her spine. Yet in the next instant, indignation kicked down the guilt. "I had a craving. What of it?"

Truvin slammed the domed cover over the plate and ran his fingers back through his hair.

Concentrate on standing your ground, Lucy, not on the overwhelming attraction to the one man who refuses to give you what you want. Project the white light. You are not weak.

"You're being selfish, you know." She walked along the wall, hands to hips. Distance between them was necessary because his scent would draw her over the edge. "Maybe you don't want to share what you have. That's what I think. You don't want to be stuck with me forever? Fine. But let me make my own choices. I'll be out of your hair if you'd—"

"Give you the one thing you think you want?" Strong hands wrangled her wrists before her. She wasn't sure how he had moved so fast, but now she had to double step not to fall off balance. "You want it, Lucy? You want to become one of *the dark?*"

"I do." No hesitation; she wasn't afraid of this.

"Fine. Then come with me."

She stumbled behind him as he marched to the door. "Where are we going? I need shoes!"

"It's time you saw exactly what sort of man you think you're in love with, darling. And what kind of life you are choosing."

Quickly, Lucy retrieved a pair of Louboutins from the box

where she'd set them beside the couch. Bless Jeeves his fashion sense.

Truvin then corralled her into a corner of the elevator, his body pressed along hers, his erection apparent as they rode to the bottom floor. "I'm not a monster, but I'm not human either. This life demands things of me. And it will make those same demands of you."

"I'm ready," she said, and felt it.

"We'll see."

He stared into her eyes, ready to kiss. Ready to take and give.

But he did not.

Lucy gasped as he drew away and turned to face the door. Just now she had desired him despite seconds ago wanting to be alone. He did have some kind of compelling power over her. That was fine; she could accept that.

But if he intended to keep her mortal, then the vampire had some explaining to do.

Gear had called moments before Truvin had entered Lucy's hotel room. He and Nathaniel had found another witch, and had her strung up, awaiting Truvin to light the tinder. She hadn't talked, but they suspected she was allied with the priest because she wore a large cross around her neck. Most witches did not recognize the Christian symbols.

If Lucy thought she wanted something she knew little about, then it was Truvin's responsibility to open her eyes. To show her what vampires were. What vampires and witches did to each other. It wasn't a game of planned strategic moves, it was a way of life. He was *the dark*. Lucy needed to see that darkness.

He hated to do this, but it seemed the only way to convince her to be more rational with her abrupt decision. The full moon was but two nights away. She had experienced little in way of madness or visions that he had seen. She could do this. Yet, he knew the risk of madness was real. His own blood master had been insane.

"How many witches have you killed?" she asked as he directed her up the steps before the dark warehouse that Gear had given Truvin directions to.

"Two in the past year. They're not a large section of the population. The vampires outnumber them four to one. But our numbers are decreasing thanks to the witches and their strange alliance with the priest."

"Why do you think the priest is involved?"

"He believes I killed his daughter."

Lucy opened her mouth to speak, but Truvin pushed her inside the warehouse and bypassed her as he walked across the floor to where Gear and Nathaniel stood.

Another witch hung bound and her arms strung up with rope. This time they'd stacked thick branches around her feet.

Truvin felt Lucy come up behind him and grip the back of his shirt.

"Who the fuck is that?" Gear asked.

"She's all right. She's mine," Truvin said, putting as much warning into the assertion as possible. He didn't like it when a fellow vamp so much as breathed the same air as any particular woman he had claimed. And his bite had introduced his personal mark into Lucy's bloodstream. Any vampire should recognize it and beware. "She talk yet?"

"Not that easy with a strap across her mouth," Nathaniel said. "Here's the lighter." He flipped the small plastic lighter toward Truvin, and he caught it.

Pacing back toward Lucy, Truvin grabbed her gaze and while he held his features expressionless, it was not difficult to register the fear in her eyes. No, it wasn't fear—did the woman never fear?—but instead betrayal. Right now every-thing she'd fantasized him to be would be splayed open and forced into her face for close inspection. She would see that he was not a man she could spend eternity with.

And perhaps she would reconsider becoming a vampire.

This had to be done. To save Lucy's innocent soul.

"You search her?" Truvin asked his men. "Empty her pockets, strip off her boots. Be careful."

Fully suited in protective clothing, Gear stepped up and tore the witch's coat from her shoulders. She groaned as the fabric ripped and pulled from her body. It also tore the seams of her floral shirt, exposing the top of one breast. Gear shook out the pockets. Two vials of crimson fell to the floor and the big vampire jumped back.

"Blood?" Lucy whispered from over Truvin's shoulder.

"A deadly weapon," he answered. "There's one witch who has special bullets made up with her blood in them. Nasty bitch. She's still out there somewhere." And allied with Truvin's former friend.

What was the world coming to when vampires had relation-ships with witches? Married them and had children! Though, Nikolaus Drake was immune to witch's blood because he had survived a blood attack, which made him a phoenix, an inde-structible vampire lord. Truvin and he had come to a head last year. Truvin had left the tribe, not willing to speak against his friend, when he knew Nikolaus was born to lead, and would continue to command Kila well.

He was aware Drake kept tabs on him and his crew of witch hunters, but none from Kila had challenged or tried to stop them.

They all wanted the same thing. Truvin had been the one to step forward and do something about it.

Gear's cell phone rang. He answered and looked to Truvin.

"Right, I'll be there. Marcus has a bead on the priest. He and another witch were seen in the city."

Truvin could feel the man's need for vengeance, to smack his fist into the face of the witch. And yet, with him gone…

Damn it, you cannot do this, can you?

"Go," Truvin commanded. "Track him and report back to me when you've found him. I'll take care of the witch."

Nathaniel high-fived Truvin as he walked out behind Gear. He called back, "Good to see you taking the torch, man. It's a rush!"

Truvin had never torched a witch.

Nor did he intend to start.

But he had to if he wanted to prove to Lucy the dangers of her choice.

Clenching his fists, Truvin thrust back his head, resisting the innate need to destroy. The vampire did not care for life or death. Mortals were disposable.

Yet you've been careful of their lives for centuries. You do respect them. Admit it!

"Truvin?"

"Ahhh!" Huffing, Truvin twisted his head down and looked over at Lucy. He could not do it. She would see him as weak.

So be it.

Turning and leaping, Truvin grabbed the chain suspended from the ceiling, about a foot above where the hook held the witch's bound hands. Dangling there, he lifted her by one wrist, drawing the leather bindings from the hook. Her feet dangled two feet from the floor. He dropped her to land a spineless heap.

Landing, Truvin stalked toward Lucy. "I can't untie her."

"Why not? Let's cut her loose and go."

"Lucy, I…" He took Lucy's hand and pressed the back of it to his mouth. Cool, so soft and gushing with life. And he, no man but a coward. He did not deserve Lucy's affection. "You have to do it. The minute I take the strap from her mouth, she'll spit on me, and that'll be the end of this old vampire."

"Oh, right. I can do it. No problem. You run ahead and get Jeeves to warm up the limo."

"You going to be okay?"

"Of course. She can't hurt me, and she's weak." She knelt before the witch, who had passed out. "Do you have a knife or something to cut the ropes?"

Truvin drew out the blade from his boot and pressed it to Lucy's palm. Then he grabbed the back of her head and pressed a hard kiss to her mouth. "I screwed this one up royally. I had intended to bring you here to show you what a bastard I am. To make you see what the future holds for you."

"Bastards don't value human life. You do, Truvin. I admire you for that."

Her confession surprised him. How could she possibly—?

"You've changed." She smoothed her palm along his cheek. "And if you want to keep the change, I want to help you."

"I do, Lucy. I would do anything for you."

"You've already done something pretty amazing. You kept her alive."

"A man can walk away from violence, and hopefully…" He bowed his head. "Well, hopefully, he can rise above his past. I'll be right outside the door."

He strode away, and with one look back, watched as Lucy removed the leather strap from the witch's mouth. She shook her by the shoulders to revive her. The witch pushed Lucy away, but merely sat there. They said a few words to one another, but Truvin didn't stay to listen.

Outside, Gear stood waiting.

Chapter 25

Thinking to leave the witch to her own designs, Lucy tossed aside the ropes and began to walk away, when she was grabbed from behind. The witch didn't attack, instead she clutched Lucy's hand and pulled her around to look at her.

Short, stocky, yet possessed of luminescent violet eyes. A streak of blood ran through her elbow-length brown hair. The witch seemed a frail doll who had been run over by the neighborhood bully wagon.

"You're mortal, yes?" she asked Lucy.

Tugging her hand away, Lucy didn't sense immediate danger. However, she wasn't in the mood for another palm reading.

"Yes, I'm mortal." And then added, "For now."

"Don't let that longtooth change you. It's not a blessing, as you may believe."

"I don't believe any such thing." Longtooth? Must be a slur against vampires.

Perturbed that this woman would attempt to know her mind, Lucy lifted back her shoulders. Truvin had wanted to show her what vampires were about. But he hadn't been able to go through with it. He had changed—for the better. But whether his resistance to put down an enemy was good or bad remained to be seen.

"If you change," the witch said, "you mark me your enemy."

"And you'll spit on me first chance you get?"

"I will."

Did she have time to put a white light over herself? Would it protect her from a witch?

"Why can't witches and vampires live in harmony? They do their thing, you do yours?"

"They once enslaved us. Drained us to husks and reduced our numbers to mere dozens. We fought back, and we will continue to do so."

"Can't you just…let it end? Let the past be the past? You've won. You've made your blood poisonous to the vamps. You will always have the upper hand."

"Not with them pursuing us."

"Like a few scraps of bulletproof clothing are going to scare you off."

"They were the first to draw blood."

Now the witch was starting to sound like a bad revenge movie.

"Right. Well, I'll keep an eye out for you, and try not to forget my protective outerwear. I'd wish you well, but I'm not sure you'd take it."

"I will, Lucy Morgan. And I will wish you the clarity of mind to fight the hunger."

"In exchange for madness? Nice wish, lady." Lucy swept her hair from her face. "I'm going for the immortality. I hear it's much better than a padded cell."

And she strode off and out the door, only to find the dust

stirred in a cloud before her. Two men struggled. Truvin and the bigger vampire, Gear. Fists connected with flesh and bone, and bloody spittle spattered the air.

"No!" Lucy ran down the steps, but her feet left the ground. An arm clutched her waist and swung her around away from the fight. "Let me go!"

Nathaniel set her on her feet in front of him, but wrapped both arms across her chest as he stood behind her. "You'll get hurt if you try to interfere. This needs to happen."

"Let go of me!"

"No way, sweetheart. Now settle. The best vamp will win."

"That other guy is twice as big as Truvin."

"Size doesn't matter. It takes agility and power to best another vampire. And wisdom. Truvin has been around a hell of a lot longer than Gear."

"You want Truvin to win?"

"I want these two to get out their anger and part either allies or enemies once and for all."

"They've been at odds?"

"No, but Gear had a suspicion Truvin was softening. This was a test to see if he could really do it, kill a witch."

"What's so wrong with wanting to preserve life?" She wriggled. No give from the vampire's iron grip. "To take the high road!"

"I've no opinion. Maybe I do, but Gear's been good to me, as has Truvin. I'd never take sides. Now settle. They won't kill each other."

So, firmly held and unable to wriggle free, Lucy could but watch as the two vampires tore at each other. Each shove sent the other flying through the air. Loose boards nailed on the side of the warehouse creaked with the impact. But their bodies took the brunt with ease and instantly they were back on their feet and charging in for more.

Truvin was smaller, though hardly puny. To his favor, he possessed agility and dodged the brute vampire's punches with ease. He didn't back down from any blow. He stood proud and defied the other to do his worst.

Gear jumped for his opponent. Truvin flattened to the ground and kicked out a slashing leg, which knocked out Gear's balance and toppled him over. Slushy snow spattered Lucy's ankles. On his opponent like a dog, Truvin punched him in the jaw, over and over.

Gear backed off, hands up. "I concede!"

Truvin spat on the ground and lifted back his shoulders. His shirt had torn to reveal blood-smeared pecs. He inhaled a snort through his nose. A kick sent a stray board flying against the wall.

A glance to Lucy, and Nathaniel released her.

She forced herself not to run to him as if he were a little boy who needed tending. It was so hard, but he did not require medical attention, nor the embarrassment of a fussy woman.

In the distance, the witch ran away.

"So this means you're giving up?" Gear growled. He flicked away a wodge of compacted snow from his neck. "You let the witch go? That's not how it works! You lead us, man."

"I don't want to do this anymore. I can no longer do so and be true to myself."

"So you'll just stand back and watch your brothers of the blood be murdered?"

Truvin's chest puffed as he took in a deep breath. Sinewy muscle stretched up and across his delts. "I am sorry."

"What about the priest?" Nathaniel challenged.

"I can't say what I feel about the priest now."

"He'll ride you until you are forced to face him," Gear said.

"Yes. I know the priest will not stop until he's a stake in my heart. I shouldn't prolong the inevitable. I'll…" He spat bloody spittle, and swished his tongue inside his cheek. "Bloody hell,

I can't walk away yet. Nor will I allow fellow vampires to fall when I can stop this. Tonight we must end it. Give me an hour."

Gear nodded and with a hand signal, he and Nathaniel packed off, loping over a pile of railroad ties and disappearing around a building.

The Mercedes's headlights flashed. Jeeves waited.

Truvin strode past Lucy, seeming not to notice her standing there, when suddenly he stopped, did not look back, but instead, held out his hand for her to take.

She slapped her palm into his and they climbed into the back of the car.

He bled everywhere. It was as if a cat had mauled him. Must have been the loose nails in the boards that Gear kept slamming him against. Lucy tried to get him to hold still while she inspected, but he pushed her away.

The scent of his pain overwhelmed. It crept like sweet spilled wine into her senses. The glitter of fresh blood, there on his lip, enticed her to climb upon his lap. It sat like a jewel, a precious ruby, on his mouth, waiting for a thief.

"So brave and strong," she murmured. A woozy wonder dropped her voice to a husky whisper. Every part of her ached in a good, wanting, sex-hungry way. "Let me give the hero a kiss."

"Lucy, no." He shoved her off him, and she landed at the opposite end of the backseat. "I'm covered in blood."

"Of course you are, you naughty boy. You've been playing rough." She swiped a finger across his forearm. The blood was riddled with dirt kicked up from the gravel road. "I want it. Please, Truvin. It smells so good."

And despite the dirt, she licked his arm.

"Hell, Lucy, stop that. It's the hunger making you do this. Jeeves, hurry up! And toss me back your handkerchief."

A white flag flew back. Truvin caught it and began to wipe away the blood.

For as much as she tried again to climb upon his lap, he held her back with his knee until he'd wiped the last trace of blood from his lip. She couldn't believe he wouldn't allow her closer.

"Aren't I good enough for your blood?" she whined. "Yours is precious rubies fit only for—what was her name—Anna?"

"Don't you dare bring her into this. Anna died because of a vampire."

"And so will I! You deny me long enough I'll die of thirst, lover. Just let me taste—"

"You're talking crazy."

"You think this is madness?" Lucy chuckled low in her throat. Crouched before him, she looked up through her lashes. "This is desire. Can't you tell the difference? Poor, pitiful Truvin."

"Faster, Jeeves! She's unsettled, the poor thing. Just close your eyes and relax, Lucy. Concentrate on the movement of the car across the tarmac. Open a window to let in some fresh air." He hit a button on the door handle and Lucy's window rolled down. "It's the blood hunger. You can beat it."

"I don't want to beat it. I want to have it."

He literally fought to keep her from climbing on him again. Why was he so obstinate? Did he not love her? Did he not want her to touch him? The sweet taste of immortality lingered right there, so close.

"You don't like me anymore?"

"Lucy, darling, I adore you. You are mine."

"And are you mine?"

"Yes, yes."

He pressed his palm over her mouth as she gnashed at him. Lucy bit a finger, but her teeth weren't sharp enough. If only she could break skin!

"We're here!"

"Good. Drive right up to the elevator, Jeeves."

The car stopped in the darkness of the underground garage and the door swung open. Truvin swiftly vacated, and Lucy followed his scent as if a bloodhound. Once inside the elevator he slammed her against the wall.

"All right," she cooed, and tangled her fingers in his tattered shirt, "now you're getting around to the good stuff. Sex first, and then love bites?"

"Look at me, Lucy. The cuts on my arms and chest?" He tore away the shirt and dropped it to the floor. "I've healed. There is no more blood."

Indeed, there were no signs of havoc, not a single cut or scrape. Wondrous how vampires healed so quickly.

"But I could nibble on your neck. Right here. The vein is so thick. Please, it aches so desperately right here." She pressed a hand over her heart, where it seemed to have enlarged and now pounded like a heavy rock against her ribs. "Don't you love me? Would you starve me?"

"Stop being so demanding!" He pushed from her and turned away as the elevator soared up to the thirty-seventh floor.

The icy silence did little to squelch Lucy's desire, but she was leery now. She didn't like to be admonished. Made her feel small.

"What?" He turned to her and splayed out a questioning hand. "Do you prefer the previous Truvin, who knew nothing about his life? Who could not know what evils there are in this world?"

"Yes!"

"Well, so do I!"

The elevator dinged, and the doors opened. Determined to remain and ride down, Lucy clung to the steel chair rail, but Truvin twisted her fingers free and pulled her out into the hallway. "You're not going anywhere tonight. You're not safe. You could be dangerous to yourself."

"I don't see how when I've not sharp teeth or a lover who cares enough to feed me."

He opened the door and Lucy tripped on the rug, tumbling to the floor. The cold marble slid under her palms and she moved with the fall, pressing her cheek to the stone.

Truvin Stone. He was as cold as a stone.

"I need you, Truvin." It hurt to confess it, but it was so true.

"You need to ride it out." He offered a hand.

Beating a fist into the cold flatness that resisted her warmth, her needs, Lucy pushed up and sat in a cross-legged splay. "Fuck you."

"You'll thank me after the moon is full."

"Oh? From the mental ward? Is that what you want? To lock me away and be rid of me?"

"Lucy, I—" He leaned over her. Lucy shuddered, wanting only a tender touch. "I'm sorry."

He knelt before her, and bent his face into her hair. "You're not being rational. Perhaps because you are incapable. There are forces—forces of the moon—working within you right now. Making you crave beyond all reason."

She clung to him. So warm, not cold or dead. Hot with life. With sweet gorgeous blood.

She ran a fingernail over his chest. Truvin flinched away from her.

Damn, it didn't cut through.

"Go sit on the couch," he said through a tense jaw.

"But—"

"Just do it, Lucy. Right now."

Some kind of angry, needy beast clawed inside of Lucy. It wanted blood. And it wasn't concerned if it scrambled her wits in the quest for the blood.

He had done this to her.

What right had he to condemn her? Wasn't really a condemnation, was it? Sure, the lost sunlight and drinking blood was a trade-off for extended life. And strength. And freedom.

Lucy wanted freedom. The ability to create a life that would ultimately serve others. He should not deny her that.

Her limbs twisted on the couch as she moaned and fought the animal need for blood.

I embrace my madness.

A voice from his past. A wicked memory of what Lucy could become if he did not overcome his reluctance.

The moon had begun to fade over the treetops.

"Dawn soon comes," announced Damien, perched upon a broken fence post behind Truvin. "We must away to that cottage down the road."

Startled, Truvin jumped as the vampire appeared at his side. Manic green eyes told tales of insanity and greed.

"Why didn't you let me die?" Truvin could not summon the strength to rail at the bastard who had changed his life with a bite and a bloody rampage of murder. "Just…leave me in the sunlight to die."

"Absolutely unthinkable!" Damien danced a weird trill before Truvin, the tails of his frock coat flapping the chill air. "I saved you from the madness that is my own. You should be thanking me." He stretched up his arms in display. "Rise, you feeble waste. Or better yet—"

Gripped by the neck, Truvin was lifted from the ground and he began to soar over the glittering snow that blanketed the countryside. Toward the cottage. And the horrors that lay waiting. They were…flying. The vampire could fly.

"A trick you'll master soon as you steal it from a witch," the vampire said. "I tried to fly to the moon once. She is a cruel mistress. Only aggravates me when she's full. Other times during the month, I am quite sane. I would not even think to

kill. Of course, Roxane would be horrified to discover my bloody messes. You've lucked upon me at a most inopportune time, you. Fancy that?"

Truvin struggled against the vampire's grip, and he relinquished, dropping Truvin. He flailed, but then ceased. Perhaps the landing would break his neck. And then he could be with Anna.

Snow cushioned his fall, though it did jar his neck and spine. Truvin landed right outside the stables of the cottage. The scent of blood was thick in the air.

"We've but moments to dine before the sun chases us into hiding."

Sitting to look after the vampire as he danced toward the cottage, Truvin cursed this night and he cursed the moon. He'd been changed by an insane vampire. What hell was this?

"She will not have hell," Truvin said now.

He had not been listening to Lucy. This is what she wanted. Who was he to say it would not be good for her?

"It is what she will have."

Bending over the couch, Truvin pulled Lucy up to cradle in his arms. "I will do it, Lucy. I won't deny you, and I most certainly will not be responsible for your insanity."

"Yes?"

"Yes." His cell phone rang.

Vacillating between answering, and pushing away his past, Lucy was the one who finally dug his phone from his pocket and handed it to him.

"They're headed toward the chapel," Gear reported. "Can we count on you?"

"Yes," Truvin answered by rote. He snapped the phone shut.

"What is it, lover?"

"They've found the priest."

The elation slid from her face. "You need to go."

"Yes, but…"

"I'll be fine until you return."

He glanced out the window. The moon appeared full, but he knew there was yet two more days for that. "Will you?"

"I will. But, you will return? Oh my God, Truvin, what if they kill you?"

There was always that risk. And if he did die, then Lucy would be left to fend on her own. "You can take any blood, you know that. Don't wait beyond the sunrise. If I'm not home by then…"

She kissed him. "You will be. I won't believe anything else."

Chapter 26

Dressed in full protection gear, Truvin slipped the goggles over his eyes and he marched up the steps to the chapel. He fisted the chin of a stone angel perched on the balustrade, wings spread and ready for heaven, and pushed through the unlocked doors.

The scent of anger and urgency assaulted the air. No fear present. Both sides knew exactly what they wanted, and would fight to get it.

Quick tally sighted Gear and Nathaniel.

There were three witches, all females. Just because they were women Truvin would not discount their strength, if not their capability to use the elements—and their own blood— against him in a wicked magic.

Abigail must be present. He remembered her scent, smoky and cold. But he didn't take the time to figure which was she, as reconnaissance was quick.

At the altar stood the priest, wielding a huge gold cross that took two hands to hold. He wore the white robe, smeared with dirt, and beneath, black leather biker boots with silver buckles.

"There is the vampire I seek!" the priest announced grandly, and he stepped down and took the aisle in long strides.

"Take a number, Priest." Now that was Abigail. Clad in white leather and long, straight black hair flowing to her elbows. She hadn't changed in appearance, nor obviously, had her thirst for vengeance.

Gear kicked in the back pew and it clattered against the one before it. "Let's do this!"

The vampires were suited up for battle. Gear lunged for the first witch who leaped toward him. She might have flown.

Nathaniel bent and swept out a leg to topple the witch who dived for him.

A blast of wind thundered into Truvin's chest. His shoulders hit the wall behind him. Abigail laughed at her control of the elements. No, she cackled. Damn air witch; they could control the wind. The suckers could fly, too, or at least, the most accomplished ones could.

Of which, Abigail was very accomplished. But she'd lost her lovesick-stalker status about a century ago after Truvin had finally given her the rub in Berlin. Or so he had thought.

He should have flamed Abigail when he'd had a chance in the mid-nineteenth century. But when he'd told Lucy he'd never killed, he'd meant it. Much as he'd hoped to get the witch off his back over the centuries, he'd come to realize their deadly dalliance had grown into a sort of game. Abigail knew he'd not the stomach for murder. He had known she would never turn him to ash, for her demented attraction to him always kept her wondering if maybe, just maybe, he could develop a change of heart.

Truvin snapped his head to the side and stomped toward the bitch who currently gathered up a ball of fire in her palm.

The priest, he kept in the corner of his eye. Right now the holy man simply presided over the chaos, cross held high in judgment. Best place for him. Truvin didn't want harm coming to one who should have never become involved in this war.

Putting up a fist to punch through the ball of flame aimed for his head, Truvin then leaped atop a pew and ran over the backs of three in a row. He kicked the witch who'd sent the flame at him in the head. She did a reactionary backflip and landed in a crouch near a stained-glass window that featured Christ washing one of the apostles' feet.

"Delicious blasphemy," Truvin muttered.

A satisfied smirk cut into his facade. This sort of challenge made his blood rush, and he enjoyed it immensely.

To his right, Nathaniel succeeded in reversing a fireball and it ignited the witch's hair. Once a witch took flame, there was little to do but sweep up the ashes. The priest shouted a blessing, crossing himself, and entreating the witch to "go with God."

One witch down. Two left to go.

Lucy had meant it when she said she could wait. But she'd no idea how difficult it would be.

No longer did a dull ache pulse in her chest, making her crave bloody meat. Her brain pounded. It was difficult to see clearly, for the intensity of the migraine blurred her vision. The very air seemed to burn her eyes. She'd closed the shades to block the cold moonlight.

"Bitch," Lucy said to the as-yet-not-full moon. "I will not go mad!"

Scratching her arm, she paced before the windows. Her forearms were red and growing raw. Blood simmered just beneath her flesh. If she drew her own blood would that begin the change?

"No," she snapped. "Don't be stupid."

The whisk of her pace fluttered her skirts between her legs.

Had Truvin been gone a long time? It felt like days. As if he had forgotten her.

"Has he?"

Clutching her elbows tightly before her, Lucy swayed in the center of the room. A birdy moan filled her throat and it bellowed out in a shriek. He'd forgotten about her. The headaches pounded that reality against her skull.

"How could he do this to me? He promised!"

Casting about, she mined the shallow darkness for something to grasp on to. Something warm and rich with life. There were but leather sofas and chairs. The glass coffee table sported a strange silver sculpture.

She shoved the silver hunk of metal off the table and it landed the floor with a muted thud. Very little satisfaction in that move.

But how to fulfill this aching need?

"I need life!"

Lucy stumbled to the door and ran down the hallway to the elevator.

Gear rushed toward Truvin, elbows pumping and fists beating the air. Just as he got to him, Truvin bent—Gear stepped onto his shoulder and soared through the air, landing a kick to the witch who flew toward him. Both went straight down, landing on the rubble of overturned pews and tattered hymnals. Gear was the first to snap back up, ready for more abuse.

"Come on, witch. Give me better than that!" He punched a fist into his gloved palm. The vampire was dangerous when he was excited. Had he a weapon, heads would fly.

Fireballs crackled through the air and windstorms raged

beneath the skeletal rafters of the aging chapel. A glint of pale light flashed in the red robes depicted on a stained-glass window.

Truvin did not fear the dawn, rushing fast toward the horizon. The DragonSkin protected. And it would be a while before the chapel grew completely light.

It seemed they could pummel one another until the end days, and he was more than willing to match every nasty magic the witches threw at him. They'd lost one, and the smell of burnt witch filled the small church with a foul miasma. The priest had blessed her ashes and then swung the gold cross about like a cutlass wielded by a Hun gone aviking.

Abigail delivered a surprise kick to the back of Truvin's knee. He wobbled but caught himself across the chest on a pew. Swinging around, he seized her by the neck. "When will I be finished with you, witch?"

Angry blue eyes sizzled brighter than the actual fireballs. "When I'm satisfied you have suffered the most, vampire."

"I never loved you," he said through the mask. "After all this time? You are still the madwoman who believes in something that was never there."

"I loved you because you were the first man to ever show me kindness." A knee delivered high to his kidney resulted in Truvin releasing her. Abigail drew out a dagger and slashed it across his chest. The DragonSkin repelled the blade. "All I wished for was a little attention."

"It's not sane to hold a grudge for so long. What do you want from me? Love? Or death?"

"Neither would satisfy if we both lived to see the end days!" Abigail's body flew to the left.

Gear stood in her place. He thrust up a hand for a high five, and Truvin, reluctantly, slapped his palm. "Thanks, man. But she's not down for the count. Take the other who's sneaking up on Nathaniel."

Sight of Abigail, struggling to push herself upright, disturbed Truvin. Despite her tough front, she was still vulnerable and misunderstood. He, the only man who'd been kind to her? It was just such a thing a lonely young woman would cling to. Kindness. And he had only in mind to trick her those many decades ago.

A few regrets would ever stain his palate. But how long must he be forced to suffer for his indiscretions?

"Which one is Stone?" the priest called out.

Silence fell over the destroyed sanctuary. Dust motes stirred in the rays of color beaming in from above. It was now or never.

If he wanted it to end, he must see to that finale.

"I am." Truvin stepped forward, stopping ten feet from the cross-wielding holy man. He pushed the goggles down around his neck and tore off his mask. Stupid to reveal flesh? Maybe.

From this moment on, he would move forward. No longer would he be forever looking over his shoulder.

"You're fighting the wrong fight, Priest. I did not murder your daughter. I may have lost my memory after you attacked me, but I've got it back, and I don't kill my victims. That's crass."

"Liar," a witch with blond tresses snarled.

"Stone doesn't lie." Nathaniel tore off his mask. "It was me, Priest. I use Stone's name when my victims demand details. I remember your daughter. She was a virgin. Sweetest taste I've had in a long time."

Nathaniel's confession stiffened Truvin into a fisted resentment. But it wouldn't due to break ranks now. If they were to get out of here alive—with Nathaniel in one piece and not as ash—they must stand united.

"You see," Truvin said calmly. "You've been chasing the wrong man. But murder won't bring your daughter back, Priest."

"It'll grant me the peace I require. Anyone shedding man's

blood, by man will his own blood be shed, for in God's image He made man!" The priest lifted the cross like a javelin and thrust it.

Truvin made a grab for it, but recoiled at the last moment. The danger in touching the cross was too great.

Nathaniel caught the heavy relic in one ungloved hand. He lifted it high. "Not baptized, Priest! You lose."

Gear moved in on the priest. And while Truvin lunged to press Gear back, he spied a witch move to his left. Not aimed for him, she was headed for Nathaniel.

As his body clashed against the solid, blocky muscle of Gear, Truvin heard a new voice enter the room.

"Truvin?"

"No, Lucy, get out of here!"

And he heard Nathaniel's maniacal cries as the witch's blood splattered him on the exposed hand.

Chapter 27

She had known Truvin would come to this chapel. The ache of her need would not allow Lucy to sit like a patient doll in the center of the stark and pristine penthouse, wondering when her master would come home to play with her.

The chapel doors were open. She stumbled through and felt warm, sizzling bits of something collide against her face and arms.

The vampire she had seen blocking her view of the inner chapel—exploded.

Groping the wall for support, Lucy cried out as a dark-haired female approached her, venom sharpening her grin. She rushed right up to Lucy, but kicked off from the wall to her immediate right, and then she did a backflip and landed on an overturned pew with the grace of an acrobat.

Swiping vampire bits from her vision, Lucy spied Truvin,

clad in the protective gear, but without his face mask. He punched a witch and dodged to avoid her bloody spittle.

What was he doing?

"Put your—" she mouthed, but everything happened so fast. She couldn't take it all in. And on top of it all she felt like ripping out her own hair with the insane need for sustenance.

To her right, Gear was brought down by a small arrow that one of the witches shot from a steel device. It broke through the goggles and pierced his skull. The vampire collapsed like a Frankenstein, all blocky and dust rising. His shoulders shook and he yowled to the merciless heavens as his flesh began to sizzle. Witch's blood must have tipped the arrow.

An explosion of bone and body and blood ended Gear's life.

"Truvin, watch out!"

"Lucy?" He started to march toward her, but a witch grabbed him from behind.

Clawing the wall to stand upright, Lucy choked on her own breath. "I need…"

"Enough!" A berobed priest scrambled to his feet amidst a tangle of toppled pews.

The air, electric with energy and blood, crackled over Lucy's skin. Frantically, she tried to brush it away.

To either side of Truvin stood a female, yet Lucy spied another at the back of the chapel, her shoulders pressed to the same wall that supported Lucy.

His white robes a travesty of blood and dirt, the priest lifted a dented gold cross over his head. "It is done!"

"He's still alive," one of the witches sneered.

"He was not the one who took my daughter's life." Pointing the cross at Truvin, the priest declared, "You did not lie to me. I have no spite for you, vampire."

Grabbed from behind, Lucy kicked the air and her arms groped the same nothingness. Before she could scream, a hand slapped over her mouth.

"The priest walks out of here alive," a witch behind Truvin commanded.

And while he felt it best to keep an eye on the two witches before him, Truvin couldn't help a glance over his shoulder.

Abigail. His bittersweet stalker. But she was not alone.

The witch held Lucy.

When had Lucy arrived? And why?

Focusing, he saw Lucy's entire body shook. Yet the witch wasn't causing her pain, only she tried to contain her. *The blood hunger.*

A glance to the stained-glass window high above sighted no moon. Dawn was soon upon them. Lucy had not yet defeated the full moon. She'd never make it.

"Don't harm her," Truvin said calmly. "I'll walk out of here, and vow never to pursue your kind again, if you'll simply let her go."

"You won't offer yourself for her freedom?" Abigail said with an implied snort.

One of the witches who now flanked the priest snickered.

"If it is what you want." Truvin reached for the upper left corner of his flak jacket and tore away the heavy-duty Velcro. He shrugged down the protective gear. Beneath he wore a thin cotton shirt. He tore that open to expose his bare chest. "Have at me."

Two witches flanking him moved in. The visceral intensity of their lust to do violence crept up his neck and tightened across his scalp.

"But you must release Lucy first," he called. "I won't go to my grave until I know she is safe."

Lucy struggled against the witch's hold. Her fingernails hooked over the witch's arm and clawed, gouging the white leather.

"She's starving for blood, you bastard," Abigail hissed. "Is this how you treat your women now, Truvin? Press them to madness?"

"Perhaps it is only because I've been pursued by the sort all my life, I cannot be comfortable without its presence."

He chided himself with a fist to his palm. *Stupid vampire. Let down your pride and let them at you.* Anything to save Lucy.

Aware of the movement behind him, Truvin checked his periphery. The witches kept their distance, but he knew one leap and the enemy would be upon him.

Didn't matter now. He needed Lucy to be safe. And he was thankful he had told her she could drink from anyone to complete the change. She did not need him.

He'd done what he could to prove his innocence to the priest—and had—yet at the expense of two of his friends.

Sunlight flashed between where Truvin stood and the witch held Lucy. A thin beam painted blue and emerald light across the dusty hardwood floor.

He and Abigail had dallied through the centuries. A mutual tease he'd grown tired of, and would not risk riposting when it could now harm Lucy.

"Please, Abigail, release her. She is undeserving of the pain you wish to inflict upon me."

"I will, Truvin. You don't believe I would be so callous as to wound another when you are the one who holds all my vengeance."

"I had not thought so, but one can never be sure."

The witch wrenched her arm tight around Lucy's neck and cracked a triumphant smile. "War is war, after all. I don't grudge you for protecting your own, as you should not when

I am compelled to protect mine. But know, you haven't won this one, Stone."

Abigail reached around and pulled something from her back pocket. She moved so swiftly, Truvin registered the flash of silver and the ejection noise as she pressed it to Lucy's neck.

Lucy cried out. The witch released her and Lucy sank to the floor.

"What the bloody hell?"

The witch sashayed toward Truvin, waggling the silver injection needle before her. "My blood now runs in your woman's veins."

"Do you know what you've done? She is close to transformation. You've made her immune to the entire race of witches."

Abigail pushed the ejector, spurting a few drops of crimson over the edge. She sneered at Truvin's sudden need to take a step back. "A worthy exchange, knowing you'll never be able to have her completely now. You can make her one of *the dark,* but you can never make her yours. Have a nice life, vampire."

And then she gripped the thin gold chain about her neck and tugged it free. Dropping it at Truvin's feet, she then strode past him, kissing the air with a hint of smoky sage and vetiver. And in what sounded like a cacophony of fluttering leather wings, the witches and the priest cleared out of the chapel, leaving through a door up by the altar.

There at his feet lay the small gold cross Truvin had once defiantly worn. It was Abigail who had taken it from him that night in the alley. She had been the one to deliver a blow hard enough to clear away his memory.

And yet…

"You've given me a new life, Abigail," he whispered.

Stepping over the cross, he dashed for Lucy, the sunlight searing his face as he passed through the beam of colored light. He plunged to his knees before his fallen butterfly.

She shuddered and moaned. The blood hunger demanded satisfaction.

"Don't touch me," Lucy murmured as he leaned in to brush aside the hair from her face. "I'll kill you. Oh, Truvin, I've become your death!"

"Shh, Lucy. It'll all work out." It wouldn't, but he didn't want her more upset than she was. The one woman he had come to love and care for beyond all things—he could never have her blood.

Abigail had secured a most fitting revenge to accompany her unintended gift.

"You can still take my blood. And you must."

And though it killed him to know he could always give but never receive, Truvin tore a fang across his wrist and pressed it to Lucy's mouth. "Quickly," he warned. "The slash will heal too soon. That's good, Lucy."

She took his blood and completed the drastic transformation that would see her one of *the dark* forever after.

He dusted a finger along her eyelashes. A part of him regretted, so deeply, he felt he would forever hold a wound for what he now allowed to happen to Lucy.

Yet another part of him rejoiced. She was his, his blood child, the only one he had ever created. The only one he desired to spend eternity with.

Yet you will risk your death every moment you are near her.

A misplaced fang, a paper cut, a fall that results in an abrasion. Her blood, now tainted by blood from the entire witch race, could kill him.

Bittersweet, this moment. Truvin clenched his jaw and fisted the wall above Lucy as she drew away from his wrist. Her head wobbled, and she granted him a woozy smile.

"Close your eyes," he instructed. "Rest for a few moments. The sun has risen, but you're safe until your fangs have completely descended. I'll call Jeeves."

He stood and Lucy slipped into a reverie, curling her arms about her legs. A sleepy, wondrous state of bliss and satiation that he knew very well. It was a new beginning. To forever.

Eyeing the open doorway, Truvin strode outside and stood in the chilly morning shadows. The stone angel snickered behind her wings at him. *She will never completely be yours. Foolish vampire, you've really fucked this one up, haven't you?*

Truvin lunged and kicked the angel's head. The stone shattered.

And Truvin cried out his rage to the world.

Jeeves arrived ten minutes later, and Truvin carried a sleepy Lucy to the car. The next few days would be spent teaching her to hunt. To sustain her life. And to live.

Could he learn the same? The decision to leave his old life behind was met with the knowledge that he could never shuck the vampire. Witches would always be his bane. As would the sunlight and now holy objects. Life was precarious.

But with Lucy at his side, life could be wondrous.

Epilogue

Three years later

Ice and snow glittered like Tiffany jewels across the frozen Venetian lagoon. A rarity, Truvin had offered as they'd gazed over the stretch of ice. Lucy loved every moment of the rare and even the mundane.

Because even the mundane held a fine point of wonder. She experienced the world with new and different senses now. Everything was new. This princess of forever had finally gotten her crown.

She and Truvin had been together for years, and had not stopped making love since that first time. Sex was exquisite, even more full and gorgeous now that her vampire senses had been mastered. Yet a measure of care had to be taken. No fangs. That was the rule.

Sure, Lucy could drink from Truvin, but she rarely did, for she could not reciprocate. Her lover's fate could be changed with a simple paper cut or a slice from a cutting knife. Lucy took great pains to be careful.

The first year Truvin had mourned the fact that he'd been denied her blood through Abigail's vengeance. But Lucy hadn't been about to allow him to wallow forever. "Suck it up, vampire," she'd admonished. "This is your life now. Love me or leave me?"

"Love you," he'd replied. "Always."

Twisting the lock open on the paned glass bedroom window, Lucy pushed it outside a few inches to draw in the cool winter air. The breeze sifted through her red silk nightgown, tickling down her body. One of the cats scampered off the bed, showing its displeasure at the introduction of the cold air.

Her lover stood by the door, watching her. She didn't have to turn around to know it. His presence gushed inside her veins. Their heartbeats syncopated. A tremendous feeling; one she felt sure to never become accustomed to, and was happier for that marvel.

"The checks were sent out with the post an hour ago," Truvin said.

Lucy nodded. After relocating to Italy, Truvin had introduced her to his accountant and she had dutifully learned how to play the stock market. Not wanting to accept any of his money, she had begun to build her own fortune. It was satisfying.

But even more satisfying was the money she could now donate to charity. It was a small start, but one that would only continue to grow. She had a lifetime to help others now. And she'd hooked up with Midge, who currently lived in Berlin, to focus some of her growing wealth toward an organization that helped war widows get back on their feet.

Midge had been right when she'd read Lucy's palm. Two lifetimes.

All her expectations about vampirism had been met. And, no, the coffin was not a requirement. All windows had been fitted with electrochromic shades, and were set on timers, so they never had to worry for the sunshine.

Which, she hadn't begun to miss. The moon offered its own brand of brilliance that dazzled Lucy into wonder each time she gazed up at it. Perhaps a tendril of lunacy had crept into Lucy's psyche, a love for the moon that went beyond the normal, but it was far from madness.

Her lover's hands slid up her thighs, shimming the slippery silk over her flesh. "You've been dabbling in the perfume oils again, Lucy, darling. What do you smell like? Some kind of summer flower…"

"Bee balm," she said. "It attracts butterflies in the summer. You like it?"

"You've attracted your own butterfly into the net. Of course I love it. But not so much as I adore you. Want to go pin some snacks?"

She smirked. Yes, indeed, stalking butterflies. It was a delicious foray.

"Not yet." She turned and sat on the windowsill. The moonlight glowed across Truvin's sharply boned visage. "How long has it been since you've last kissed me?"

He nuzzled into her hair. "An hour or two?"

"Naughty boy. I'm feeling neglected."

"How shall I ever make it up to you?"

Lucy drew up her nightgown and clasped her legs around Truvin's hips. "Let me refresh your memory."

* * * * *

Watch for THE DEVIL TO PAY, the next book in the BEWITCHING THE DARK *series, featuring Ivan Drake, the ill-fated son of Nikolaus Drake and Ravin Crosse.*

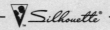

SPECIAL EDITION

A late-night walk on the beach resulted
in Trevor Marlowe's heroic rescue of a
drowning woman. He took the amnesia
victim in and dubbed her Venus, for the
goddess who'd emerged from the sea.
It looked as if she might be his goddess of
love, too…until her former fiancé showed
up on Trevor's doorstep.

Don't miss

THE BRIDE WITH
NO NAME

by *USA TODAY* bestselling author
MARIE FERRARELLA

*Available August
wherever you buy books.*

REQUEST YOUR FREE BOOKS!

2 FREE NOVELS PLUS 2 FREE GIFTS!

Silhouette®

n o c t u r n e™

Dramatic and Sensual Tales of Paranormal Romance.

YES! Please send me 2 FREE Silhouette® Nocturne™ novels and my 2 FREE gifts (gifts are worth about $10). After receiving them, if I don't wish to receive any more books, I can return the shipping statement marked "cancel." If I don't cancel, I will receive 4 brand-new novels every other month and be billed just $4.47 per book in the U.S. or $4.99 per book in Canada, plus 25¢ shipping and handling per book plus applicable taxes, if any*. That's a savings of about 15% off the cover price! I understand that accepting the 2 free books and gifts places me under no obligation to buy anything. I can always return a shipment and cancel at any time. Even if I never buy another book from Silhouette, the two free books and gifts are mine to keep forever.

238 SDN ELS4 338 SDN ELXG

Name	(PLEASE PRINT)

Address	Apt. #

City	State/Prov.	Zip/Postal Code

Signature (if under 18, a parent or guardian must sign)

Mail to the **Silhouette Reader Service:**
IN U.S.A.: P.O. Box 1867, Buffalo, NY 14240-1867
IN CANADA: P.O. Box 609, Fort Erie, Ontario L2A 5X3

Not valid to current subscribers of Silhouette Nocturne books.

Want to try two free books from another line?
Call 1-800-873-8635 or visit www.morefreebooks.com.

* Terms and prices subject to change without notice. N.Y. residents add applicable sales tax. Canadian residents will be charged applicable provincial taxes and GST. Offer not valid in Quebec. This offer is limited to one order per household. All orders subject to approval. Credit or debit balances in a customer's account(s) may be offset by any other outstanding balance owed by or to the customer. Please allow 4 to 6 weeks for delivery. Offer available while quantities last.

Your Privacy: Silhouette is committed to protecting your privacy. Our Privacy Policy is available online at www.eHarlequin.com or upon request from the Reader Service. From time to time we make our lists of customers available to reputable third parties who may have a product or service of interest to you. If you would prefer we not share your name and address, please check here. ☐

SN08R

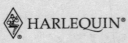

HARLEQUIN®

American ★ Romance®

CATHY McDAVID
Cowboy Dad

THE STATE OF PARENTHOOD

Natalie Forrester's job at Bear Creek Ranch
is to make everyone welcome, which is an
easy task when it comes to Aaron Reyes—the
unwelcome cowboy and part-owner. His
tenderness toward Natalie's infant daughter
melts the single mother's heart. What's not
so easy to accept is that falling for him means
giving up her job, her family and the only
home she's ever known....

***Available August
wherever books are sold.***

LOVE, HOME & HAPPINESS

nocturne™

COMING NEXT MONTH

#45 DANCE OF THE WOLF • Karen Whiddon
The Pack

On a mission to find his best friend, who's disappeared,
Dr. Jared Gies's search leads him not only to
Elena Cabrera—the woman he recognizes as his one
true mate—but also straight into danger. And although
Elena wants nothing to do with shifters, their very
lives—and those of Jared's fellow wolves—now depend on
him winning her trust.

#46 SON OF THE SHADOWS • Nancy Holder
The Gifted

War would erupt before the House of the Shadows—
unless its Guardian, Jean-Marc de Devereaux, could turn
his back on his forbidden love with Isabelle of the House
of Flames. But what surprises had their union already
wrought in this world of powerful magic and age-old
vendettas?

SNCNM0708